FLASH BURNOUT

A NOVEL BY
L. K. MADIGAN

GRAPHIA

Houghton Mifflin Harcourt
Boston New York

For NBW and NBW, my in-house dynamic duo

All rights reserved. Published in the United States by Graphia,
an imprint of Houghton Mifflin Harcourt Publishing Company.
Originally published in hardcover in the United States
by Houghton Mifflin Books for Children, an imprint of
Houghton Mifflin Harcourt Publishing Company, in 2009.

For information about permission to reproduce selections from this book,
write to Permissions, Houghton Mifflin Harcourt Publishing Company,
215 Park Avenue South, New York, New York 10003.

Graphia and the Graphia logo are registered trademarks of
Houghton Mifflin Harcourt Publishing Company.

www.hmhbooks.com

The text of this book is set in Garamond.

Library of Congress Cataloging-in-Publication Data is on file
ISBN 978-0-547-19489-9 hardcover
ISBN 978-0-547-40493-6 paperback

Manufactured in the United States of America
DOM 10 9 8 7 6 5 4 3 2 1

4500245794

FLASH BURNOUT

Too close
Too much light
The camera flashes.

I can't
See her face
In the bright glaring light.

.... CHAPTER ONE ....

Cease handling the equipment immediately
if it emits smoke, sparks, or noxious fumes.
—*Mitsu ProShot I.S. 5.3 camera guide, 2007*

When I go down to breakfast, I'm greeted by photos of bullet wounds scattered all across the kitchen table. You would think my dad would at least have the courtesy not to put stuff from work on the table where we *eat*.

Right on cue, I hear a snore from the family room. Dad must have gotten home late and decided to sleep on the couch last night. He does that sometimes so he won't wake Mom.

I shove the photos to one side, trying not to look at them, and pour a bowl of cereal.

Mom comes into the room yelling, "I mean it, Garrett. If I have to tell you to get up again, I'm going to tell you with a bucket of cold water. It's almost seven fifteen!"

Her hair is still wet from her shower, and she's running around in her underwear and a blouse. Usually she's a Zen master of calm. She *has* to be, she's a hospital chaplain, but every morning she turns into a spaz. She's always setting down half-finished cups of coffee and throwing things into her briefcase and searching for her shoes.

"Morning, sweetie," she says, leaning over to hug me.

"Morning."

She glances at the photos and turns away to pour herself a cup of coffee without so much as a raised eyebrow. Just another cheery morning in the Hewson household. "Did you feed The Dog Formerly Known as Prince yet?"

"No."

"Don't forget." She drinks some coffee, studying the front page of the newspaper.

"As if."

"It's too early for snide and snappy, Blake. I can listen to it later, but not right now, okay?" She peels off her blouse, her face red and sweaty. "Aarghh, hot flash!"

"Jeez, Mom! People are eating here!"

She fans herself with the newspaper. "I swear, it's starting to happen every morning! Could it be the coffee?" She shakes her head. "I don't care. I am never giving up coffee."

I keep my eyes on my cereal. It never used to bother me when my mom ran around half dressed. But now that I have an actual girlfriend whose actual bra I have seen in person, it makes me feel kind of squicky to see my own mother in her bra.

Dad shuffles in from the other room. "Morning." He perks up when he sees Mom standing there half naked.

"Hi," says Mom, putting up her hands. "No, don't hug me, I'm having a hot flash. What time did you get home?"

"Around one." Dad holds his arms out in a pretend hug and pats the air around Mom. "I couldn't sleep, so I worked on my presentation for a while."

"Yeah, Dad, thanks," I say, flicking the photos farther away from me. "Can't you remember to put stuff like this away? I've already vomited at the sight of it."

Dad chuckles.

Ahhh, the first laugh of the day. I'm going to be a comedian when I grow up, so I keep a log of how many times a day I make people laugh. Garrett says it's ass to keep a log, but it is *not* ass. It is analytical.

"I'm going to dry my hair," says Mom, exiting the room. "And if Garrett is not up—"

I can hear her muttering, "He will rue the day" as she disappears down the hall.

I finish my cereal and stuff my books into my backpack, whistling a line from the new Gingerfred song, "I'm angry at my backpack, I hate how much it weighs."

As I slide my photo homework into my portfolio I think, *These are good.* No more listening to Mr. Malloy say, "Technically fine, Blake. But where's the heart?" *Phhft.* He gave me a C last year. Who the hell gets a *C* in photo?

Dad sits with a cup of coffee, studying the bullet wounds.

"How come you were late last night?" I ask.

"Shooting. Downtown. The cops shot a homeless guy. They say he charged them."

"Oh."

"Bystanders heard the guy raving to himself, though, so he was probably mentally ill." Dad rubs his face. Even though he's a medical examiner and his job depends on there being a supply of dead people, he would prefer that people not kill each other so randomly. "I wish the police could figure out a better way of dealing with the mentally ill than shooting them." He takes another sip of his coffee. "Especially eleven times. That's not for public knowledge, Blake, by the way."

I nod.

Garrett comes into the room, The Dog Formerly Known as Prince at his heels. Garrett is The Dog's favorite; he sleeps in Garrett's room. I don't know how The Dog can stand it—the room reeks of sweat and stale farts. Maybe that's perfume to a dog.

I pour two big scoops of kibble into The Dog's food dish, and he tears himself away from Garrett's side long enough to notice that yes, *I* am the one feeding him. Without so much as a mercy wag, he buries his snout in his dish.

I check the clock—just enough time to text Shannon:

Hi GF, can't wait to see u. What r u wearing? heh. BF

"Haul ass, Studly," says Garrett. "We're out in five."

4

Garrett started calling me Studly after I acquired an official Girl-Friend. I guess it's better than Ass-wipe, my previous nickname.

"You're the one who's late," I say.

Garrett's big jock hands clench into fists, but he just looks at me.

I brush my teeth and head out to the driveway. Garrett's not there yet. I lean against the hood of the car, checking my cell for a text from Shannon. No reply.

When Garrett finally shows up, I say, "What happened to hauling our asses?"

"If you don't get yours off my car, you're going to have it handed to you," he says.

"What?"

"Your ass. Get it off. My car."

I step away from Monty, a 1964 Mercury Montclair Marauder that Garrett and Dad fixed up. My dad is a grease monkey at heart. When he's not cutting up dead people, he's usually in the garage dinking with pistons and valves and crankshafts and whatever-other-shafts make engines run.

Garrett leans over the windshield and studies it like a judge at a car show. Then he whips out a bandanna. No, I'm not kidding, he carries a bandanna around in his back pocket, not because he's a gang member, but because he likes to cover up his shaved jock head when he's in the sun. He polishes a speck on the windshield, then unlocks the door. We get in, and he backs out of the drive-way without saying a word.

I flip on the radio and tune it to our school's radio station.

The last yell ("Hehh!") of a James Brown song fades out, and a girl's voice comes out of the speakers: "Good God, y'all! I'm Chick Trickster, flicking you some slick discs *live* from the Wild West studio at West Park High. And what a flippy, trippy, overly hip school this is! Just right for this chick. Pleased to meet you and greet you, don't make me cheat you. Speaking of which, Franz Ferdinand is 'Cheating On You,' right here on 88.1 FM—KWST."

"Hey, it's a girl," I say.

"What?"

"It's a girl on KWST."

"So?"

"So I've never heard a girl DJ on there before."

Garrett grunts. "She's probably a dog."

"What? Why would you think that?"

"Why else would she be on the radio? Hot chicks don't go sit in a little studio and hide their hotness behind a microphone. They do cheerleading or the drama club or the dance team."

"Right, Gare. Every single hot chick in the world wants to be a cheerleader." I shake my head. "Maybe she *likes music*."

"Yeah. We'll see."

We don't talk the rest of the way, which is a relief.

Shannon is standing with Kaylee and Jasmine on the quad when I get there. She's sooo luscious in her little white top—it barely reaches the waistband of her baggy shorts. There are "no bare midriffs" allowed at West Park High, but I can see a few millimeters of silky skin between her top and her shorts. I want to touch her like a junkie wants his drug.

"Hey," I call.

She doesn't wave and smile when she sees me, which is my first clue that something's up. Kaylee and Jasmine kind of slip away without speaking to me as I approach, which is my second clue.

Uh-oh. Maybe I can joke my way out of it, whatever *it* is.

"Houston, we have a problem," I say. "Shannon is not smiling. Repeat: not smiling."

Shannon continues to not-smile.

Hmm. "Baby?" I say, tilting my head at her.

"You know what?" she says.

"What."

"I am so done with the word 'baby.'"

"Ohh-*kay.*" *Who are you and what have you done with Shannon?*

"Not just you. Everyone! Guys calling each other baby. It's enough already." She crosses her arms, as if disgusted by all slang.

Houston, a little help here? I think. *Crashing and burning is imminent. Over?*

The Houston in my head yells, *Abort, abort!*

"What's going on?" I ask.

She doesn't answer right away, just stares off into the distance with her cool blue eyes. Then she says, "You really don't know?"

Oh. Mygod. I just wanted to get a little sugar before class! It's waaay too early for this drama. "I'm, uh, *wrong* somehow? I've

7

done something wrong. And I'm really, really sorry." I pause. The Houston in my head whispers that maybe I could risk a joke now. "Baby," I add.

Her lips twitch into a smile, and for a second I think I've made a spectacular landing. Houston and I start to congratulate each other.

Then she makes this bitter-beer face, like she's mad at herself for smiling. "I can't believe you!" she says, and storms off.

Wow. From bullet wounds at breakfast to girlfriends gone wrong. And it's not even eight o'clock.

·············CHAPTER TWO·············

There are always two people in every picture:
the photographer and the viewer.
—*Ansel Adams, American photographer (1902–1984)*

Shannon actually *storms off.* I've never seen anyone do that . . . leave in a way that you could call storming off. Her hair flips around her shoulders and her legs stretch out in big, pissed strides. Her whole body yells, *Get out of my way.* I picture innocent bystanders getting knocked to the ground by the sheer force of her storming.

Sweet.

Our first fight! She must be crazy about me. Why else would she get this emotional? I run to catch up with her.

"Shannon, wait," I say, putting my hand on her shoulder.

She stops. "What."

I fondle her perfect shoulders. I know it's weird, but I love shoulders almost as much as the really good parts. "Just tell me what I did, okay?"

"Why didn't you call me last night?"

Blink. Blink. Wait. "I did! I did call you last night! What do you mean? Did you forget? We talked about your mom . . . and . . . *Dracula*! Remember?"

"I don't mean that time, Blake. You were supposed to call me *after dinner.*"

Ohhhh. I forgot. Riley called me after dinner and I went up to the skate park with some of the guys. It was dark by the time I got home, and I guess I forgot about the After-Dinner Call. "Oh. Sorry. I forgot." I decide to leave out the guys and the park. "Why didn't you just call me on my cell? Or text me?"

"I'm not going to call you on your cell every five minutes!" Now she's raging. My nuts recoil in fear. "I'm not going to be *that* girlfriend . . . who calls her boyfriend to check up on him all the time! You said you would call me after dinner, and you didn't. Fine. I guess you didn't really want to talk to me, or you wouldn't have *forgotten.*"

There are tears in her eyes. This blows my mind so much that I don't know what to say. "Are you actually crying?" seems wrong.

She leaves before I can come up with the right words. This time she doesn't storm off, she just walks.

I lope along behind her. A couple of jokes pop into my head, but I don't say them. I may not be the brightest bulb on the string of party lights, but I can tell that my humor is not required at the moment.

Shannon and I don't have any classes together until English. At the door to her class, she stops and wipes her eyes. Then she takes a deep breath and walks in, not even saying goodbye. Oh no she *didn't!*

Fuming, I head for biology and spend half the class coming up with one-line zingers to greet her with next time I see her: "You better straighten up, missy, or I will turn this thing around!"

That's, uh, the only one I come up with.

Next is U.S. history, with the criminally boring Ms. B. She's so dull I can't even remember what the B stands for. At least I don't have her class after lunch. So many people nod off during that class it's known as History of Naptime.

I flip open my cell and start to text Shannon. That's the one good thing about Ms. B. (Blandish?), she's so oblivious that she never notices people texting during class. I type,

```
shan i'm sorry i forgot to call,
```

then I hit the cancel button and flip the phone shut. I just flashed on something Garrett said to one of his jock friends the other day: "Get some balls, man. Did you just *hand* them over to Reese when you started going out?"

When Ms. B. (Buford?) finally releases us back into the wild, I hurry to English class, figuring I can catch Shannon outside for a minute and make up. It's been two hours. How long are BF-GF fights supposed to last, anyway? Does the duration vary based on the severity of the offense?

As I turn the corner, I see Shannon walk into English. Not

even waiting for me! Okay, now *I'm* getting pissed. That shit is not right.

Riley comes up behind me. "S'up, Flake?"

Again with the nicknames. But I call him Viley, so it's fair.

We roll in, and Mr. Hamilton says, "What's up, Riley? Cool shirt, Blake."

I nod at him, then see that he's wearing the same LOST IN SPACE shirt as me, and I start laughing. He's the only teacher at West Park High who has a modicum of cool. I learned that word from him, by the way, when he told me I had a modicum of comedic talent. He's wrong, of course. I have a maximum of comedic talent.

Shannon goes straight to Moody Corner. That's a big chair in the back of the room reserved especially for premenstrual head cases . . . I mean people who feel "sad, mad, or generally unable to deal," according to Mr. Hamilton's sign. But so far I've seen only girls sitting there. Coincidence? I think not.

Mr. Hamilton starts talking about *Dracula,* the book we're reading. "Okay, so who can tell me what an epistle is?" he asks.

"A piss what?" I say, and everyone laughs.

Score! Two confirmed laughs so far today and it's still early.

"Oh, Blake . . . Blake," says Mr. Hamilton, shaking his head. "Never go for the piss joke. Don't just go for the easy laugh. George?"

Oh. Well, that still counts. It would have been bonus points if the teacher laughed. I glance over at Shannon, and she's staring out the window, arms crossed, clearly not amused.

But Marissa is smiling. I tally an invisible point in the air, and she rolls her eyes at me.

Marissa and I met last year in intro photography. We were the only ninth-graders in the class, so we kind of huddled together in a clump of freshman nervousness.

I try to pay attention while Mr. Hamilton talks about *Dracula,* but I keep wondering what I'm supposed to do about Shannon. Are we broken up now? Is that *it?* Should I try to talk to her after class, or write her a note, or leave her alone, or what? I look over at her a couple of times, but she has her head down, scribbling something.

I wait for Shannon after class, like always. Lunch is next, and we usually eat together. But then Ellie goes over to her. Ellie is Mr. Hamilton's daughter, by the way. Which makes her totally cool by association. But even if she didn't have a tattooed, music-loving English teacher father, Ellie would still be cool. If she decided to start wearing canned vegetables pinned to her clothes, by the end of the week half the girls in the school would be pinning canned veggies to their clothes, too.

Ellie and Shannon whisper.

I lurk.

Shannon glances up at me as if I'm a waiter standing by to take her order. She says flatly, "I'll see you later, okay?"

I stare at her, frozen.

No. She did *not* just dismiss me! Oooh, she will rue the day!

I don't storm off, but I don't slink away like a bitch-ass punk, either. Just when I get to the door of the room, I hear Ellie say, "Hey, Blake?"

Now my whole exit is busted. I have to stop and turn around. "Yeah."

"If you see Manny, will you tell him I'll be there in a minute?" asks Ellie.

"Yeah."

I don't see Ellie's boyfriend Manny anywhere, but I do see her friend Dez. She's one of the hottest chicks in the whole school, even though she's only in tenth grade, like us. I admire her heart-shaped ass for a couple of seconds, since Shannon isn't around to catch me looking.

If there's one thing I've learned since getting a girlfriend, it's that you don't look at another girl for more than a hyper-second. You learn to take a quick sip, then savor the flavor of the after-image in your head. About a week or so after Shannon and I became official, she noticed me noticing a girl, waited patiently for a few seconds, then said, "Okay, finish up now."

I said, "What?"

She said, "Finish up checking out the other girl. That's long enough."

Ha! How lucky am I to get a girlfriend with a sense of humor?

Well, most of the time, anyway. I don't know what kind of pod person took over her body this morning. I half expected her to reach up and unzip her forehead so the alien inside could escape, like that Doctor Who episode with the Slitheen (Season One, Episode Four).

I join Marissa in the pizza line.

"What's up with Shannon?" she asks.

"I don't know. I guess I forgot to call her for the hundredth time, or something." Then I instantly feel like a traitor. "Nah, we just had a misunderstanding."

Marissa's so easy to talk to, I sometimes wish that we had hooked up. But it's not that way with us. We're always going to be just friends. I still remember our first assignment in intro photo: shoot and print a series of black-and-white portraits of another member of the class.

As the only ninth-graders, Marissa and I were paired up by default. We took the city bus up the hill to Washington Park, where we shyly pointed cameras at each other. Studying her through the lens, I realized that she had the most heartbroken eyes I'd ever seen. You don't notice it most of the time—she's usually smiling. And she's got a little jeweled stud in her nose, so your eyes automatically go to that.

Marissa smiles at me now and says, "Bye. See you in photo." She grabs her pizza and leaves.

Two slices of pepperoni and a large vanilla shake later, I'm looking for a place to sit down. I see Manny as I'm heading for the tables. I open my mouth to tell him Ellie will be here in a minute, then I think, *What am I? Message boy? HELL no!*

Riley and some of the other guys are getting up a game of poker at one of the tables. I make my way over.

"Flake, you in for some Texas hold 'em?"

"Hell yeah, Vile."

I'm juggling my pizza and a pair of aces, and feeling mighty good, when someone touches my arm. Shannon.

"Hi," she says. She gives me a tentative smile.

"Hi," I say.

She stands there looking expectant. I realize that she wants me to leave the game and talk to her. I look down at my pair of aces. Have I ever held a pair of aces before? I *could* say, "Just let me finish this hand, Shannon," but I'm ninety-seven percent sure that would be the wrong thing.

I lay down my cards, saying, "Fold," and get up to leave.

Riley coughs the word "pussy."

We walk away from the table, and Shannon takes my hand. "Sorry I freaked out," she says. "I was feeling, I don't know—" She struggles to find the right word.

Hormonal? I almost suggest.

"Anyway, Ellie told me I was being stupid." She smiles and shrugs. "Will you forgive me?" After a second she adds, "Baby?"

Whew. She's back. Making a mental note that Ellie is my new best friend, I lead Shannon out to the bleachers for a little privacy, where we can forgive each other more thoroughly.

·····

I am full of Shannon after lunch. Her sweet, round shoulders and her thin, freckled arms that break out in goose bumps when I stroke them and her ohmygod luscious lips that I could just stay attached to for hours, and *man,* did I want to get her into the back seat of Garrett's car. But (a) I know Garrett would punish me repeatedly if he found out, and (b) we had to go back to class, and (c) no way would Shannon agree to it.

For some reason, our photo teacher, Mr. Malloy, feels that he must wear a beret on his bald head and a goatee on his receding chin, like some kind of French poser. Seriously? We're too embarrassed on his behalf to even give him shit about it.

"Let me see your series," I say to Marissa.

She hands me her portfolio. Our assignment over the weekend was to shoot a series of color photos featuring monochromatic subjects. Mr. Malloy wanted us to find subjects to photograph that were mostly all one color, or preferably lacking in color, except for one contrasting bright spot that would draw the eye.

Marissa's first photo shows an expanse of green lawn with one yellow dandelion sticking up. "I was lying on the ground for that angle," she says.

The next one is a close-up of a gray stone birdbath with a flock of tiny grayish-brown birds splashing around in it. Her contrast is a blue jay, midflight, swooping down to the birdbath. Some of the tiny birds have already started to take off. She must have been sitting there forever waiting for that shot. "What are those—sparrows? No, they're too little."

"Bushtits," she says.

"Bush-*scuse* me?"

She giggles. "That's what they're called."

"Nice," I say. "Your grandma's backyard?" Marissa lives with her grandma.

"Yeah, and it was really cloudy out," she says, "so the background is gray, too."

Her next shot is an arrangement of milky white vases, all empty except for one holding a red rose. The last photo is an extreme close-up of her black cat, sleeping, with just a glint of its pink tongue showing.

"No people," I say.

She pauses. "Huh. You're right. I never noticed, but I hardly ever shoot people." She frowns a little, then shakes her head. "Whatever. People are hard. Besides, Wizard Kitty is almost like a person."

"Right," I say. "A person covered in fur and claws."

She snickers. "Let me see your shots."

I hand her my photos. I took the bus downtown really early Saturday morning, before people and cars were all over the place.

I wanted some lonely shots. My first one is a wide-angle shot of the brick sidewalk on Broadway, stretching out clean and pinkish-red in the early morning light. The contrast is one crushed blue ticket stub. Then I have a close-up of black pavement where someone scattered a bunch of white petals. It made me wonder if some girl was picking the petals, saying, "He loves me . . . he loves me not . . ." or if some guy got stood up by a girl and was ripping up the flowers as he walked away.

My favorite shot is the one that's the most depressing: a woman, dressed all in black and gray, is passed out against the side of a dirty gray building. Even her pale arm looks dirty and gray, with a tattoo of a snake slithering down it. The only color in the shot is a streak of bright purple in her hair.

Marissa grabs that photo and holds it closer to her face. She gasps, a ragged sound that breaks through the murmur of other people. "That's my mom!"

CHAPTER THREE

You are hereby forbidden to shoot any scene that could be called a *cityscape*.
The world doesn't need any more of those. Look for street portraits,
with a subject that cries out to be immortalized
and a surrounding environment that compels the shot.
—*Spike McLernon's Laws of Photography*

Marissa's hand shakes as she grips the photo. "Where did you take this?" she asks, her voice shaking, too.

"Um, down by Flink's."

"*Where* by Flink's?" she says, suddenly loud.

People are staring at us. Mr. Malloy heads our way.

"Um, off of Burnside and Third. You know where Flink's is." Flink's is a club in Old Town. Not a month goes by that my dad doesn't do an autopsy on some drug OD from Old Town—or Tweaker Town, as he calls it.

"I mean *which* street? *Exactly* which street?" Marissa is nearing meltdown.

"I don't remember! I think it was Burnside."

Mr. Malloy ambles up, cocking his head at us. "What's going on here?"

Marissa drops her eyes. "Nothing."

"Oh," I say. "We were, um, just talking about the homework."

"Let's see." He holds out his hand.

Marissa hesitates for a second, then hands him the photo of her . . . ohmygod *her mom?* I hand him the rest of my shots.

"Gritty," Mr. Malloy remarks, glancing through them. He reaches for Marissa's photos and examines them. "Pretty," he says. "You two are predictable. I'm going to call you the Pretty-Gritty Team."

I give him a fake smile. Marissa's gaze fastens on the photo of her mom, and as soon as Mr. Malloy walks away, she takes it out of my hand. "*Where* on Burnside?" she whispers. "Tell me exactly."

"Marissa, I told you. I don't remember." I stare at her while she stares at the photo. I want to say something, but I can only think of veryveryvery lame phrases. *Sorry?*

"What day was this?"

"Saturday. Early."

Her eyes fill up with tears, and her lips tremble like a little kid's. On a scale of good reasons to cry, Marissa's reason suddenly outranks Shannon's ten to one. I pat her arm a couple of times. She keeps her head down for a while until she gets herself under control.

I have an overwhelming urge to study the photo of the woman passed out against the wall—*Marissa's mom?*—but I don't want to take it out of her hand. Besides, I can picture it in my head. The woman's face was mostly obscured by her straggly mud-colored hair, except for that bright purple streak in it. But the snake tattoo on her arm shows up clearly in the photo. That must be how Marissa recognized her.

Marissa sits for the rest of the hour like she's in a trance. She hardly moves while Mr. Malloy talks about light and shadow. He makes us write down the word "chiaroscuro" and tells us our homework is to look it up and write a paragraph about how to use it. Then, one at a time, he looks at everyone's homework photos. I can hear him murmuring comments to people, like, "Try a slow synchro next time" and "Good depth of field." Since he's already looked at our photos, he doesn't stop by Marissa and me.

When the bell rings, I figure Marissa will want to ask me more questions, but she just grabs her stuff and jets out of the classroom. She still has my photo, but I don't want it now, anyway.

I'm standing at my locker getting out my Spanish book when I see Marissa heading for the door.

"Mariss!" I slam my locker shut and catch up to her. "Where are you going?"

"I have to go down there," she says. She doesn't need to explain where "down there" is.

"But that was two days ago! She won't be there anymore," I say, baffled.

"She might. When she crashes, she sometimes sleeps for days." Her heartbroken eyes bore into mine for a long moment before she turns away.

. . . . .

Shannon has soccer practice after school—roughly forty-seven thousand times a week, plus one or two games thrown in to mix it up. But as I'm heading for Ottomans with Riley, she catches up to me.

"Ms. Faraci had some last-minute emergency," she says. "She called off practice for today."

"Great!" I say.

"Later," mumbles Riley, dropping his skateboard and stepping on, heavy backpack and all. He pushes off, rolling down the sidewalk.

"She's going to kick our asses at practice tomorrow," says Shannon.

"She *said* that?"

"No!" She giggles.

At Ottomans, the beanbag chair that looks like a giant soccer ball is free. We juggle our milkshakes while we squish in together. Ottomans is a shop near school that sells drinks and snacks. It's not the cheapest place around, but it's ours. Not many adults want to sit on beanbags, footstools, or ottomans. All of the tables are low to the ground, too.

I love the feel of Shannon against me. I love her pretty round kneecaps poking out of her baggy shorts.

I love the way her long hair grazes my arm like feathers. It's shiny and soft, and seems to glow with every shade of blond you can think of.

I love her belly laugh. We laugh a lot when we're together.

We met over the summer, both of us working as "coaches" for the kids' day camps at the community center. Mornings we spent doing arts and crafts or playing various ball games with six-year-olds. Tuesday and Thursday afternoons were swim days. I'd seen Shannon around school last year, but she's kind of quiet, so I didn't know her very well. But when I saw her laughing and splashing in the pool in her little black bikini, I had a sudden urge to get to know her *very* well.

Shannon squirms around in the beanbag, trying not to spill her shake, her hard hipbones moving against me. I'm still getting used to being this close to her. I can practically count the cinnamon sprinkle of freckles across her cheekbones.

Shannon's cell phone rings. She hands me her shake while she pulls the cell out of her pocket. "Dang," she says, checking the display. "It's my mom."

"How does she know you don't have practice?"

"I don't know! She's spooky." She flips open the phone. "Hi, Mom." Pause. "Oh. It was canceled." Shannon widens her eyes at me and pretends to smack her forehead. Apparently her mom didn't know practice was canceled; she just called to leave a message.

"Right now? Why?" says Shannon, shifting her delicious weight against me. I feel like groaning. She's practically in my lap. Little Guido is waking up in my boxers. "Oh," she says. "Okay. I will."

She hangs up. Her grandma is in the hospital, and they need to go visit her, blah blah blah. "Sorry, big fella," she says with a little sigh against my neck, then wrestles her way out of the bean-bag. "Do you want us to drop you at home?"

"Uh . . . no. I'll call Garrett." Shannon's mom makes me nervous, and besides, I'm not going home yet.

She gathers up her stuff. "I'll call you later." She gives me a quick kiss, and I watch her walk away.

I flip open my cell and hold down 4 until it auto-dials Garrett.

"Studly. What?" he says.

"Can you drive me downtown?" I ask.

"No." I can hear jock talk and metal music in the background.

"Garrett, come on. I need to go downtown."

"Why?"

"It's important."

"Blake, I'm busy," he says.

I sigh. "Fine. And hey, Garrett? Could you make sure to keep crushing my spirit under your boots of indifference?"

A moment of silence. "You've already used that line, man."

"Oh. All right, see you later."

I walk to the bus stop. I really don't want to ride the bus downtown for thirty minutes and wander around with this hulking backpack weighing me down, but I can't stop thinking about Marissa.

She had to know that she wasn't going to find her mom still passed out on the sidewalk in broad daylight two days later. Even if her mom does sleep for days after she crashes, some policeman would have called the drunk wagon by now.

Oh my God. What if her mom was not just passed out in that photo, but *dead?* I never stopped to consider that before. What kind of cold, heartless bastard would stand around taking pictures of a body lying on the ground without even checking to see if the person was alive? What if she'd had a seizure or something and just needed an ambulance?

The rest of the way, I worry about being a heartless bastard. I get off the bus at Burnside and start walking. Within two blocks I am offered an assortment of contraband: chiva, jelly, Tina, and ice. Don't ask *me*—I'm not even sure what they are. I'm kind of surprised no one tries to sell me any plain old weed. On the third block, heading my way, I see a scary-looking woman with bulging eyes and a short skirt. I cross the street. Flink's is on the corner of Third, and I head in that direction. As I pass the public men's room at the edge of Fountain Park, I smell puke. Nice.

I walk around for probably an hour, but I never see Marissa. I stand at the bus stop waiting to go home. It's rush hour now, so people in business suits and students from the culinary college are waiting at the bus stop, too. It's more comforting to have people around when the gutter punks start asking for spare change. I give away all of my change except for what I need to ride the bus home. My dad tells me never to give street people money, but sometimes it just seems easier. I know they're ninety-nine percent definitely turning right around and using the money to buy their next hit, but what about that one percent that maybe really does just want to buy food? I know there are missions and places where they can get free meals, but what if they're really in the mood for a bacon cheeseburger?

. . . . .

My mom is playing the piano when I get home. It's all heavy downer chords, like we're at a funeral. I swerve away from the living room. She always plays that song when she's in a bad mood. Since my mom is a hospital chaplain, even though she's around living people most of the time, she's frequently with people *when* they die. It's kind of weird, in a way, that my mom spends time helping people die . . . and my dad spends time figuring out *how* people died. You would think my parents would be the most depressing people on earth. But they're not, they're both pretty cool.

After trolling around downtown for so long, I feel filthy. I head upstairs to take a shower while Mom is pounding on the piano. The Dog Formerly Known as Prince follows me. Even he must be feeling bummed out by the song.

When I finish showering and go downstairs, Mom is sitting at the kitchen table doing a crossword puzzle. Something that smells good—like garlic and onions—is simmering on the stove.

"Hi, honey!" she says, perfectly cheerful. "How was your day?"

"Good." I grab a bag of Chex mix and start munching. I love that my mom never says, "Don't eat that now, you'll spoil your dinner." She understands that sometimes you're just starving and you have to eat right then.

Dad comes in the back door, his hair bushed up like Albert Einstein. He ploinks the ear buds out of his ears, and leans over to kiss Mom. "Smells good in here," he says.

"It's just a so-awse," Mom says, putting on her best Bronx accent. She frowns slightly at Dad.

"What?" he says.

"Did you have a stinky decomp today?" asks Mom. A stinky decomp is a corpse that has started, you know, decomposing.

"Ohhh, I did! Sorry, I'll go shower." Dad hands me his iPod. "Check out the new Gingerfred," he says, and lopes away. He prides himself on being all hip to the new music. He doesn't know that he's always about six months behind, God love him.

Suddenly my throat feels tight, like I might cry.

My parents seem like a miracle.

CHAPTER FOUR

When wearing camera on neck strap, avoid entanglements.
—*Mitsu ProShot I.S. 5.3 camera guide, 2007*

"That chick is not a dog," Garrett says.

"What?" We're Marauding to school, and we just drove into KWST range. A moldy oldie is playing "Lips Like Sugar" by Echo and the Bunnymen, and I'm zoning out, thinking that Shannon's lips *are* like sugar.

"That chick on the radio," says Garrett. "I saw her yesterday. She's not a dog."

"Oh. See? I told you."

"In fact, she's kind of smokin'."

"Yeah?"

"Yeah. I don't know why. Just—" Garrett lifts his hands from the steering wheel for a second, as if fondling an invisible female. "Something about her."

Thus ends our discussion on women for the day.

"Scrof, what are you doing?" snaps Garrett.

"Wha—? Nothing. And what's scrof?"

"Looks like you're getting ready to open that granola bar in my car. Don't." He stops at a red light. "Short for scrofulous. I shouldn't have to explain every damn word to you."

"I'm starving!" I slept through my alarm this morning and didn't have time for breakfast. "I'll be really careful."

"Do not. Eat. In my car."

I shove the granola bar back into my pocket.

·····

When I walk into English, I fully expect to see Marissa huddled in the big chair in Moody Corner. But the chair is empty. I turn to look at Marissa's desk. Empty. I walk slowly to my own desk.

"What's wrong?" says Shannon. "You've got a funny look on your face."

Oh, I was wondering if Marissa is okay, is my first response. It gets shot down by Houston, landing harmlessly in my brain's trash can. Am I allowed to worry about other girls? Besides, then I would have to explain why I'm worried, and I don't want to tell Shannon about Marissa's mom. That's nobody's business.

"I was thinking about *Dracula,*" I say.

"What about it?"

"About how, uh, it was like, the first horror story." *Lame.* I'm not even sure that's true. I wait for her to call me on it.

She doesn't. "Oh. Hey, did you start your journal last night?"

"No. I forgot." In *Dracula,* they were always writing these long-ass letters to each other, which is how the author advanced the plot. See, I do pay attention in class. Anyway, Mr. Hamilton wants us to keep a journal or write letters—*epistles* (heh)—in the journal. With a *pen* instead of on the computer. Come on, man! George even asked yesterday if we could just do blogs or vlogs instead, but Mr. H. wouldn't go for that.

I glance at the door. The bell hasn't rung yet, so Marissa might still show up. I hope everything is okay.

· · · · ·

Shannon has an appointment with some ass kicking, I mean *soccer practice* after school, so I head over to Ottomans for a smoothie by myself. Bree, one of Marissa's friends, is standing in line in front of me.

"Hey, Bree," I say.

She turns. "Hey," she says uncertainly. We don't really know each other.

"Have you heard from Marissa?"

"What?" Bree stares.

"Just that . . . she was absent today, and I was wondering if, you know, she's sick or something." I pause, then add, "We're in photo together. I'm Blake."

"Oh, right. Blake. Yeah, I talked to her last night. She's sick." The line moves forward, and Bree turns away to place her order.

After I order, I join Bree at the waiting-for-your-drink area. "Did she say when she's coming back?" I ask.

Bree studies me, frowning. "No."

Did you know about her mom? I want to ask. *Is that why she lives with her grandma?*

But maybe Bree didn't know.

We wait for our drinks in awkward silence, then Bree grabs her cup and leaves.

· · · · ·

No one is home yet at my house, so I save the world from aliens a few times with my Extermination game on the Mindbender. Then I zone in front of the tube, munching a mix of cheese-and-caramel popcorn, my favorite. After channel-surfing through nothing but mind-numbing junk for almost an hour, I realize that I'd rather do my homework than zombie out in front of the TV any longer. My mom is right: we have two-hundred-plus channels of crap available 24/7.

I stare at a blank piece of notebook paper for a long time, trying to think of something to write for Mr. Hamilton's dumb-ass journal assignment.

All I can think to write is, *Dear Marissa, I hope you're okay. I hope your mom is okay.*

Finally I give up and decide to do my photo homework: "Define the word *chiaroscuro,* and suggest ways to implement the effect."

I walk over to the desk to look in the dictionary, and I find myself digging through the stack of phone books instead. One of them is for West Park High students. I flip to the F's: Marissa Fairbairn. Her grandma's name is listed below hers: Mary Stanmore. Hey. Mary . . . Marissa . . . I wonder if she was named after her grandma.

I pick up the phone to dial the number, then just stand there for a long time, trying to figure out what to say. *Hey, Marissa, how are you?*

What can her answer possibly be except "messed up"? I hang up the phone, put away the phone book, and open the dictionary to C.

· · · · ·

The next day when I walk into English, the first place I look is Marissa's desk. Empty. *The hell?* My heart starts tripping a little. Okay, maybe she really is sick. Maybe it's a female thing, really bad cramps or something. Do girls have cramps for days and days?

I go up to Mr. Hamilton, who's in the middle of greeting people. "Hey, Riley. What's up, George? Morning, Yoon. Morning, Dez. Hi, Ellie."

"Hey, Mr. H.," I say.

"Hey. How are you, Blake?"

"Good. I was wondering." I hesitate, then lean closer and lower my voice. "If you, um, know why Marissa is absent."

"No, I don't. Sorry." He gives me an apologetic look.

I spend most of English in a place far, far away. My mind does, anyway. My body sits there like a good dog. Why would Marissa be absent two days in a row unless something was really wrong? A small, sick part of me is starting to wish I'd never taken that photo of her mom passed out on the street.

KWST plays a bunch of head-banging songs during Loud Lunch that annoy the crap out of me, Riley won't shut up about some new Mindbender game, and when I get to photo, Mr. Malloy doesn't know why Marissa is absent, either.

Even Shannon's sugar lips fail to distract me the rest of the day. In fact, I'm kind of glad she has soccer practice today.

I stop at Ottomans for a smoothie, then head for the bus stop. Half a block from the stop, I find myself veering into a phone booth. I flip through the falling-apart phone book till I get to the S's. Luckily, there are only five Stanmores listed: Gina, John, M, Wm, and Wyatt.

M for Mary. "M. Stanmore" is on 521 Azalea Road. I go back into Ottomans, muttering, "Five two one Azalea." I find an empty WiFi and Google Map the address. It's only about a mile and a half from here.

Feeling sleuthlike, I head for a different bus stop. It's a short ride to the right neighborhood and a two-block walk to Azalea.

As I approach 521, I see a woman in the front yard. She's kneeling on one of those foam rubber garden things that's supposed to keep your knees from hurting while you work, and there's a pile of weeds next to her. But she's not working; she's just sitting there staring off into space. I check the address on the house against the piece of paper—yep, it's 521. She looks the right age to be Marissa's grandmother, too.

I walk closer; she still doesn't notice me. Finally I move into her line of vision and say, "Um, Mrs. Stanmore?"

She jumps a little. "Yes?"

"Sorry. I didn't mean to scare you. I was just wondering if Marissa's home."

The woman puts her hands on the metal grips of the garden thing and pushes herself to her feet. "Yes." She takes off her sunglasses, and I see that her eyes have big shadows under them and the same heartbroken look that Marissa's eyes have. Must be hereditary. "Who may I tell her is calling?"

"Oh. My name is Blake. We know each other from school."

Marissa's grandma gives me a small smile. "Hello, Blake. I'm Mary. Nice to meet you." She glances at the front door, as if deciding whether or not to invite me in. Then she nods and walks up the front steps. She opens the screen door, waiting for me to follow her inside.

I stand awkwardly while Marissa's grandma goes into the hallway, calling, "Marissa, honey, there's someone here to see you." She turns the corner, and I hear her saying, "His name is Blake."

I wait, afraid Marissa is going to shuffle out, her eyes all red and swollen from crying. Or what if she's all bruised up from getting mugged in Old Town? Maybe that's why she hasn't been to school. Or worse, what if she's really pissed that I tracked her down and just showed up at her house without calling first?

But Marissa comes into the room beaming and glowing. "Hi!" she says. "What are you doing here?"

She looks so happy that I feel stupid saying, "I was worried when you weren't at school."

"Ohhh."

We stand there for a minute while we try to adjust to the weirdness of me standing in her living room; then Marissa says, "Want something to drink?"

"No." Pause. "Well, okay. Just some water." Sleuthing is thirsty work.

She leads the way into the kitchen and pours me a glass of water and herself a glass of iced tea. Then she opens a cupboard and brings out a bag of cookies. "That's so sweet that you were worried."

"Well." I wait for her to sit down. "Last time I saw you, you were kind of . . ." I let the sentence trail off.

"Oh, right. God, that seems like a year ago. I can't believe it was only three days." She munches a cookie. "I found my mom."

I stare. "You're kidding. Was she . . . was she still there?" I'm horrified to picture Marissa's mom passed out in the street for all that time.

"No! Not where you took the picture. But she was in Old Town. I found her." Marissa looks so proud.

"Where is she now?" I glance down the hallway.

"She's in the family room. Do you want to meet her?"

No, I think. "That's okay," I say.

"No, really," she says, straightening up. "In fact, it's thanks to you that I found her. I want her to meet you."

I shrug. What if *I* don't want to meet *her?*

"Also, it's thanks to you that she's going into rehab."

"What?"

"She was saying she wasn't going to go into rehab. Then I showed her that picture you took. How could anyone look at that picture and say they don't have a problem?"

"Oh." I gulp some water. "That's good."

Marissa stands up. "She's, um, she's having a really hard time right now."

"Okay."

"She's not going to rehab until Saturday. They didn't have a bed open till then. It's a thirty-day program. So she's just having a really hard time."

"You know, I don't have to meet her right now." I stand up, too.

"No, it's okay. I just wanted to warn you."

Oh crap, I really don't want to do this. What was I thinking, stalking Marissa all the way to her house and barging in during the middle of this thing with her mom?! I just wanted to see if she was okay. Now I want to leave.

I follow Marissa down the hall to a big room where there's a TV playing, and two big couches, and shelves full of books and DVDs and games.

"Mom?" she says.

A figure huddled on the couch turns, and I have to force myself not to gasp.

CHAPTER FIVE

Whatever disrupts a pattern will get your attention.
—*Spike McLernon's Laws of Photography*

The woman on the couch is so skinny that she could be mistaken for a child. She sits up, clutching a blanket around her shoulders. The purple streak in her hair looks out of place, like a flag on a desert island.

"Mom," says Marissa gently.

The woman seems to shrink inside the blanket, her eyes cast down.

"This is my friend Blake. From school. You know, the guy I told you about? The one who took the photo?"

Marissa's mom looks up at me then, her eyes huge and haunted. Oh shit. She's crying now. She stands up, the blanket falling off her shoulders, and takes a step in my direction.

She looks so fragile, like she might fall, that I move toward her, holding out my hand.

"I'm so glad to meet you," says Marissa's mom, and takes my hand in both of her bird-bone hands.

"Me, too," I say. She's standing still, but her whole body is fluttery and jangly as she holds my hand.

"I'm—" she says. "I'm sorry you saw me like that."

"Oh," I say. Now that she's close to me, I can see a tattoo on the side of her neck, slithering down into her shirt. Whatever it's supposed to be, it's got claws. How much would it frickin' hurt to get your *neck* tattooed? Her breath is fairly rank.

"I'm going to get help. I really don't want to be like this anymore." Tears keep running down her face, and I feel like running for the door. I've never been in a situation like this, and it's clear that I suck at comforting people.

Hey, wait. My mom does this all day every day. I picture my mom comforting this woman, and I say, "I'm sure you're going to be okay."

She grips my hand harder and says intensely, "Thank God you were there that day. Thank God you took that photo. Marissa came looking for me, and now I'm going to get help. Thank you."

I nod. I'm ready to take my hand back, but it seems rude to pull it out of her grasp. Luckily, she seems to have finished. She drops my hand. Next to me, I hear Marissa exhale.

So.

Okay.

Now what? Usually, uncomfortable silences are my cue to crack a joke. But I have never felt less like joking in my life.

But we're all standing there like people waiting for the light to turn green or something. My monkey mind flings a piece-of-shit joke at me, and I catch it gratefully: "I'd better be getting home so I can polish my Good Samaritan badge now."

Marissa and her mom laugh. Except . . . oh no. Marissa's mom is missing a tooth. Wait. Make that teeth. Two of them.

You heard me. *Teeth.* The one right next to the top front teeth, and the one next to that. What are those called? Cuspids? Bicuspids? Cuspidors? Whatever. There are two of them no longer residing in her mouth.

Okay. It is definitely time to go. "It was nice meeting you, Mrs. Fairbairn."

"Anne."

"Anne. See you later," I say. Good God, she's crying again. I mentally subtract my joke from today's score. Oh well, it *was* a piece of shit. I head for the hallway.

"Thanks, Blake," Marissa says when we reach the living room. "That was really nice of you." She adds, *again,* "She's having a really hard time right now."

"Sure." I look longingly at the front door.

"The doctor told us that people going through meth withdrawal—"

I gulp.

"They don't go through physical withdrawal, like people on heroin. But they feel really sad. They don't feel *normal* without meth, you know what I mean?"

"Wow." *What about her teeth?* I want to ask. "So are you coming to school tomorrow, or what?"

Marissa makes a face. "My grandma told me I have to go. I hate to leave my mom right now, but I can't stay home again. I'm just so happy to have her back that I don't want to let her out of my sight."

"Really? How long since—?" I stumble and stop. *How long since you've seen your mom?* sounds weird.

But Marissa seems to know what I was about to say. "I haven't seen my mom in almost a year."

"Oh."

"She was living in Seattle for a while. She came back to Portland about three or four months ago, she told me. But she didn't come see us. Because, well, she wasn't thinking straight."

Your mom left you for a year? I think. *But you don't want to leave her for a few hours?* "Well, I guess I'll see you tomorrow, then," I say. I cross the room and open the front door.

"Hey, Blake? Um, could you not—" She pauses.

"I won't tell anyone," I say.

She smiles, relieved. "Bye," she says, turning back to the family room.

Marissa's grandmother is out front, sitting on the porch swing. "Nice to meet you, Blake," she says.

"You, too." I hurry down the steps and glance back from the sidewalk. Marissa's grandma is staring off into space again with her heartbroken eyes.

· · · · ·

42

Dad is in the garage when I get home, sitting on a stool with wheels, peering down at some greasy piece of metal. He's got his bushy hair pulled back in a bandanna, and he's muttering, "I can't believe this gasket doesn't fit the crankcase." He looks up at me with a puzzled look. "The manufacturer sent me the wrong gasket. Can you believe it?" Then his gaze sharpens, and he pushes his glasses up. "Hey, funny man. What's up?"

I must have a stunned look on my face or something. "Nothing." I pretend to take an interest in the pieces of . . . engine? . . . on the worktable in front of him. "What are you doing?"

"Oh, this? I'm trying to fix a lawn tractor."

"A lawn tractor? We don't have a lawn tractor. Do we?" My dad is notorious for picking up junk at garage sales and buying stuff off craigslist. So it's possible that we do have a lawn tractor now.

"No, Neil's lawn tractor blew a gasket, and he asked me to help." Neil is our neighbor, and you only have to look at him to know that he would never be able to fix a lawn tractor. Metro (cough)sexual. My dad is studying me now instead of the greasy part. "You okay, man?"

"Yeah. I'm fine. Where's Mom?"

"She had to work late tonight. How about Thai food?"

"Sounds good. I'm going to take a shower."

"Okay. See you in a minute."

I head for the door. Then I turn back and try to ask as casually as possible, "Hey, Dad?"

"Yeah, bud."

"What makes people's teeth fall out when they use meth?"

My dad blinks. "Oh. Well, actually, we're not really sure what causes meth mouth." He takes off his glasses to polish them, then puts them back on and studies me. "Why do you ask?"

I could say, "No reason," and keep moving. But I answer, "I saw someone whose teeth are messed up. I've heard she uses meth."

"A student?"

I shake my head.

Dad slips into Dr. Hewson mode. "Well, one theory is that the abuse of stimulants like methamphetamine causes a cessation in saliva production. Dry mouth. Saliva aids in breaking down bacteria in the mouth. If you don't have saliva, the bacteria build up. See the connection?"

"Yep." I nod and go inside the house.

.............CHAPTER SIX.............

<u>Chiaroscuro:</u>
It's an Italian word, so I plan to use it casually in a sentence next time
I talk to my grandparents. It literally means "lightdark," and in photography
it means using both elements in one composition. I plan to experiment
with darkened rooms and directed angles of light to achieve chiaroscuro.
I would also like to try shooting a photo of the full white moon through
black tree branches on a clear night, if I can figure out the shutter speed.
—*Blake Hewson, homework, Photo II*

"I saw your brother with a girl yesterday," says Riley, skidding to a stop in front of me. He grabs his skateboard and stuffs it in his pack before a teacher can show up to accuse him of skating on school grounds.

I'm standing with Shannon and her friends before the first bell. "Yeah?" I say. "Has she been blind since birth or did she lose her eyesight when she looked at him?"

"Oh, stop!" says Shannon. "You know your brother's got that scholar-jock thing going on. Brains *and* brawn."

I give her a betrayed look while Jasmine and Kaylee giggle, and Shannon adds, "But he's not funny like you are!"

"He *is* totally cute, though," chimes in Jasmine, giggling some more.

"I don't think he's that cute," says Kaylee.

"So who was she?" I ask Riley. "This scholar-jock-loving girl."

"It's that new girl. The one who moved here from Oklahoma."

I must look clueless, because he continues, "On the radio? Calls herself Bitch Trickster or something?"

"What does she look like?" I'm remembering Garrett's detailed description: not a dog.

"She's okay. Streaky hair, not too tall, not too short. Kind of skinny."

"Huh." That's new for Garrett. He's a curves guy. "Give me something to grab *on* to," I've heard him leer.

"Where did you see them?" asks Kaylee.

"It was late yesterday," says Riley. "Garrett was coming out of auto shop, and Cappie—that's her real name—was coming out of the radio station. I was waiting for Carter."

"Who's Carter?" asks Kaylee. Why is she so red all of a sudden?

"My brother. He's in Radio Club, too."

"Is he the one with the funny T-shirts?"

Riley nods. "Yep." He hardly looks at Kaylee; he's busy telling his story. "So this Cappie chick says something to Garrett and he walks over to her, and they start yakking like they're old pals."

"Cappie?" I say. "That's her name?"

"I guess."

"Is she a captain?"

Everyone laughs. Points!

"So they were talking," I say. "So what?" Verbal intercourse. Where's the intrigue?

"Then she kissed him," says Riley.

· · · · ·

As soon as we drive into KWST range the next morning, I turn to Garrett. "So."

He keeps driving.

Let's see. How shall I go about messing with my brother today? "I like the stuff they've been doing at KWST."

Nothing.

"That new girl really adds something."

Not even a grunt.

Wait. Is that a millimeter of a smile? One thing I can say about Garrett is that he doesn't kiss and tell.

"Why are you getting all up in my business?" Garrett asks, then adds, "Studly. That reminds me. I've been meaning to tell you."

"What."

"I've been hearing how you're all over your girlfriend like a desperate housewife."

"What?!"

"Yeah, man. In between classes, during lunch, after school at Ottomans . . . you're constantly pressing the flesh."

Is it wrong that this makes me feel the tiniest bit proud? My moves have been getting some play. "Whatever," I say. "Like it's anyone's business."

"It's *my* business if I have to be shamed by your pathetic puppy dog thing."

Okay, now I'm mad. Who does he think he is to judge my style? I'm getting a reputation as a hotblooded stallion while he's Scholar Jock Man. "Jealous much?" I ask.

"Jealous?" He starts laughing. "Listen, Ass-wipe, I'm going to let you in on a little secret. Girls don't like it when you're too much into them."

This is so untrue it almost hurts me to correct him. "Garrett," I say kindly. "Yes. They do. Girls *do* like you to be way into them. Trust me. The more into them you are, the happier they are. There's no such thing as *too much* into them."

"Yeah. You're an expert now. One chick takes pity on you, and all of a sudden you're giving *me* advice about women!" Garrett shakes his head. "Haven't you ever heard the phrase 'too much in the sun'?"

"Wha—?"

"It's from *Hamlet*."

"And it means?"

"Figure it out, man." Garrett turns up the radio.

· · · · ·

48

Marissa smiles when I walk into English. I nod. It's a relief to see her back at school. Now I can stop worrying about her and get on with my life.

I sneak glances at Marissa a couple of times during class. Looking at her, you would never guess that her mom is a meth head. Marissa is cute and clean and gets good grades. *Normal.* I guess that's due to her grandma. Props to Grandma Mary!

Shannon has some club meeting at lunch today . . . Music Club, maybe? . . . so Riley and George and I get up a game of cards. I like having a GF, but I like having things the way they used to be, too. Spending some quality time with my boys. Seems like I'm supposed to spend all of my breaks and lunch with Shannon now.

Mr. Malloy writes a date on the board at the beginning of photo class: <u>March 12.</u> "Third Thursday Gallery is sponsoring this year's photo contest," he says. "It's not until March, so you've got plenty of time to compile your best work."

Then—I am so not kidding—he looks right at me and says, "Plenty of time to improve and polish your work."

Burn!

No one else seems to notice, though, so I just stare down at my desk while blood gushes into my head and heats up my face. I glance at Marissa. She does a little sympathetic thing with her lips. *She* noticed.

"Every student who enters the contest will have an opportunity to show their work at the gallery for one night," Mr. Malloy goes on. "The winner will have a month-long showing at Third

Thursday. If the winner chooses to offer his or her photos for sale, the gallery will suggest a price range."

Marissa and I look at each other.

"Are you going to enter this year?" she asks.

"Why? Apparently I suck too much."

"Come on. He didn't mean anything."

"He said, 'Improve and polish, or DIE, *Blake.*'"

She laughs.

"He said, 'People will turn away in revulsion and vomit into their shoes, *Blake.*'"

"Shush. Let's enter," says Marissa. "I will if you will."

"Fine," I say. "I'll show Beret Boy 'improve and polish.'"

· · · · ·

Garrett's car is in the driveway when I get home, but he's nowhere to be seen. His bedroom door is closed and music pulses behind it. Wait. Is that a voice? Is he talking to himself in there?

I'm sprawled on the couch, channel-surfing and scarfing down my special blend of cheese-and-caramel popcorn when I feel the hair on the back of my neck prickle.

There's a girl standing in the doorway.

"Whoa!" I yell, and the popcorn goes flying. I sit up. "What the fuck?"

"Hi, Blake."

I can't speak, because I'm in the middle of a heart attack. Finally I manage to answer. "Who are you?"

"Cappie." She's barefoot, with long, tan legs and short black hair with blond streaks in it. "Can I have some?" She moves closer and points to the half-spilled bowl of popcorn.

"Sure."

She grabs a handful and munches it, then plops down next to me on the couch.

"Um, yeah. Won't you sit down?" I ask. She's way too close for someone I just met and almost shit myself in front of.

"What's on?" She grabs the remote and starts flipping channels. *Bold*. That's a dangerous move . . . taking a dude's remote.

"Where's Garrett?" I ask.

She doesn't answer for a moment, and I stare at her. She's got some killer green eyes. "Who?" she says.

Blink. Blink. "My brother. The guy who lives here."

She munches more popcorn. "Oh, that's right. Garrett. I call him Caveman."

"*Cave*man?"

"Mm-hm. He's so big and strong, he could drag me away by my hair."

Riiiight. We sit there in silence for a minute, because really, what kind of thing is that to say? There's no answer to it. Finally I say, "And where is, uh, Caveman?"

"Asleep."

"Asleep." *What did you do to him,* I think, *that he's passed out in the middle of the day? And can you teach Shannon how to do it?*

"Well, just FYI," I say, "his name is Garrett. Garrett Hewson."

"Hewson? As in Paul Hewson?"

"Uh . . . ?"

"That's Bono's real name. Don't tell me no one's ever told you that before!"

"Oh, right," I say. "Uncle Paul. We like to keep that quiet."

She smirks at me and grabs some more popcorn.

After a couple minutes of watching TV in silence, I ask, "So are you that new DJ?"

"Chick Trickster. Yes."

"Cool. So how did you meet Garrett?"

"I like to think of it as fate." She stands up, and I realize I don't want her to go. She's weirdly fascinating. "Wait. Where are you going?"

"Do you have anything to drink around here?" She heads for the kitchen like she's lived here all her life. I hear the refrigerator door open. "Oh, good. Beer."

I leap off the couch. If my parents come home and find some strange girl chugging brews in their house, we will *all* suffer the punishment of a thousand lectures. I stumble into the kitchen, where I find Cappie pouring herself a glass of milk. She grins, raises the glass in my direction, and drinks. I grin back and pretend to clutch my heart.

"Listen, Blake," says Cappie.

"Yes?"

"Consider your lips sealed."

"Huh?"

"This was just a play date. A free hookup." She drinks the rest of her milk, then says, "I don't date jocks. So your brother and I are not going to be the new cute couple on campus. I don't want you telling people I was here."

I stare at her. She doesn't blink, and finally I say, "Fine. Like anyone cares."

"Great!" She swoops past me, brushing my arm lightly.

"Hey, where is everyone?" I hear Garrett calling.

I hear nails clicking on the floor, and The Dog Formerly Known as Prince appears in the kitchen. He must have been in the room with Garrett and Cappie. He looks surprised.

··········· CHAPTER SEVEN ···········

I really believe there are things nobody would see
if I didn't photograph them.
—*Diane Arbus, American photographer (1923–1971)*

I saw my first dead body when I was nine.

Not the whole body. Just the elbow. I'm not even sure if it was a man or a woman, because it was covered up, chilling in the cold room. One of the arms was sticking out a little, so the body must still have been stiff. (They stop being stiff after a while.)

Dad has always been so, you know, *blunt* about corpses that I wasn't even freaked out. It's like growing up with a doctor—they'll talk about things at the dinner table that would make most people run out of the room with their hands over their ears. My dad is a doctor, too, of course. But his patients are, um, metabolically challenged.

I remember the day when I saw The Elbow. My dad needed to stop by his office, and Garrett and I were with him. He told us we could wait in the car, but we wanted to go with him. He led us through the big tiled "cutting" room, which was empty, and past the sliding glass door of the "cold" room, which was not.

We got really quiet after that.

Dad grabbed what he needed from his office and introduced us to some coworkers, and we were out of there in less than five minutes.

"You guys okay?" he asked once we were in the car.

"Yeah," said Garrett.

"Blake?"

"Yeah," I said unconvincingly. Maybe I was a *little* freaked out.

"Did it seem weird, going through the back way?" he asked.

"Yeah," we both mumbled.

"You know what my job is, right?"

This is kind of embarrassing. I remember I started crying.

I remember wishing my dad had a normal job.

My dad opened his car door and came around to the back seat. He opened the door and got into the back seat with me.

Garrett was trying to look like a tough guy, like "Jeez, that Blake, what a baby." But I remember that he looked a little squicked-out, too. My dad put his arm around my shoulders and said, "You know what, guys?"

"What," I snorfled.

"I think it will help if you guys think of me as the last doctor these people go to. It's my job to find answers for them, even if they're not around to know about it. If someone did something to hurt them, even *kill* them, it's my job to find the evidence so the police can catch that person. Or if someone died mysteriously, it's my job to find out how. Once I know the answer, the dead person's loved ones can have peace of mind."

Right then I stopped wishing my dad had a normal job and decided he had the coolest job ever.

Not that *I* want to be a medical examiner. But I'm glad he does, because he's wicked smart.

So today is Sunday. Mom has informed me that I can accompany her to work and study in her office while she gives a sermon in the hospital chapel, or I can go with Dad.

"Mom! What am I, five years old?"

I can almost see her putting on her Homework Police hat. "If you'd done your homework yesterday, my friend, we wouldn't be having this conversation." She raises her eyebrows at me. "You'll get more studying done away from the TV and the Mindbender."

Gee, thanks. Trust me much?

To review: my choices are dying people and their sad relatives . . . or dead people down the hall.

It's not even close . . . the dead people rock.

"How come Garrett gets to stay home?" I ask.

Before my mom can answer, Garrett pipes up, "Studly, I'm coming with you."

You heard me: Garrett doesn't have to come. He *likes* it there.

He is just that twisted. I have never watched an autopsy. Hi, can you say *morbid?* Not only has Garrett watched a bunch—he wants to learn how to be a *diener.* That's what they call the morgue attendants—it's pronounced *dee-ner.* I love that word because it means "servant" in German. Those wacky medical examiners!

When we get to Dad's office, Garrett grabs the bottle of Dead Guy Ale from Dad's shelf and pretends to chug it, like he always does. I snag some candy from a skull candy container. My dad collects these Mexican folk art things that are used to celebrate Dia de los Muertos. You know, Day of the Dead? Doesn't everyone's dad collect that kind of thing?

I crash on Dad's beat-up old office sofa with my copy of *Dracula* while my dad goes to change clothes.

"Dad, can I watch today?" asks Garrett.

"Let me see what I've got," says my dad.

Garrett sits down at the desk and logs on to the Internet. A couple of minutes later my dad reappears. "Not right now, Garrett. It's an infant."

My dad has *some* limits.

"There's a boating accident after that. You up for that one, bud?"

"Sure."

Trying to blank out the images that go along with "boating accident," I open *Dracula* and start reading.

"Just two cases today, guys. We should be out of here in a

couple of hours," says my dad. He clomps away in his clogs. Some people wear clogs when they garden. My dad wears them when he goes cadaver diving.

About forty-five minutes later I wake up when Dad clomps back into the room.

"Ready, Garrett?" he says.

"Yeah!" Garrett logs off the Internet and jumps up.

"Dad," I say.

"Yeah, bud."

"What happened?"

He knows what I'm asking. He doesn't sugarcoat things. "Shaken baby syndrome," he answers, and walks away.

· · · · ·

Mondays used to be a slow boat ride through the bowels of hell, until I hooked up with Shannon. But now I actually look forward to Mondays, especially if I haven't seen her over the weekend. I know, right? Looking forward to *school*. But I can't wait to get there and feel her up, I mean ask about her weekend.

We kiss and cuddle on the quad for a few minutes before the first bell, then head off to our separate classes.

I'm even looking forward to English today, and not just because Shannon's in my class. This book, *Dracula*, is pretty good. Sure, it's got all this veddy British writing in it, but come on. It was written forever ago, and it still has a great creep factor. Things keep getting worse and worse for the people trying to hunt down the vampire.

When I walk into English with Shannon, I'm busy getting my stuff out and answering Riley, who just asked about my weekend, when I notice Marissa.

She has a black eye.

CHAPTER EIGHT

When you really need to fill up your frame,
there's no better lens than the fisheye.
—*Spike McLernon's Laws of Photography*

I stop in the middle of my sentence, staring. Riley turns to look where I'm looking.

"*Damn,* man, what happened to her?" he says.

I can feel my heart thumping in my chest. What *did* happen to Marissa? Wasn't her mom supposed to go to rehab this weekend? Did they have, like, a *brawl?*

Marissa glances over at me. And grins.

I look away really fast, embarrassed to be caught staring.

"Oh my God, what happened to Marissa?" asks Shannon. She turns to me for an answer.

I shrug.

"Aren't you going to go talk to her?"

I shrug again, staring hard at my desktop. Somehow I can't get out of my chair.

Shannon gets up and goes over to Marissa.

"Okay, everyone," says Mr. Hamilton, clapping his hands in his oh-good-it's-a-new-day way. "Settle in. We've got vampires to dissect. Metaphorically speaking, of course. Jasmine, good morning. Shannon, take your seat, please."

Shannon comes back to her desk and sits down. I look questioningly at her.

"Hurtle," she says.

"Hurl?"

"No. Hurtle."

"Hurdle? She was at a track meet?"

"No! Hurtle, with a *t*." Then she shakes her head at me to indicate I should shut up. Mr. H. is looking right at me. I shut up.

WTF? *Hurtle?*

I spend half the class wondering what "hurtle" stands for. I doodle on my paper:

Hork Until Real Tears Leak out of your Eyes
Hairy Underwear Risks The Loss of Ejaculation
Hurkin Unwashed Road Trout Look you in the Eye
Horny Uber Risk Takers Like Elevation

I tune back in to class, and in honor of the book under discussion, I scribble:

Horrible Unclean Renfield Takes Living things and Eats them

I sneak another look at Marissa. She seems like her usual self, despite the black eye. Not like someone has been smacking her around.

After class, I turn to Shannon. "What's hurtle?"

She looks puzzled for a second, then says, "Oh yeah. Marissa. Hurtle is . . . *you* know. That biking thing. Where they start at the top of Tower Hill and go hurtling down that steep, winding road. People crash all the time." She gathers her stuff. "Are you ready?"

I follow Shannon, then stop at the door. "Shan, I'll catch up to you in a minute. I'm just going to check in with Marissa."

"Okay." Shannon gives me a crooked smile and says, "Don't be too long." She flirts one last look over her shoulder at me as she leaves.

Huh. Not sure what to do with that. Does she mean I'll be in trouble if I talk to another girl for too long? Or that she can't stand being apart from me? I need a translator!

Marissa finishes zipping her backpack as I walk up to her. "Dude, what the hell?" I say.

"What? Oh, this. It happened during Hurtle. My grandma was *so* upset."

"But what happened? I didn't know you did that Hurtle thing."

"I've never done it before. My brother invited me to go," she says, walking into the hall. She says it as casually as she might say, "Bree and I went shopping." I've known Marissa a whole year, and she's never mentioned brothers or sisters.

"You have a brother?"

"Sure. His name's Gus."

"Really? How old is he?"

"Eighteen. He lives in a house with a bunch of other guys. He's a bike messenger. Anyway, I called him to tell him about"— she glances around at the streaming students, then lowers her voice—"our mom. I asked him if he wanted to come see her before she went to rehab, but he said no." She frowns.

We've arrived at the cafeteria. There's an awkward moment where we look at each other, then into the caf madhouse. We're supposed to go our separate ways now—me to join Shannon, Marissa to join her girls. I wish we hung with the same group. Then I could hear more about this Hurtle thing.

"Your poor eye." I can hardly stop looking at it, all the purple and green shades. I kind of want to take a picture of it.

"I know. I thought my grandma was going to cry when she saw it. And she's got enough on her mind, you know what I mean?"

"How did it happen?"

"It was at the very beginning, so I didn't even do the Hurtle. A bunch of other riders were pushing and shoving for a better spot. I was right next to them, and one of them elbowed me in the eye. *Jerk.* You wouldn't believe how many people there were."

Just then Riley bumps into my shoulder as he jogs past, calling, "Flake, you in? It's the Texas hold 'em finals today. Or do you need to join the little woman?"

"I'll see you in photo," Marissa says, and walks away to join her friends.

I enter the caf. *Do* I need to join the little woman? And do I have to ask permission to play poker?

I search the crowd for Shannon. Ah, there she is—standing with Ellie and Kaylee. What's she *doing*? The other girls are giggling while Shannon makes this face: her upper lip is pulled back weirdly above her front teeth, and she's kind of hunched over, twiddling her fingers. *What the—*

As I approach, Shannon straightens up and grins at me, her cheeks reddening.

"Hey," I say.

"Hi."

"I'm, uh, gonna go play poker with the guys today." I point to Riley's table. "Okay?"

"Sure," she says. "I'll see you later."

As I walk away, she mutters, "*Ex*-cellent."

The other girls bust out laughing.

Ahhh. She was doing Mr. Burns. Who knew my girl could do impressions, too?

· · · · ·

That afternoon at photo, I sit down next to Marissa and we pick up right where we left off. "How come I've never heard of this Hurtle thing?"

She considers. "It's kind of fringe. A bunch of bike messengers started it a couple of years ago. Nowadays anyone can show up. They start at the top of Tower Hill every Friday night and race down Laurel."

"That's so insane! Laurel is . . . what do they call it? *Hairpin* turns all the way down the hill."

"Right. And sometimes people crash, which is partly why they call it Hurtle. I mean, yeah, you're *hurtling* crazy fast, but you might also get *hurt* really bad."

"And you did."

"Phhft! This is nothing! A black eye from just *sitting* there. Stupid biker and his stupid elbow. Some people end up with broken bones and half their skin peeled off."

"Erghh. Doesn't anyone wear protective gear?"

Marissa laughs. "Listen to you, Mr. Safety First. Nah, not really. A few. The hardcore hurtlers are extreme biker types. Like my brother."

Mr. Malloy sets down the chalk and turns from the chalkboard. He looks out over the class, freezing for a moment when he sees Marissa's black eye.

She smiles, and he raises his eyebrows.

"Hurtle," she says with a shrug.

Oddly, Mr. Malloy seems to understand her immediately. "You crashed?" he asks.

She shakes her head. "No. I never made it down the hill."

"Ahh. Okay, everyone. I've written another term on the board.

'Saturation.' I want you to look up the definition and write down some ideas about how you can use saturation in your photos. We'll discuss it Friday." He starts fiddling with the overhead projector, and I whisper, "Marissa."

She looks at me.

"Can I take a picture of your eye?"

"No!" But she laughs.

"Come on," I whisper.

"*You* come on!"

"Dude, I don't get to see many black eyes up close. You look like a fighter. A tough chick."

"I *am* a tough chick."

"A tough chick would let me take a picture of her eye."

"Blake. Marissa," says Mr. Malloy. "The discussion is up here." He taps the overhead projector.

We stop talking and focus on the image on the screen. After a second I scribble a note to Marissa: *Come on.* I pass it to her, and she scribbles back, *You come on!*

I add: *I'll let you take a picture of* my *eye.*

She covers her mouth with her hand to hide her grin. After a moment she writes a longer message, then passes the note back to me: *Do you have a garden? I'll let you take a picture of my eye if you'll let me take pictures in your garden. You know I love to shoot flowers.*

I read the note and hesitate. *Do* we have flowers? I try to get a visual of our backyard. Yep, I'm pretty sure we have flowers.

Seems like my mom is always sticking some blooming thing in a vase. I write back: *It's a deal. My camera is at home. After school, I will immortalize your battle wound. Then you can shoot flowers.*

She reads the note and nods.

Cool. I can't wait to get my pixels on her face.

CHAPTER NINE

Macro photography is usually associated with nature.
—*Mitsu ProShot I.S. 5.3 camera guide, 2007*

"I don't understand," says Shannon. "You're going to take pictures of her?" We're walking to the bus stop.

"Of her eye, yeah! I can't wait! I might even do a series—you know, take pictures of it every day while it's changing colors."

"Huh. And she's going to your house?"

"Yeah. She likes to shoot flowers."

"Shoot flowers?" says Shannon.

"Take pictures of them. She's going to take pictures in our garden."

"But—"

"But what?"

Shannon shifts the straps of her backpack. "But I mean, even *I've* only been to your house once."

"You've only been—"

"I know it sounds stupid, but I'm your girlfriend, and I've

only been to your house once. Now Marissa gets to go?" Shannon's lower lip trembles a little bit.

I'm not following this at all, but she seems to be getting upset, and I can feel things moving into Not Good Land. "Wait," I say carefully. "What do you mean 'Marissa *gets* to go?' What's the big deal? You can come over to my house anytime you want."

She crosses her arms. "Uh, no I can't, Blake."

"Why not?"

Okay, now she's getting *mad* instead of sad. I'm trying to keep up.

"I was taught to wait for an *invitation* to someone's house, rather than inviting myself over."

"Oh." I feel like crossing my arms, too, and mimicking, *I was taught to myeh myeh myeh myeh myeh*. I take a deep breath. "Shannon?"

"What."

"Would you like to come to my house?"

"When? Today?"

"Sure. If you like. With Marissa and me. She won't care."

"I have soccer!"

"Blow it off."

"I can't blow off *soccer*." She looks truly appalled.

We're stuck. I'm pushing, she's pulling. The door won't budge.

"How about tomorrow?" I say.

"I've got—"

I reach out and pull her close. "I know. You've got soccer. But you also have an *open* invitation to come to my house. Okay? So if you ever want to blow off soccer and come home with me"— I put my lips close to her ear—"I would love that."

She relaxes against me. I inhale her flowers-and-rain scent. "I wish I could," she says. "You know my mom would kill me, though."

"Why?"

"She worries about us being alone together."

I squish her against me even closer. "Are *you* worried?"

She shakes her head, her hair tickling my neck.

"Forget Marissa," I say. "Why don't you and I sneak away someplace?"

Ahh! Turns out that's the right thing to say.

· · · · ·

No one is home yet when Marissa and I get to my house, so I dig my key out and unlock the door. The Dog Formerly Known as Prince dances around and whines his welcome-home song. Marissa pets him gingerly; it's clear that she's a cat person.

"What's his name?" she asks.

"Well, it used to be Prince," I explain. "We got him from the Humane Society. But he didn't seem like a Prince to us, so we decided it should be The Dog Formerly Known as Prince."

She looks blank.

"You know, like the singer?" I say. "Never mind, it's a lame family joke."

"Wow, you guys have a piano," she says. "Do you play?"

"Nah. My mom made Garrett and me take lessons, but they didn't stick. She plays, though."

"I wish I could play an instrument."

"Let's eat, I'm starving." I head for the kitchen. We power down some milk and cookies, like hungry kindergartners, and Marissa looks around the room rather than at me. She gets up to examine a photo hanging on the wall by the window over the kitchen sink— it's Garrett when he was a baby. His face is covered in some kind of orange baby food—carrots? squash?—and he's clutching a little spoon. My dad is at the edge of the frame, grinning at Garrett.

"Cute," she says. "Is that your dad?"

I nod.

"Look at his hair! It's so big and *springy*."

"Yep. It still looks the same." I munch a cookie, thinking that Marissa never talks about her dad. I'm just about to say, "What's your dad like?" when she comes back to the table and reaches for the package of cookies. "Do you mind if I take some of these?"

"Take them where?"

"For later."

"Oh. No. Take as many as you want."

She wraps up a handful of cookies in a napkin and slides them into the pocket of her backpack. *Strange.*

"Okay, tough girl. Let's get started," I say.

The walls in the kitchen are pale yellow, perfect for a neutral background. I shoot a bunch of pictures of Marissa's eye from various distances and angles, then take her outside for a few photos in natural daylight. I even attach a telephoto lens for some of them, so the bruise will really fill up the frame. These are going to be good.

Marissa borrows my camera, since hers is at home, and wanders around the backyard shooting close-ups of plants. There's not a ton of stuff blooming, since it's September, but she finds some frilly girly purple ones and a few tall white ones. She asks me for a ladder, which I'm pleased to locate in the garage—who knew?—and climbs up a few rungs to take pictures of an abandoned bird's nest in a tree. After she takes a couple of pictures of the nest, she stares at it for a minute, then takes off her rings and bracelets. She arranges the jewelry in the nest and takes photos of that.

"Do you have any glass animals?" she asks suddenly.

"What?"

"You know, little glass figures? Or ceramic. They give them away in those boxes of Red Rose tea."

I look at her blankly.

"Never mind. My grandma drinks Red Rose tea, and she saves the little ceramic figurines that come in the box. I was thinking I could put a hen or some other animal in the nest. Oh! A cat would be funny."

I have an idea. "Wait here," I say.

I go inside the house and head for my mom's desk. Sitting on the windowsill above her desk is a little ceramic angel I bought her for Mother's Day about five years ago.

I carry the ceramic angel outside to Marissa. I hold it up for her to see. "Will this work?"

She gasps and says, "Ohhhh!" She stares down at it for a moment, then reaches into her jeans pocket. She pulls out a tiny silver-gray charm. Pewter, I think it's called. "Look."

I take it from her. It's an angel.

"Whoa," I say, and hum the *Twilight Zone* music. "Do you always carry this around?" I examine it more closely. Engraved on the back of the angel's wings is a word: KAT.

"Kat?"

She doesn't answer, and I glance up at her.

Her eyes . . . they've got that heartbroken look really bad right now. "Um, I don't feel like talking about that. But yeah, I always carry my angel around with me." She holds her hand out for the charm, and I give it back to her. She puts it in her pocket.

"Here," I say. "You can use this one for your photo." I hold out the ceramic angel.

"Maybe we better not."

"Why?"

"I'm scared I might drop it."

"Just be careful. Here."

She takes it out of my hand and positions it as carefully as if the fate of the world rested on that angel being safe in the nest. Then she zooms in and out, trying various distances for effect.

"Hello," calls my mom from the back door. "What's up?"

Marissa jumps so hard the ladder shakes.

"Easy!" I say.

"Oh, no! Is that your mom? She's going to be mad!"

I steady the ladder. "What? No, she won't."

"We took her angel!"

"It's okay. Hi," I call back to Mom.

"Oh. A girl is what's up," says my mom. "What are you guys doing?"

"Taking pictures."

"I see." She comes outside and squints up at Marissa. "Hi. I'm Benita."

"Nice to meet you," says Marissa. "I'm Marissa." She giggles at the awkwardness of her position and comes down the ladder to shake Mom's hand.

"Don't stop what you're doing on my account," says my mom.

"No, we're finished," says Marissa. "Blake, do you need help with the ladder?"

"What? No! No, I got it," I say, stepping forward to take the ladder into my capable hands. "Go on inside."

My mom and Marissa go into the house while I wrestle the ladder into the garage, bruising both shins in the process. Right after I hoist the ladder onto its pegs, I remember the angel sitting in the nest. Shit. I'll go back for it later.

By the time I get inside the house, Marissa and my mom are standing in the Hall of Shame. It's the hallway leading from the living room to the family room, where about a dozen photos hang from the walls. "Who took all of these?" asks Marissa.

"Mostly me," says my mom.

They're all color shots, framed with white matting in black frames. Marissa examines them. My mom stands next to her, adding comments like, "That was our trip to Japan four years ago. We're standing in front of the Big Buddha. That's really what it's called, isn't that great? There's Garrett in his Little League uniform. Look at him getting ready for the pitch. Doesn't he look kind of terrified and focused all at the same time? He was about seven in that one. There's Blake meeting Captain Hook at Disneyland. See how he's posing for the camera with his hand on his hip, just like Captain Hook? He loved Captain Hook."

Marissa doesn't make polite oohs and ahhs like most of the captives who are forced to look at the Hall of Shame. She studies each photo intently, as if they're images of some primitive tribal culture.

"Of course, there's the obligatory wedding photo," says my mom, waving her hand at the eight-by-ten of her and Dad. It's not one of those posed wedding shots, though. It's a casual shot of the two of them grinning at each other, pieces of wedding cake in their hands. They look as if they're about to paste each other with cake.

"I'd better get going." Marissa turns to me suddenly. "Thanks for letting me take pictures in your garden."

"Thank *you* for letting me take pictures of your eye," I say.

"Oh, Blake," says my mom. "Did you really?"

I realize that my mom has not even asked about Marissa's eye. She's got mad diplomatic skills! "She got an elbow in the eye," I explain.

"Oh, dear."

Marissa zips up her backpack. "I'll see you tomorrow," she says, then turns to my mom. "Nice meeting you."

"You, too, Marissa. Do you need a ride home?"

"No thanks, I'll take the bus," says Marissa. "Blake, will you e-mail me those photos?"

"Yep."

"Great!" She heads for the door. "Bye."

My mom follows her. "How far away do you live? I'd be happy to drive you."

Thinking about Marissa's grandma's house reminds me: I keep forgetting to ask about her mom going to rehab. But I don't want to ask in front of my mom.

"It's okay, Mrs. Hewson," says Marissa. "I can read on the bus."

"Benita. Call me Benita, please."

"Benita. Thanks. Bye."

And Marissa is gone.

CHAPTER TEN

Aside from being a guitar player or an athlete, there's no better profession than that of photographer for attracting women.
—*Spike McLernon's Laws of Photography*

Have I mentioned how much I love summer?

Okay, technically, September is not summer, it's back-to-school time. But we've been having a heat wave lately, so it feels like summer. Girls are wearing small clothes, and that is beautiful.

Summer is bare legs in shorts and painted toenails peeking out of sandals and *yesss* . . . shoulders. Shannon's shoulders are the only ones I'm allowed to touch, but there are so many others to admire. Ahh.

As long as I'm discreet.

"Think they're real?" asks Shannon.

"Wh-what?"

She puts her face about an inch from mine. "That girl by Coffee Jones. The one in the white top. Nice rack, huh?"

I feel my eyes wanting to roll wildly, like a spooked horse, because I know I'm trapped. "Uh—" *Houston, we have a problem. Please advise.*

"That girl you were looking at," she clarifies.

The Houston in my head reminds me that the best defense is an offense. "Oh, *that* girl!" I exclaim, smacking my forehead. "Yeah. *Nice.*" I waggle my eyebrows. "You want me to see if I can find out her name? Maybe we can get her number!" I start to move in the direction of Coffee Jones.

"Blake!" says Shannon, grabbing my arm.

But I keep moving, saying loudly over my shoulder, "Good eye, baby! You're right, she does have a nice rack!"

Shannon gasps and giggles, clawing at me. "Stop! Blake, stop!" she whispers. "Come back!"

"Excuse me," I call. The girls in front of Coffee Jones look over at me. "Hi," I say. "My girlfriend was wondering—"

Shannon squeals and races around in front of me, laughing and trying to cover my mouth with her hand.

I stop, and she falls against me so hard we almost end up on the ground. The girls by Coffee Jones turn away.

"I can't believe you!" Shannon is cracking up—a big belly laugh that fills up a space in my heart as well as the control center in Houston.

We stand there for a minute, just holding on to each other and grinning like loons.

Then she squeezes me tighter and says, "You're so fun. I love you."

Gulp.

The first "I love you."

I open my mouth.

There's a silence that is stuffed full of hope and dread and held breath.

"I love you, too," I whisper.

.....

I go quietly insane the rest of the day.

My mom has been on a rampage about chores lately, so she makes me wash The Dog when I get home. I'm up to my elbows in soapsuds and wet dog when I suddenly think, *Ohmygod, I said I love you to a girl!*

Houston seems to have been shocked into silence.

Then my mom forces me to help her fix Nonna's famous minestrone for dinner. While I'm chopping carrots and green beans and leeks (heh . . . leeks), I'm thinking, *Ohmygod, I told Shannon I love her!*

Oblivious to my inner turmoil, Mom is frying bacon.

Maybe I should tell her.

Then again, she's been unnaturally cool about the whole girl-friend issue. I still remember what she said last month when I told her that Shannon and I were officially boyfriend and girlfriend: "That's great, honey. Can you hand me the USB cable?"

Here I'd been thinking we were going to have a soft-focus Mother-Son Moment. I'd confess I had fallen in love, and she would hug me. Maybe even cry. Then she'd tell me she was happy for me and couldn't wait to meet the young lady, and we would share a plate of cookies while we talked about Love.

Instead she asked me for the USB cable. She wanted to update her iPod, and I was blocking the drawer where we keep the cables.

"Hi," says Garrett, strolling into the kitchen.

I look at him. I wonder if *he's* ever told a girl he loves her.

"How was school, sweetie?" asks Mom.

He opens the refrigerator and grabs an energy drink. "Good." He chugs his drink, then strolls over and gives her a hug. "Mmm, baaaacon," he says in a Homer Simpson voice. "What are you making?"

"Blake is helping me fix Nonna's minestrone," she says. "It will be ready in about an hour."

"Nice," he says, and sidles up to me. *"Mommoni,"* he whispers. (That's "Mama's boy" in Italian.)

I kick him, but he leaps away just in time. For such a big dude, he's fast.

The Dog Formerly Known as Prince barks, excited by the scuffling.

"Next time, *you* wash The Dog and make dinner," I say. "I have to do everything!"

"Blake," says Mom. "Garrett does his share around here."

Garrett bumps me hard on his way out of the kitchen. The Dog follows him.

I fume, chopping carrots.

Then the love thing smacks me in the head again: *Ohmygod, I told Shannon I love her!* A new worry is attached: *Does this mean I'm supposed to say it all the time now?*

Mom would probably know the saying-I-love-you rules. I should ask her.

I heave a big sigh. "What a day," I say.

Mom lifts each piece of bacon out of the pan and lays it on a paper towel.

"Wow," I add.

She glances at me, smiles, and goes over to the sink to start washing a bunch of kale.

"What a really, really crazy day," I say.

Mom turns off the water and puts the kale in her salad spinner. She does the spinning thing to get all the water off. It makes a lot of noise, so I say a little louder, "Man. What a—"

"How's it going, Blake?"

Finally. The suspense must be killing her.

"Good," I say. So how should I tell her? *Mom, you probably don't remember your first love, but—*

"Almost finished?" she says, wiping her hands on a towel.

"Uh—"

"You get the beans and tomatoes. I'm going to fry the veggies in the bacon drippings." She takes the cutting board full of chopped veggies and dumps them into the pan.

I grab cans of pinto beans and tomatoes from the cupboard and open them.

"Thank you, Blake. You've been a big help. I can take it from here."

"ItoldShannonIloveher." It comes out in a rush before I even know I'm going to speak.

Mom stops moving and smiles at me. "Honey. How wonderful." She turns off the stove.

Silence.

"So did she say she loved you back?" she asks after a moment.

"No! I mean yes. She said it first. Then I said it."

"Ah."

My mom can mean a million things with that one syllable. She reaches out and gives my cheek a mom-like caress. "My young man. How do you feel now?"

I shrug and open my mouth to make a joke.

Nothin'. I got nothin'.

I hope this is a temporary condition, or I have no future as a standup comic.

"Well, I'm happy for you, sweetie. Love is such a treasure."

I'm still trying to figure out how to word my question—*Am I supposed to say it to her every day now?*—when Mom asks, "I was wondering how your friend is doing. Marissa."

"Marissa?" I say, puzzled. "Fine."

"How's her eye?"

"Oh! Cool!" I say, brightening. "It's all healed now, but I got some amazing shots of it. Wait till you see."

A look of professional patience comes over her face, and she says, "I was wondering if you think she's really okay, Blake. Does she have a boyfriend?"

Blink. Blink.

"Someone who might have a temper? I was wondering if you believe her when she says she got that black eye from someone bumping into her."

Ohhhhh.

"Mom," I say, relieved. "Yes. She wouldn't lie to me. She went to that Hurtle biking thing."

My mom's expression remains skeptical.

"Really. Don't worry. She doesn't even have a boyfriend."

"All right," she says. "That's good to know. I'm glad she's got you for a friend. I'm sure you would know if things weren't right with her."

"Um. Sure," I say. Is now the time to tell my mom about Marissa's tweaker mom? Or would that be breaking my promise to Marissa?

· · · · ·

Marissa's the first person I see at the football game.

"Hey," I say.

She's sitting with her friend Bree and a couple of other girls I don't know. "Hey," she answers. Her face is blank and empty, as if the real Marissa has gone away.

I scan the rows of people in the stands. Shannon texted me that she was sitting with Riley and a bunch of other people. I glance back at Marissa. "You okay?"

"Shhure," she slurs.

I look at Bree, who gives me a challenging stare. "Her cat got run over," she says.

"Your cat got run over?" I say, looking back at Marissa.

Her face stays blank; she doesn't look at me. "She was old," she mumbles.

In my mind I see a picture of a black cat with a pink tongue. "Wizard Kitty died?"

Marissa's face crumples, and Bree throws an arm around her shoulders. "Don't make her talk about it," she says.

"Okay," I say. "Sorry."

Bree pats her coat pocket. "Don't worry. We're getting her drunk on."

I stand there for a second. "Sorry," I say again, and move away from them.

I wander around for a minute, looking for my peeps but thinking about Marissa. *First a tweaker mom, now a dead cat. Could you possibly give her a break, God?* I think. And now her friends are getting her hammered. I hope she'll be okay.

I've only been drunk once before. I yakked all over Riley's dad's car, which made the fun-drunk part seem less fun.

Then I see Riley and George and Bald Jake and oh! hottie Dez and Aisha and . . . my heart does a trembly thing I've never felt before . . . Shannon.

She's sitting between Aisha and some guy I don't know. I feel a spurt of Neanderthal possessiveness. Both girls are turned toward the strange guy, but they look polite, not fascinated. Probably like, "Hi, what's your name again, what school do you go to, etc."

I make my way up into the stands. When Shannon catches sight of me, her face lights up.

I'm not even kidding.

One minute she's normal, the next minute she's beaming light. Even the strange guy notices and turns to see what she's looking at.

Me. That's right, Guy We Don't Know. *I* made her look that happy.

Is she going to say it again? Are we going to say I love you all the time now? I'm not sure I'm ready for that.

But I can't wait to get to her.

CHAPTER ELEVEN

Saturation:

The dictionary definition says, "to soak, impregnate, or imbue completely." That's not what we're talking about in photos. The brighter your colors, the more saturated they are; the duller your colors are, the less saturated they are. Get it? You can adjust those levels in Photoshop, but try not to get them pregnant, especially the skin tones, because you can wind up making people look weird.

—*Blake Hewson, homework, Photo II*

Ahh, the weekend.

Time for sleeping in, racking up new high scores on the Mindbender, and hanging out with friends in RL instead of IM. Unless you've got a mother like mine, who is *way too involved* in your schoolwork. Then the weekend involves being woken up before you're ready, fed a healthy breakfast, and herded toward your desk. Tyrant!

I slump at my desk, flipping through my homework assignments. Biology . . . *so* don't care . . . history . . . *zzzz* . . . photo . . . hey. I wonder how Marissa feels today after getting tanked at the game last night. I pull out my cell phone and scroll through the names, looking for her phone number. She doesn't have her own cell yet; she uses her grandma's land line, like some kind of pioneer girl trapped in the 1990s.

She answers. "Hello?"

"Marissa! Hi. How are you?"

"Fine. Blake?"

"Yeah. I wanted to see if you were okay."

"I'm fine. Why?"

"I just thought, you know, you might be feeling bad today." A thought strikes me. "Do you even remember talking to me at the game last night?"

"I talked to you? Oh." She gives a bitter laugh. "No, I don't remember. I barely remember being at the game."

"Dude, I'm sorry about Wizard Kitty."

Silence. I'm about to ask if she's still there, when I hear a quiet sound that makes me realize she's crying. "I had her a long time," she says finally. "I got her when I moved in with my grandma."

"Oh, Mariss."

She takes a big breath and gets herself under control. "Sorry," she says. "I didn't mean to bawl all over you."

"It's okay."

"I just miss her. I keep thinking I'm going to turn around and she'll be there."

"Yeah." I look around for the Dog Formerly Known as Prince. I have a sudden urge to pet him.

"And I miss my mom!" she bursts out.

"Aw, dude, sorry." It's weird to think that Marissa misses her mom, even though her mom was gone for so long before. "Can't you call her at"—*rehab,* I almost say—"that place?"

"No. She's not allowed to have calls."

"That sucks."

"I know. Thank God for Grandma. She helped me"—Marissa struggles with her voice for a second—"bury Wizard Kitty. In the garden."

"Aww."

"So at least she'll be near flowers and stuff." She chuckles a little. "Her ghost can haunt the birdbath."

"Does your grandma, um, know that you got loaded last night?"

"No," says Marissa. "She was asleep when I got home. I had the bed spins for a while, but I didn't throw up."

"Whew!" I say. "That's good. You wouldn't want to wake up dead from choking on your own vomit!"

"Uh . . ." says Marissa uncertainly.

"Of course, better your *own* vomit than someone else's."

Pause. *"What?"* she says.

"It's a line from *This Is Spinal Tap*."

"What's that?"

I clutch my head. "What's that? Don't tell me you've never seen *Spinal Tap*."

"Nope. Is it a movie?"

"Marissa," I say. "Get your ass over here right now. You need to see this movie. It is pure comic genius, and . . . and I can't even talk to you until you've seen it."

She laughs.

Ahhh. I made a sad girl laugh.

She asks for a rain check on the movie, and we say goodbye.

·········CHAPTER TWELVE··········

You are hereby forbidden to clutter up your shot.
Unless the shot demands chaos.
—*Spike McLernon's Laws of Photography*

Talk about gritty. Mr. Malloy calls my photos gritty, but he's never actually been to the grit-a-palooza that is Hurtle.

I'm surrounded by bikers. Not the ponytailed, leather pants–wearing, Harley-driver kind. The kind who ride flimsy, naked-looking *bicycles* and, for some reason that is still not clear to me, want to go kamikaze-ing down this steep, winding hill so fast that if anything goes even the slightest bit wrong, they will end up as red smears on the pavement.

Marissa convinced me to come. She wanted to see her brother Gus again, and she knew he would be at Hurtle.

"Are you going to do it? Ride your bike down that crazy hill?" I asked.

She looked at me like I had asked something completely random, like "Are you really a female?"

"Of course," she said. "But you don't have to. Just bring your camera. It's wild. You'll love it."

She was so right. I do love it. I couldn't take a boring photo here if I tried.

I zoom in on a trio of skateboard dudes with baggy pants and scabby legs. I guess people on skateboards can Hurtle, too. Then I shoot a tall blond goddess girl who looks like she should be granting wishes or frolicking in a meadow instead of pushing her bike through a crowd of tough guys. Here comes a bunch of people with a combined total of piercings that could stock a small jewelry store. There's a guy with his whole face tattooed! I inhale audibly over that.

"What?" says Marissa. She's sitting astride her bike, hanging back with me. After the elbow in the face, she's decided not to go near the front.

I flick my eyes in the direction of Tattooed Face Boy.

Her eyes widen and we exchange appalled looks.

There's a grandmotherly type of woman pedaling sedately around behind the scary hardcore types. Who in the what now? What is Granny thinking? She's going to be toast once these people take off.

"Oh my God," I say.

"Now what?"

"Some people brought their kids!"

I see parental types milling around with little kids whose bikes still have training wheels on them. Some of the kids are even on *tricycles*.

"What the hell?" I say.

"Turtle," says Marissa.

I blink at her.

"It comes after Hurtle. People who don't want to Hurtle can Turtle."

"Wha—?"

She grins. "Even you could Turtle."

"All right, enough with the digs at Frosty!" I say, patting my snow-white bike. "And I get it. Turtle is for geezers and little kids. But no way. It's still a steep hill, no matter how slow you're going!"

"Blake, the people who do Turtle turn off at Roseway Drive and circle the park. They don't blitz down the hill." She gives me a friendly punch on the shoulder. "You could follow behind and get some string-cheese shots."

I make a face at her. We call photos of little kids and old people doing cute things string cheese, because they're cheesy and they tug at your heartstrings. Marissa kind of likes it when she comes across a string-cheese photo op. I, on the other hand, would lose my gritty reputation if I took shots like that.

"I'm going to wheel on home after everyone takes off," I say. "Thanks for bringing me."

"Sure."

"So where's your brother?" I ask.

"I don't see him yet," she says. "But he'll be here. He's always here on Fridays."

I train my lens on a couple of wiry-looking guys in yellow bike shirts bending and contorting really slowly. My mom does yoga, and that's what it looks like.

"Who would put their kid in a shirt like that?" says Marissa. "Get a shot of that little boy. Poor kid."

I aim in the direction she's looking and see a cute kid, maybe five years old, wearing a black T-shirt and sporting an unfortunate haircut—you know, the kind where the hair is short in front and then there's a "rat tail" hanging down in back. The shirt says V.I.M.F. in big silver letters. I can think only of one interpretation for that: Very Important Mother . . . well, you get it.

The kid is accompanied by his . . . dad? . . . a tough guy with a shaved head and hooded eyes. Where's the mom? Oh, there she is: standing a bit farther back smoking a cigarette and fidgeting. Her eyes jump all over the place, and she nods nervously every few seconds. I shoot some photos of the happy family, then turn to Marissa.

"Poor little—" I start to say, but stop. Marissa is staring at the mother, tears welling up in her eyes. "What's wrong?"

"Nothing," she whispers, and turns away. "I wish the thing would start."

I glance away from her. *Should I ask her again what's wrong? Or leave her alone?*

Marissa lifts the front of the bike by the handlebars and slams it down again. Before I stop to think about it, I raise my camera and snap a picture of her.

She turns back to me, rolling her eyes. "Okay. That's enough." She gives a little smile. The moment has passed.

"Do you see your brother anywhere?"

Marissa scans the crowd again. After a moment she grins widely. "There he is!"

I look in the direction she's focusing on. "Which one is he?"

"See the tall guy? The one with the messenger bag with the sticker on the back that says FREE TIBET?"

That guy? He's *huge.* Must be six three and built like a lumberjack. But he wants to free Tibet, so maybe he's nonviolent.

"Gus!" yells Marissa, and I can't help thinking, *Don't call him over here!*

The guy looks our way, and when he sees Marissa, he gives a grin that looks just like hers. He pedals over to us.

They both lean across their bikes and hug. Marissa looks doll-size next to him.

"This is my friend Blake," says Marissa after they separate.

"'S up," says Gus, no longer smiling.

"Hey," I say. "Nice to meet you."

He doesn't answer, just studies me. "Nice bike," he says finally.

I stand there. I know that's a cut . . . but I don't know how to respond.

"How do you know my sister?" he asks.

"Gus," says Marissa.

"We go to school together," I say.

"Yeah? Are you trying to hook up with her?"

"Oh my God!" says Marissa. "Gus! Blake is my friend from photo class. We're not *together.* Be nice to him." She turns to me. "Sorry."

Gus nods. "All right. Nice to meet you, man." He holds his right fist out, and I bump knuckles with him, hoping never to see those knuckles again.

"Hurtle's about to start," says Gus. "See you later, okay?" He pulls a pair of sunglasses out of his front pocket and raises them to his face.

I see some tattoos on his arms, and I look closer. I love tattoos, I just don't want to get one. There's some kind of bird and some flames . . . maybe a phoenix? And a Celtic cross. And . . . wait. That doesn't look like something a tough biker would have tattooed on his arm for the whole world to see. It looks like . . . an angel.

I must be staring kind of obviously at his arms, because Gus says, "You got any tats?"

"Um," I say. "Not yet." I lean closer. Since he brought them up, it must be okay to stare. "Is that an angel?"

Gus glances down at the small tattoo on his right forearm and nods. "Yep. I got that where I can always see it." He holds his arm out, and I can see the word scripted inside one of the wings: KAT. "It reminds me to take care of the people I love."

"Gus," says Marissa in a soft voice. "You did."

He nods at her. "Naw. But I was just a kid, right? At least I took good care of *you*." He smiles and gives her shoulder a squeeze, then pedals away.

Marissa watches him go. When she turns back, her expression is distant.

Is Kat a person? I want to ask, but I don't. I'm starting to think I don't want to know.

After a minute she says, "Sorry about the . . . you know, the thing he said. About us hooking up."

"It's okay."

"He was my protector when we were little. So he thinks he still has to watch out for me."

"It's cool. He's your brother. I get it."

She faces me. "No, you don't. We went through a lot together. He used to sleep in my room with a baseball bat."

"Oh. Why?"

A shutting-down look falls over her face. "Never mind. Sorry. I don't wanna— He's a good guy once he gets to know you."

"Okay."

We look around at everyone but each other, until finally I say, "Who decides when the hurtling starts?"

She points to the front, where people jostle for position. "See the guy with the hair?"

Yep. You can't miss him. It's gelled up into foot-long black spikes with green tips. "I see him."

"Watch."

I watch. Pretty soon he raises a black, leather-covered arm in the air and waves madly. Then he gives a long, loud whoop and drops his arm. He and the people in front take off in a blur of spinning wheels. I snap photo after photo of the crush.

"See you," says Marissa. She pedals off into the crowd.

"Bye," I say. "See you Monday."

I take a few more photos, but most of the riders have rounded the first bend and disappeared. Then I see some girl with a bunch of blue feathers in her hair pedaling along behind everyone else.

Cappie?

Wait till I tell Garrett his friend-with-benefits was here, rolling with the bikers and skate punks.

CHAPTER THIRTEEN

Use gaffer tape, not duct tape. I use it for everything,
even taping down cords. Don't leave home without it.
—*Spike McLernon's Laws of Photography*

"I just got the best asphyxia by hanging *ever*," says my dad.

Garrett looks interested. "What happened?"

"We're eating," I say.

"No, Blake, you'll appreciate this," says my dad. "It's kind of funny."

"Please pass the salad," says Mom. She's sitting there in her bra, fanning herself after a hot flash. It's a typical Hewson family dinner.

Dad hands her the bowl. "So there's this guy. He likes to go out to the bars on Friday night and get drunk."

I pretend to crack up. "Oh, that *is* hilarious!"

My dad grins and keeps going. "Only problem is . . . he keeps losing his keys while he's drunk. His *house* keys, not his car keys. At least the guy doesn't get in his car and drive home. He goes to the bars within walking distance of his house. So anyway, he starts keeping his house key on a cord around his neck."

Uh-oh. This guy just became a candidate for the Darwin award, I can tell. The Darwin awards honor excessively stupid deaths.

"So Friday night he comes home and tries to unlock his front door. He gets the key in the lock, but then he must have passed out. Which gives new meaning to the phrase 'falling down drunk,' by the way. The next morning his neighbor finds him hanging from the cord. Which is still attached to the key in the lock."

Garrett is nodding and chuckling like the ghoulish little *diener* he aspires to be.

"Is this your way of keeping us from ever drinking?" I ask.

My mom laughs so hard that bits of crouton fly out of her mouth.

That gets Dad going, and Garrett says to me, "Double points, right, man?"

I nod happily. If I make food fly out of someone's mouth, I get double points for the joke. If it's milk and it comes out of someone's nose, triple points.

After we finish dinner, I carry my plate over to the counter and jet out of the room so I can check my e-mail and phone messages. Shannon and I are supposed to meet up at Ottomans later.

"Not so fast," says Mom.

Garrett is halfway down the hall, too.

Shit, he mouths.

We trudge back.

"Your turn to do the dishes, guys."

"Okay," I say. "One second. Just let me—"

She shakes her head. "No. Not one second. Now. The quicker you do them, the quicker you're free."

"Washing!" I call. I hate drying.

So does Garrett, for that matter. He scowls. "Fine. You load the dishwasher, too, then."

"Thank you, men," says Mom. She heads for the family room, calling back over her shoulder, "Someday your wives will thank me for training you properly."

"What if they're husbands?" I call after her. "Don't assume."

Garrett and I snicker, waiting for her response.

After a moment we hear, "Whatever makes you happy."

I squirt dish soap into the sink and run water. Garrett snaps the towel at me.

"Ow! Cut it out!"

"Ow," he mimics. "Here." He hands me the wooden salad bowl.

I wash it in the sink. Mom has been careful to teach us which things do *not* go in the dishwasher ever since I ruined some of her fancy china teacups in there. It's not like they were a total loss. She used the shards to make mosaic steppingstones.

"How's your girlfriend?" I ask.

"She's not my girlfriend, man," Garrett says. "I told you."

"Oh, right," I say, handing him the salad bowl to dry. "I saw her last night."

"Last night? Where?" he says. Too quickly.

I've been saving this up alllll daaaay. I drag out the pause until it feels like I'm blowing up a balloon that's about to pop in my face.

"Hurtle."

"Hurdle?" Garrett looks blank.

"You know. That biking thing."

He shakes his head. "What biking thing?"

"You know. A bunch of people meet at the top of Tower Hill and go blasting down Laurel on their bikes."

"Oh." He thinks for a minute. "Yeah. I guess I have heard of it. But it's mostly guys, isn't it? What was Cappie doing there?"

"You tell me. She's *your* girlfriend."

He moves toward me, and I jump back, squeaking a little. His big fist appears in front of my face, then moves past my head. He opens the cupboard door and puts the salad bowl on the shelf, purposely crowding me. Then he turns away. "Hurry up. You're taking forever."

So that's it? I saved up this juicy tidbit all day and he's not even going to bug me for more details? "She had feathers in her hair," I announce.

No answer.

"And she wasn't wearing a helmet." I widen my eyes. Dad is manic about us always wearing helmets.

Garrett hands me a casserole dish, shaking his head and smiling slightly. "You can't tell her what to do."

This is so unsatisfying.

"And what were *you* doing at this Hurtle thing?" asks Garrett. "Did you limp old Frosty down the hill?"

"As a matter of fact, I was there in my capacity as photojournalist," I say. "Marissa showed me—"

"Ah yes," he interrupts. "Your *other* girlfriend."

Must. Not. React. He knows Marissa is just a friend. He's yanking my chain about her because I'm yanking *his* chain about Cappie. But I'd like to wrap that dishtowel around his thick neck and pull until his eyes bug out.

We work in silence for a while.

I finish loading the dishwasher, knee the door closed, and punch a button on it.

Garrett finishes drying the chopping knife and makes a few fake jabs in my direction with it, like he always does. I dodge out of reach, like I always do. Well, ever since that first time.

He slides the knife into its slot in the wooden block and hangs up the dishtowel. "Guess I'll have to ask Cappie about the Hurtle thing when I see her tonight." He grins and turns to leave the room. "What are you up to, Stud? Which of your lovely ladies gets the pleasure of your company tonight? Or are you all alone with your scintillating self?"

I open my mouth to put him in his place but get stumped wondering what "scintillating" means.

"Oh, *snap*," he says, and he's gone.

If I don't pick up the pace with the clever retorts, I'm doomed. The hecklers will shred me.

.........CHAPTER FOURTEEN..........

After taking several pictures in a row, do not touch the flash,
as this may result in burns.
—*Mitsu ProShot I.S. 5.3 camera guide, 2007*

"I see you survived Hurtle," I say to Marissa on Monday.

"Oh, it was great! I can't wait to go again next Friday."

"It was nice meeting your brother."

She gives me a look.

"What. It *was*."

"He'll be nicer once he gets to know you," she says.

"I look forward to it." I open my portfolio to take out our assignment.

Marissa points to my photos. "Let's see."

I hand her some pictures. We've been working on motion.

Motion? What's so hard about that, Obi-Wan Hewson?

It's harder than you think, my young Jedi. I'm not talking about motion like a shot of someone running, all blurry and speedy. I'm talking about shooting a subject that is *static*—not moving—in a way that makes your brain think *movement*.

Mr. Malloy has this great photo on the wall of huge red rocks with curvy lines etched into them, swooshing around from one side of the frame to the other. It's so cool I could stare at it all day. *That* kind of motion.

"This is great." Marissa laughs. She's looking at the stuffed-snake photo.

I know, it sounds lame. But the snake looks like it could start slithering at any second. My mom was taking care of Sammy, our neighbors' little kid, the other night while his parents went out for their anniversary. He carries his favorite stuffed animal, a green and purple snake, with him everywhere. I did a little "art direction" with it by arranging it on the floor in a snake-crawling pattern, then shooting it at eye level. I'm kind of proud at how it turned out.

The second photo is a close-up of my mom's hair. I had her sit on the couch, with her long hair cascading over the back of the couch like a . . . well, a hairy waterfall, I guess. I set a lamp nearby to make a "hair light" and shot the photo from above. She has a few gray hairs mixed in with the brown and black—they look like little sparks.

Marissa studies the picture of my mom's hair without speaking. Suddenly she looks up at me and says, "Blake."

"What?"

"Will you take a photo of my mom when she comes home?"

"Um." *Random.* "Okay."

"It's just—" She looks down at the picture of my mom's hair again. "I mean, the last photo that was ever taken of my mom was of her passed out like a bum. You know?"

I nod.

"And you took that photo. For some reason, I need you to take a photo of her looking normal. That would make me feel better."

I get it.

. . . . .

I've come home a couple of times now and found Cappie there with Garrett. I don't know how my brother manages to make sure neither one of my parents is going to be around, because they don't work nine-to-five-type hours. Either he's been lucky, which he always is—*dick*—or he's researched their schedules.

I decide that his luck might work to my advantage. So when I walk into the house one day and find Garrett sleeping on the couch in the family room (what does she *do* to him?) and Cappie sitting at the kitchen table with a slice of pie and a book propped open in front of her, I waste about two seconds saying "hi," then I pick up the phone to call Shannon on her cell.

"Shannon! No soccer practice today, right?"

"Right. Why?"

"Want to come over?"

"Now?"

"Yeah! My parents aren't home."

"But how would I get there?"

"Umm." I hadn't really thought that far ahead. I pictured Shannon in all of her fondle-ability, then I pictured her magically *here*.

"Maybe my brother could pick you up. Where are you?"

Cappie is shaking her head, not even glancing up from her book.

"Or maybe not. What about . . ." But I'm flat skint of ideas. I sigh. "Never mind. It was a long shot."

She sighs, too. "See you tomorrow."

I hang up and flop down at the kitchen table. Cappie's got blue streaks in her hair these days, like a blue jay. I picture her flitting in to bang my brother, eat our food, and boss me around before flitting off again, and suddenly I'm mad at her. "Can I get you another slice of pie?" I ask in a sarcastically helpful voice.

She glances up, registers my tone, and smiles widely. Uh-oh. She makes me nervous when she shows her teeth. "Blake, right?" she says, like she's still learning my name. She holds up her plate. "That would be great. And some milk. I get so *thirsty*."

I blow some air out between my lips and get up to leave.

She's standing next to me in a flash, and I have to admit, I flinch a little. I barely saw her move from her chair, and now she's up in my face. "Shannon, right?" she asks.

"What?"

"The girlfriend. Her name is Shannon, right?"

I stare, then nod.

Cappie walks to the counter to cut herself another slice of pie.

I'm almost out of the room when I hear her say, "And Marissa?"

I stop.

"She's the other one, right?" Cappie opens the refrigerator and pulls out the milk.

I turn. "*What* other one? She's just a friend."

Cappie nods vigorously. "Right, right. Just wanted to make sure I get the names straight. What's her last name again?"

"Fairbairn. Why?"

"Just doing some fact-checking."

Before I can figure out what the hell she's talking about, Garrett shuffles into the kitchen, looking dazed and amazed. "You're still here!" he says in the most lovesick, un-Garrett-like voice I've ever heard.

"*Cave*man," growls Cappie, walking toward him with her arms out.

I flee the kitchen like my hair is on fire. I do not want to see my brother and his *not*-girlfriend hooked up like a circuit.

· · · · ·

It happens at lunchtime.

It's the Love Gone Wrong show, which is when listeners are allowed to make requests. People love it because most of the requests are anonymous, so we all get to speculate about whose love has gone wrong. Cappie is DJing.

"Welcome back to Love Gone Wrong lunch hour, divine diners," says Cappie. "We've enjoyed a buffet of songs, now here's a delicious dessert by Nora No, 'You Say She's Just a Friend,' going out to Blake, from Shannon." The first few notes of the song—about a jealous girlfriend—pour over the loudspeakers, and Cappie says, "Tell it, sistah. Beware of fair bairns."

I'm so shocked it's like I go deaf. I turn to Shannon.

She looks disoriented. As if from a great distance, I hear her ask, "Did she just say *my* name?"

Fucking Cappie. I flash on her saying, "Just wanted to make sure I get the names straight."

The Nora No song keeps playing, and it's like knives in my ears.

"I can't believe this," says Shannon. "Blake, I didn't—"

"I know," I say. "I know you didn't do it." People are looking at us now. They must think it's real. They must think Shannon is jealous of Marissa. I look around the cafeteria until I locate Marissa. She's sitting with her friends, and they're all huddled together in a knot of wide eyes and giggles, whispering.

Marissa sees me looking at her and looks away really fast.

Gahh! Now Marissa thinks it's true, too.

How could Cappie do this? There must be rules! You can't just broadcast stuff on the radio that's not true! Can you? It's slander, or libel, or something.

"What should we do?" asks Shannon. Her cheeks are pink.

All of a sudden I'm totally furious. My girl didn't do anything to Cappie. She doesn't deserve to be embarrassed in front of the whole school. If Cappie wanted to get back at me, she sure as shit should've taken it up with *me*.

I stand up. "I'm going to the radio station," I say.

"Blake, wait," says Shannon, her eyes going wide. "Don't. You'll just make it worse. Don't leave me right now, anyway. People will think it's true."

I stand there steaming. "Fine. I won't leave. But we have to go tell Marissa. Come on."

Shannon stands up and takes my hand. I feel like I'm walking across a stage in front of an audience full of people munching pizza and burritos.

As we reach Marissa, I hear a couple of people murmur, "Oooh," as if a fight is about to bust out.

I open my mouth to speak, but Shannon says in a rush, "Marissa, I didn't do it! I didn't request that song. I would *never* do something like that."

Marissa exhales, "Oh, thank God! I couldn't believe—"

"I *know*. I couldn't, either. Blake looked like he was about to faint," says Shannon.

Both girls are all giggly and gossipy now, and I close my mouth. Problem solved. I call out in my best policeman voice, "Okay, move along, people. Nothing to see here. Go back to your lives, citizens."

I'm itching to get my hands on Cappie, however. This is not over. Oh, no. Not by a long shot.

"I'll see you guys later," I say to the girls.

"Don't, Blake," says Shannon. "He's going to the radio station," she adds to Marissa.

"Oh, no," says Marissa.

I leave them fretting over my manly determination.

Garrett catches up to me as I'm halfway to the Bomb Shelter, which is what the radio jocks call the station.

"Blake, where ya goin', man? Don't you have a love triangle to manage?"

"Shannon did not request that song!"

"No?" Garrett chuckles. "That Trickster cracks me up."

"I'll crack *her* up," I mutter.

"What? What did you say?"

"I said I'LL CRACK HER UP!"

Garrett studies me. Finally he says almost gently, "Dog, you're taking this way too seriously."

"She said on the *radio*—for the whole world to hear—that my *girl*friend is jealous of my girl *friend!*" I rage.

"I know. I'm just sayin'. Getting all up in her face is the exact wrong thing to do. She'll kick your ass without even breaking a sweat."

"What?" I stop. "She would *fight* me?" Now there's an appalling thought: getting beaten up by a girl.

"No, man. I was speaking metaphorically. That means—"

"I know what it means!"

He nods. "So you *understand* that she may not lay a finger on you, but she would still kick your ass."

I stop walking and glare at him for a long moment. Finally I say, "Why do you go along with it, Garrett?"

"With what?"

"She's using you, man. Coming over to the house . . . doing whatever it is you guys do . . . eating *our food* . . . then acting like she doesn't even know you at school."

Garrett laughs. "Is she cutting in on your share of the food, little guy?"

Oh God, what I wouldn't give to be about four inches taller and forty pounds heavier, so Garrett would never be able to call me little again. "You know what I mean," I said. "It's like she's messing with your head."

"Aw, it's not that way," says Garrett.

"How is it then? Explain it to me."

He shifts his gaze to a point behind me, not answering for a minute. The cocky grin on his face slips a notch. "It's like a game," he says. "We're hiding in plain sight. Walking around school like we don't know each other, when all the time we're, you know." He trails off, gazing into the distance. "She likes games. And hell, I'm free to see other people, if I want. She told me that right up front."

"Really." From the look on Garrett's face, I wonder if "we" like this game, or if it's just Cappie.

"Yeah." He shakes his head, as if clearing away a nagging doubt. "She's cool. Not like other girls."

I'm still steaming, so I don't even care that I'm venting on my brother. "You know what she told me the first time I met her? That she was having a play date with you. A free hookup. That she doesn't date jocks." I stalk away from him, calling back over my shoulder, "So it's a good thing you're cool with the game."

"Blake."

I keep going. *Hate.*

"Blake!" Garrett raises his voice. "Stop or I'll have to come after you."

I don't stop. I don't care if he—

Ow!

My brother just punched me.

.........CHAPTER FIFTEEN..........

The telephoto lens has an inherent compression of space.
—*Mitsu ProShot I.S. 5.3 camera guide, 2007*

All hell has broken loose.

Shannon is sitting across from me in a booth at Juke's, and she's crying.

So yeah, that bites, and I've had an assful of this kind of drama.

But the fun doesn't end there, folks!

Cappie is here. With a guy.

Who is not Garrett.

Oh, and did I mention that Garrett is here, too?

He came rolling in after the game with his pumped-up football peeps, all rowdy and proud because they won. They settled at the biggest table to receive their admirers, and sure enough, a couple of cheerleaders landed there first thing.

I saw the exact moment when Garrett caught sight of Cappie. He was smiling at something that Willow, one of the cheerleaders, had said, when he glanced over her shoulder. It's hard to miss Cappie tonight: she's got those blue streaks in her hair, and she's wearing a teeny tiny black dress with her legs going up to her ears practically. (*Niiice* stems, though, I gotta say.)

Anyone else looking at Garrett wouldn't have noticed him change expression. He's a stoic dude. But I've been looking at him for fifteen years, so I can tell when his smile kind of freezes and his eyes go tight.

I rub my shoulder gently. It feels blue and green and purple. The color of a new bruise. But I don't have any desire to photograph it.

I *was* going to throw a punch back at Garrett after he hit me, but I didn't, uh, want it to turn into a fight in the middle of school. So I just called him every dirty word I could think of while he stood there looking at me. When I ran out of words, he said, "Dog, I'm sorry, but I did tell you to stop. Now . . . I was *going* to say that I'll talk to Cappie for you."

"Oh."

But I refused to say thank you.

I guess he went to find Cappie after that, and I don't know what he said to her, but she's all over some other guy right now. He's a DJ at the radio station, too, so they must spend a lot of time together. He's got some sick dreads. Stone is his name, I think. He's looking kind of dazed, like he's not sure what to do with this bundle of Trickster, who's now licking salt off her fingers while she stares into his eyes.

So, okay. Garrett and Cappie are doing the friends-with-benefits thing. They're not a couple. Whatever. But how cold is that? Hooking up with someone else in front of the person you're quote-unquote dating? Does she want to get back at him for some reason?

At this very moment—I shit you not—Cappie turns her killer green eyes on me. And winks.

In the meantime, I've got Shannon sitting across from me all teary-eyed and red-nosed. If I'm not trying very hard to make her feel better, it's because I am worn out with the effort of knowing what to do all the damn time.

"I can't help it," she says again.

"Yes, you can," I find myself snapping. "You can just stop crying."

Which only makes her cry harder.

I made the un-fucking-believable mistake of telling her I was worried about Marissa. *Bad call, Houston! Being honest with GFs appears counterproductive.*

These were my exact words: "I'm worried about Marissa. She was getting hammered at the game. Again! I hope she's not turning into an alky."

A slow but steady undertow of misunderstanding proceeded to drag my ass out to sea.

Shannon analyzed each word out of my mouth, then deconstructed the meaning behind my words, searching for hidden code in those innocent little sentences. By the time we got to Juke's, she was sniffling. All of our friends fled to safety, leaving us alone on our raft of tragedy.

When Cappie and Stone make their exit, the buzz in the room goes quiet for a minute, then ramps up after the door closes behind them. I check Garrett; he has his chair pulled close to Willow and is leaning in to whisper something in her ear.

Scholar-jock boy will be fine.

Around eleven thirty Garrett stands up, and Willow follows. He comes over to my table and says, "Let's go, man. Shannon, do you need a ride?"

Shannon has moved out of her sad and into her mad. "No, thank you," she says. "Kaylee's mom can take me home. See you Monday." This last line is flung without even looking at me. She stands up and walks away.

Let's see, I can go after her and be the bigger person blahblahblah and apologize for something that is still unclear to me, or I can get the hell out of Dodge and wrap up this shitty day. Not only is my girlfriend mad at me and my arm is throbbing like a bitch, but I haven't made anyone laugh the entire day.

"Get me out of here," I snarl, and bang out the door.

· · · · ·

When I wake up, I check my cell for messages first thing. There's only one, from Riley:

Flake u left behind a pissed GF and bald jake's friend—i dunno his name—tried to hit that. But she went

home w/kaylee. Dog ur my hero—don't cave!!!
Rile

My blood begins to simmer. Guy We Don't Know tried to get with my girl? He will *rue the day!*

Except . . . wait. Maybe she's not my girl anymore. In which case, I can't be mad that some other guy tried his luck.

Except . . . wait. She left with Kaylee. In which case, maybe she *is* still my girl.

Houston advises me to stop orbiting Uranus and see if she sent me an e-mail.

I boot up my laptop and check my e-mail. Nothing but spam.

Huh.

Maybe we *are* broken up.

So what should I do, call and grovel at her feet?

I don't *think* so. She caused a scene over *nothing*. If she's going to be that high maintenance, then fine. *See* ya.

I go downstairs to breakfast.

And you know what? I don't care what kind of hormonal hell Shannon dragged me through yesterday because I said I was worried about Marissa. I'm still worried, and *she's* the one I'm going to call first.

. . . . .

"Be serious," says Garrett. He's standing next to my mom. More like towering over her.

My mom's eyes narrow. She moves farther into Garrett's personal space. "I am completely serious, Garrett Thomas."

Uh-oh, the middle name's out. I stop at the kitchen door, frozen in midstep. I can still back away.

Garrett falters in his cockiness. We don't like to get Mom mad. She can stay calm way longer than the average person, but once she snaps, she can inflict major damage. But Garrett doesn't back down. "I'm awake, aren't I? It's not like I'm still in bed. I'm up and ready to go."

"It doesn't matter whether or not you're awake. When you break your curfew and come home at two in the morning, you should expect repercussions. Actions have consequences."

Garrett's glance skips over to me. We hate that phrase. We are *allergic* to that phrase. We have vowed to each other *never* to use it on our own kids.

"Mom. I'm sorry. But please punish me later. I'm supposed to go observe at the ME's office this morning."

"Maybe you should have thought of that last night."

Uh. Right. In the middle of "driving Willow home," Garrett is going to say to himself, "Golly, I'd better not be late or Mom will refuse to let me go look at dead bodies." I stifle a snort.

Mom glances at me, and I turn to stone. Remain. Perfectly. Still. Maybe she will forget I'm here. "Did you want to comment, Blake Daniel?"

"No! Nonono. Sorry." Making Mom laugh when she's pissed earns me triple points, but it's a verrrry tricky stunt. I am not about to risk it just for *Garrett*.

She turns back to him. "I realize you had plans today. I'm sorry you will have to miss them."

Now she moves past him to the kitchen sink.

Garrett clenches his fists. I can see sweat breaking out on his shaved jock head. "What am I supposed to tell the ME on duty? I can't come because my *mommy* won't let me go outside to play?"

"If you like." Mom rinses her coffee cup and puts it in the dishwasher.

"Mo-om! It's a job! I mean, not a paying job, but I'm supposed to show up when they tell me to."

"That's not strictly true, honey," she answers. "You're still observing. You're not training. And if you're too embarrassed to call, your dad can do it."

Garrett slams out of the kitchen; I jump out of his way just in time. I'm thinking that now is not the time to ask him what happened with Cappie.

The Hewson boys are not having a good weekend.

· · · · ·

"Hello?"

"Oh, good," I say. "You didn't choke on your own vomit last night."

Pause. Then Marissa says, "Or anyone else's."

We crack up.

"Dude," I say after a minute. "Are you, like, turning into a drunk?"

"No! God, Blake!"

"Well?"

"What are you, the party police?"

"No, ma'am, I'm not." I put on a cop voice. "I'm merely a concerned citizen. Just the facts, ma'am, if you don't mind."

Marissa sighs. "Partying with my friends on the weekends doesn't make me a drunk. And it's not like it's every weekend, anyway."

"You sure about that, ma'am?"

"Yes, I'm sure. Shut up! I can't believe you. Besides."

"Besides what?"

"I like catching a little buzz. Things seem easier."

Before I can answer, she says loudly, "I'm not like my mom!"

"What?"

"Having a couple of drinks or a few hits doesn't mean I have a problem."

"No." I can't agree fast enough. She's sounding mad, and I've never made Marissa mad before. I'm still trying to figure out what to do when I get *Shannon* mad. Do all girls get mad in the same way, or are there endless varieties and levels of girl anger? "Mariss," I say. "Come on. I didn't mean anything. I was just joking around."

"Okay. Good."

"Good."

"So," she says. "How are you?"

"Good."

"Good."

We giggle again. We keep talking, and the next thing I know, I'm telling Marissa about the fight I had with Shannon. I manage to leave out the fact that the fight started over Marissa.

"You should call her," she says when I finish.

I shake my head, as if she can see me. "Uh-uh."

"She was probably just having a bad day."

"Maybe."

We keep chatting. She's so easy to talk to. Somehow we end up on the subject of my parents. "How wild is it that your mom and dad have been married all this time?" she says, like it's a *Guinness Book of World Records* event. "I hardly know anyone whose parents are still together."

There's a question I'm dying to ask her, but it's so nosy. But she's my friend, and I finally decide it's okay to ask.

"Marissa? Um . . . where's your dad?"

Silence.

"I mean, I know about your mom. But I was wondering what the deal is with your dad. Why you live with your grandma."

I breathe, waiting.

She says so low I almost can't hear her, "He's in jail."

.........CHAPTER SIXTEEN.........

Camera: Latin for "room."

Shannon's parents are sitting in the living room when I arrive, interfering with my plans for a make-up make-out session.

My girl called *me* today. She said she was sorry! I didn't even have to grovel. She said she didn't know why she was so emotional last night.

So I begged Garrett to drive me over to Shannon's ASAP, but he flat-out refused. Dickwad. I can't wait till he needs a favor, so I can shut him down.

My dad took pity on me but made me wait till he was done with whatever unimportant thing he was in the middle of. Grrr. I'm craving my driver's license.

Now I'm rotting in Shannon's living room while her parents pretend they don't hate me.

They always put on a show of niceness, but I know they want me to go away so they won't have to worry about their daughter having sex.

We're not.

But we might, you know. If things were different. Okay, a lot different. We both know people our age who are having sex. I think parents like to believe that that's *not* happening, but sorry, olds, it is. I'm not clear who it helps if parents are in denial, but whatever.

Shannon's mom watches me like a hawk. When I catch her staring at me, she gives this pained smile, like she's got bad gas.

Mr. DeWinter is really old. Like fifty, I think. He's out of touch with life in general, but he does like football. In fact, when we first met, he thought I was Garrett. "So you're the halfback, eh?" When I had to admit that he was thinking of my brother, his expression soured and has never changed since.

"Have fun, honey," says Shannon's mom. "Take a sweater. You're going to freeze in that shirt."

No, she won't, I think. *I'm going to have my hands all over her.*

Shannon grabs a jean jacket. "Bye," she says to her parents, breezing out the door.

I try to smile reassuringly at Mrs. DeWinter, but I have a feeling my smile looks as pained as hers.

My dad is waiting in the car outside. He drops us off at the Meriwether Mall, where we walk around for a while, holding hands; then we go to a movie, pushing up the armrest between us so we can squish closer together.

I couldn't even tell you what the movie was about. I was in a state of Shan-toxication through the whole thing. My nads must've been the color of blueberries.

We go back to my house for some dessert before Shannon has to be home.

"Mom, we're going to have these cookies in my room," I say, heading for the stairs.

My parents are cool enough to allow us to be in my room alone, but they make a point of clomping past my door every so often. We can tell when my mom is going to make an appearance: the piano playing stops. With my dad, it's loud humming.

"Why don't you take that thing down?" asks Shannon, glaring at my poster of Rose Tyler, the girl from *Doctor Who*.

"What? Why?"

"She's not that pretty."

On what planet? I feel like asking. There's no way I'm taking my Rose off the wall. She's my good-luck charm. I fondle that poster every morning before I leave the room.

"She just wears a lot of makeup," says Shannon, wandering over to my desk. She picks up my model of Doctor Who's TARDIS (Time And Relative Dimension In Space), holding it carelessly.

"I never noticed," I say. I take the TARDIS out of her hands and put it back on my desk. I spent hours assembling and painting the Doctor's time machine; I wouldn't want anything to happen to it.

Shannon doesn't wear much makeup. She's not flashy and sparkly and turning heads every time she enters a room, but she has a deep well of hotness.

"Why do you need a picture of some other girl in here?"

Shannon straightens her school photo, which sits framed on my desk.

I feel like saying, *Come onnnn! You must be joking! It's a poster.* Instead I reach over and take Shannon's hand, pulling her down next to me on the bed. "Don't be jealous," I say.

"Blake," she says. "Your parents."

"They just made their rounds. We should be good for a few minutes."

She looks at me from under her lashes and leans closer. "Listen," she whispers.

I listen. I don't hear anything except the sound of the piano.

"That song," she says, moving her lips to my neck. "Isn't it pretty? I've played it. It's called 'My Heart at Thy Sweet Voice.'"

Then, well, we do what we can with our limited privacy. I hope my mom goes on playing that song forever. After a while I forget where I am, and Shannon reminds me by taking my hand in an iron grip and removing it from its softandgorgeous destination. She sits up and moves away from me.

I groan and bury my face in the pillow. "Give me a minute," I mumble. When I finally sit up and look over at Shannon, she looks kind of glowing and breathless, and I suddenly comprehend that primal urge to grab and *take.* Roughly.

But I would never grab and take from Shannon. Or any girl. God! What kind of animal would do that?

Still. This urge, this *drive,* feels like the most powerful thing in the universe. So the meaning of life is . . . sex?

That can't be right. All of this heavy thinking is helping me decompress, anyway. My heart rate and other functions are returning to normal. Whew. I'm less likely to do something macho now.

"Maybe I should go," says Shannon.

"I guess so," I say. I don't hear the piano anymore.

She stands up and adjusts her shirt. "Don't you have a mirror in here?"

I look around my room. I never thought about it before. "No," I say. I make a mental note to add a mirror, just for occasions like this. "You look perfect," I say.

She curves into my arms again, but then we hear someone coming down the hall, and she jumps back.

My mom treads heavily past the room, carrying a stack of towels.

"Hi, Mom," I say.

She turns and gives an innocent smile, like, *Oh hello . . . didn't realize your room was right there . . . just on my way to the linen closet, la la la . . .*

"Could you give us a ride to Shannon's house?"

"Sure. Just let me put these towels in the hall closet," she says.

"Right," I say.

As Shannon and I exit the room, she gives Rose Tyler a playful slap and growls, "Watch out. He's mine!"

•••••

"Blake, can you help me with something in the garage?"

My dad is standing in the doorway to my room, wearing his grease monkey coveralls. His wild hair flies free, somehow looking even more electrocuted than usual.

Uhn? My dad never asks me to help him in the garage. He gave that up when I was about twelve years old. And sure enough, I hear Garrett call from his room, "What do you need, Dad? I'll help."

"No thanks, bud. I need Blake at the moment."

"Are you sure?" Garrett appears in the doorway to his room, cell phone in hand. "Hang on a minute," he mutters into the phone, then looks at Dad. "What are you doing?"

My dad shifts from one foot to the other. "It's, uh"—he gives a weak smile—"I just need Blake. Come on." He turns and heads downstairs.

Garrett watches him go, a look of disbelief on his face. "Must need a midget for comic relief," he says, and goes back into his room, shutting the door.

Crap on toast. What the hell?

I go to the garage, where my dad is standing near his huge rolling toolbox.

"What do you need help with?" I ask.

"Oh, um," he says, and turns to rifle through the toolbox. He hands me a screwdriver. "Here."

"Thanks." I examine it as I would a fossil.

My dad grabs a wrench and sits down on his stool, peering at . . . a motor? a rotor? . . . on his workbench. This seems to mellow him out. "So, Blake."

"Yeah?" I wait for him to point at whatever I'm supposed to screw.

"Your mom tells me it's time for the Talk."

"Wha—"

"She says you and Shannon are getting very close."

"Uh . . ."

My dad reaches forward and twists something with his wrench. He breathes deeply, going to his Zen place. "So I wanted to touch base with you about safe sex."

Ohhhhh . . . .

. . . . Noooooo!

"Your mother and I gave you the birds-and-bees talk a few years ago."

Something which scarred me for life, yes.

"But we didn't address the birth control issue, because, well, it wasn't appropriate at that point."

I stare down at the screwdriver, wishing it were a key to unlock a door to a parallel universe where I could go to escape this conversation.

"Dad, Shannon and I aren't—"

"Let me finish," he says.

But he doesn't. He takes a big breath and says nothing. Poor guy. He would be perfectly comfortable describing a severed spine or something.

"No means no!" he bursts out. "You understand that, right? Your mom wanted to make sure we talked about that. Never force a girl to do anything. Okay?" Now he's staring hard at me, and I nod.

"Don't even try to *persuade,* okay, Blake? No gray areas! Got me?" He looks like he's about to pop a vein, and I nod in alarm. "Okay," he continues. "Sorry, but that needs to be crystal clear. And you'll know when it's right. Shannon, or whoever . . . *someday* . . . will know, too."

I open my mouth to protest, but I close it again. Maybe if I stay quiet, this will be over faster.

"Sexuality is a powerful force. Maybe the most powerful urge we have as humans." He keeps looking at me, and I want to curl up into a ball of embarrassment. But also? I'm fascinated. He's saying stuff that I was thinking *just last night.* "The thing about being human, though," my dad goes on, "is we have the ability to reason. We can choose to do the right thing, even when we don't want to."

Uhn? Does he mean that having sex with Shannon is wrong? Or *forcing* Shannon to have sex would be wrong? Which . . . *duh!*

My dad studies his motor thingie and applies his wrench to it again. This seems to help him focus. "Anyway," he says, "I know you'll do the right thing. Just wanted to be clear on that. How-

ever. When you do decide the time is right, I want you to be prepared. I'll show you where we keep the box of condoms in a minute. I had this talk with your brother a couple of years ago."

Where we keep the box of condoms? My head almost spins off my body. So does Garrett just shuffle in and grab a condom whenever he needs one, and my parents can tell when some are missing?

"In fact," says my dad, forging ahead, "in a perfect world, your girlfriend would be on some form of birth control, too. So you're protected from pregnancy *and* disease. Both of you."

"Dad." I so seriously cannot take any more of this. "Thanks. Really. But you don't have to worry. Shannon and I are not, um, ready."

A look of pure relief washes over his face. "Good! I'm glad to hear it. You're both very young. But even if it's not relevant now, it's important to get this stuff out in the open. And you can always talk to your mom and me. You know that, right?"

I nod. I look down at the screwdriver in my hand. I set it down on the workbench. "Can I go now?"

"Sure." He claps a hand on my shoulder, then pulls me close in a hug. "You're a good guy, Blake. I'm proud of you."

"Thanks," I say into his shoulder. We break apart, and I head for the door to the house.

"Hey," he calls.

No no no no no. "Yeah?"

My dad opens a cabinet above his workbench. "The condoms are in here, bud."

"'Kay, bye."

"In fact . . ."

WHAT?!

"Take one to go, why don'tcha?" He takes one out of the box and tosses it to me.

.........CHAPTER SEVENTEEN.........

Fear of what other people think should never dictate whether or not you get your shot. So what if someone sees you crawling on your belly or hanging from a tree? Do you think Margaret Bourke-White cared what other people thought when she became the first woman allowed to fly on a combat mission?
—*Spike McLernon's Laws of Photography*

Mr. Malloy is in a bad mood. Not sure why. Maybe his beret is too tight.

"Rudimentary," says Mr. Malloy, examining my Hurtle photos. Rudi-*wha*—? Does that mean I'm rude? And . . . mentary?

He notes my blank expression and says, "Gritty as usual, Blake. I get that. You've mastered stark and startling. These subjects are easy to shoot. They're interesting in themselves. You don't have to work at setting up the shot or layering the elements. I'd like to see you take bigger risks with your work."

If Mr. Malloy doesn't think photographing some of these thugs was risky, he's out of his shiny head.

I just nod and slide my photos back inside my portfolio. If I get another C in photo, it's really going to bust up my GPA. Why didn't I take drama or some shit like that?

Mr. M. reaches for Marissa's homework, and I tense. He's not going to bitch her out, too, is he? Because I might come unglued if he gets up in her face. This girl has enough trouble. A dead cat, a dad in jail for God knows what, and a meth-head mom. The last thing she needs is some asshat ripping on her work.

"Pretty," he says, examining her flower photos. He smiles. "As usual." He pauses over the shots of the ceramic angel in the nest. "Interesting composition," he adds.

Marissa shrugs happily. "It was kind of a weird idea," she says.

"I like it." He hands her back her photos. "Pretty-Gritty. What am I going to do with you two?"

After Mr. Malloy moves on to offend some other people, Marissa leans closer to me.

"My mom's home," she says quietly.

"She is? That's awesome. How's she doing?"

"Good, good." Marissa nods, but her eyes slide away from mine.

"Yeah?"

"Yeah." She fiddles with her notebook, extracting homework. "Well."

"Well what?"

"She's still, um, kind of down. It's a long process."

"What is?"

"Getting straight."

"But she was gone a month."

"I know. But getting straight takes longer than a month. Especially from meth. It's a whole life change. You can go to rehab and get clean, but you can't stay there forever. You have to come out and live your life. That's when the *real* hard part begins."

I can't help thinking to myself, *But she's alive. Dead is even harder.*

"When do you want to come over?"

"What?"

"When do you want to come over and take some photos of my mom? Remember?" Marissa pins me with her stare. "You promised you would take some pictures of my mom when she got out of rehab."

I hesitate.

"Well, it wasn't a promise," she says hastily. "I asked, and you said okay. But I'd really appreciate it."

"Sure," I say. "When's a good time?"

"How about tomorrow?"

Tomorrow? I was thinking she would say this weekend or something. Hmm. Shannon will be at soccer practice. It could work. I wonder if I *have* to tell her I'm going to Marissa's.

· · · · ·

Marissa's mom still looks sad, if you ask me.

She may be clean and sober, but she's not very happy.

And truthfully? She reminds me of twigs and dried leaves . . . like a strong breeze could blow her away.

Marissa bounces around her mom, saying, "Come on, Mom— it'll be fun."

"I don't want my picture taken." Marissa's mom is on the

133

couch, staring at the TV. She's surrounded by empty candy wrappers.

"Why not?" A whine enters Marissa's voice, and she grasps her mom's arm with both hands, giving it a slight tug.

"Well, my teeth, for one thing," says Marissa's mom. She bows her head and—oh, here we go—starts to cry.

Marissa shoots me a look, like, *I know this sucks, just bear with me.*

I shoot her back a look that says, *Can I please go now?*

"Mom," she says gently. "Come on. You don't have to smile with your teeth showing. But I want a new picture of you to go with your new life."

Marissa's mom heaves a sigh that comes up from the bottom of her scraped-clean soul. "I don't see why you had to drag your friend into this." But she stands up. "And I don't even have any makeup on. Why don't we do this another time?" She's almost pleading.

Marissa doesn't bend. "No. You know we'll never do it another time. And it's important to me. Okay? Can't you just do this for me?"

Marissa's mom turns to me, but her head remains bowed. "Where do you want me to stand?"

I unlock my lips to say, "Um, how about—"

"Let's go outside," says Marissa. Keeping hold of her mom's arm, she heads for the door.

I'm reminded of a mother dragging a stubborn little kid along, but this time it's all backwards. The kid is dragging the mother. I

134

follow them outside. *Let's do this,* I think. *The quicker I get the shot, the quicker I'm out of here.*

"Over there," I say with some authority, pointing to a big tree trunk. "I like that texture of the bark. It will make a nice contrast with your skin."

The truth is, I don't give a flying monkey's ass about texture and contrast. I just want this over.

Marissa's mom steps off the grass and goes to stand next to the tree. It's a big evergreen. A fir or something.

"Isn't it too dark under here?" she asks.

"No," I say sharply. "I'm going to use some fill lighting, anyway."

"What's that?" she asks.

"Uh, it just means I'm going to turn on the flash to light up your face so the tree doesn't add shadows."

I shoot a few photos of Marissa's mom. She doesn't smile until Marissa prods her, but that's almost worse. She stretches her pinched lips into a parody of a smile. The most colorful part about her is the purple streak in her hair, but even that is faded and washed out. All of her tattoos are covered up.

I review my shots on the tiny screen. Even with the flash, Marissa's mom has shadows under her eyes. Whatever. "Looks good," I say. "Thanks. I'll e-mail these to you."

"How about some over by the birdbath?" asks Marissa.

I don't even answer. I just walk in the direction of the birdbath and wait. Marissa positions her mother next to the gray birdbath like some life-size garden sculpture, and I snap a few more shots. "Okay!" I say. "Great. Thanks. I've got to get going. Mariss, see you tomorrow at school." I smile in the general direction of Marissa's mom and turn to leave.

"Blake," calls Marissa.

I keep walking. "Yeah?"

"Thank you."

I pause and glance back at her. She looks so grateful that I can't stay mad. "No problem, dude," I say.

.... CHAPTER EIGHTEEN ....

My portraits are more about me than they are about the people I photograph.
—*Richard Avedon, American photographer (1923–2004)*

Of course Shannon found out.

Because if it wasn't for bad luck, I'd have no luck at all. Like the song says.

We had one whole day of peace before my trip to Marissa's house came back to haunt me.

Why didn't I just tell Shannon about it? A smarter man would have.

We were all cozied up in the soccer beanbag at Ottomans. No soccer practice or sick grandmas for Shannon. No bitchy tricksters or troubled buddies for me. Just a squeezable honey with her hair tickling my arms and her eyes magnetized to mine. Isn't love like a drug? I know: a song says that, too. *Somebody* has already said everything.

Shannon has my camera and is taking photos of me. "You be the subject, Blake. I will immortalize you."

I strike some goofy poses, and she snaps away, giggling. I get out of the beanbag and do a couple of big pratfalls.

She laughs so hard that other people can't help looking at us and smiling. I feel like I've scored a hundred points with Shannon's beautiful belly laugh.

"Here, I'll show you how to do a mini-movie kind of thing," I say. "I'll do a bunch of poses where I move, like, an inch at a time, and you shoot the photos, then we'll review them really fast and it'll look like stop-time animation. That's how they do claymation, like *Wallace and Gromit*."

We screw around with that for a few minutes, laughing at the movie of me pretending to trip and fall.

"Hey!" she says. "Let's get someone to take our picture." She climbs out of the beanbag and asks a girl nearby to take a picture of us. The girl nods and waits for us to snuggle back into the beanbag. She takes a couple of photos and hands the camera back to Shannon. We peer into the review screen; we look shockingly cute.

I turn the camera on her. "Do Mr. Burns for me."

She goes shy. "What?"

"Your Mr. Burns impersonation. Come on. I'll take some shots. In fact," I say, flipping the button to MOVIE, "I'll even make a movie of it!"

"Nooo."

"Why not?"

She shakes her head. "You have to earn Mr. Burns."

"What?!"

She's laughing now. "I don't do Mr. Burns for just anyone."

"Shannon!"

"Nope." She's really getting into this now. "Mr. Burns is reserved for my most trusted inner circle."

"*I'm* not in your inner circle?"

She's laughing so hard she can hardly speak. "I'm reviewing your application."

I tickle-attack her. "I'll review *your* application!"

While we're engaged in beanbag battle, a few of our friends breeze in—Riley and Caitlin and Dez and Bald Jake.

I stroke Shannon's arm. She may not be curvaceous and bodacious like Dez, but I wouldn't change her. Guys are constantly ogling Dez. I would hate it if guys were doing that to my girl.

Riley pretends to climb into the beanbag with us. "Move over, Shannon," he complains. "You're hogging the sweet spot."

She giggles and pushes him halfheartedly. He does a big pratfall, just like me! I taught him that.

It warms the cockles of my socks to see my best friend and my girlfriend joking around. Shannon has always felt a little shy around Riley, so it's cool to see them starting to become friends.

I'm floating along in blissful ignorance when it happens.

"Did you get some good photos at Marissa's yesterday?" asks Caitlin.

Shannon stiffens.

I blink. "Yeah," I say.

"Her grandma is really nice," Caitlin adds.

Houston, I think. *Oh shit.*

Houston maintains radio silence.

I don't think Caitlin has any idea that she's ruining my life. She probably thinks Marissa and I were innocently working on a photo assignment together; I doubt she even knows about Marissa's tweaker mom.

"Yes. She is. Mary," I say, stumbling along. "Her name is Mary. She *is* nice."

A rigid smile is fixed on Shannon's face, and her body has gone wooden.

Everyone hangs for a while, eating and drinking and goofing. Shannon does her best to act normal, but her body is no longer curved against me. She has gone stiff and spiky.

Finally it's time to make our way home. I struggle out of the beanbag and hold out my hand to her. She takes it without smiling.

We walk out to the bus stop. Not talking.

Finally I say, "You're mad, aren't you?"

"No," she says.

But she doesn't look at me, and even though I may not work at the Genius Bar, I can tell she *is* mad.

We walk in silence for a minute.

After what feels like a year, I ask, "Are you sure?"

"I'm not mad." She pauses. "I'm wondering."

"Wondering what?"

More walking in silence.

Finally she says, "Wondering whether or not I can trust you."

Ow! I get an image of the Mr. Burns Circle, with me standing outside of it. "You *can* trust me. I've told you a hundred times that Marissa is just a *friend.*"

"I know. But I can't help wondering."

I clutch my head. *Houston, please translate . . . Stat!*

Shannon watches me for a moment, then puts her hand on my arm. "It's just, I don't understand why you wouldn't tell me you were going over to another girl's house. Don't you see that it looks kind of sneaky?"

Well. When you put it *that* way.

"Yeah. I can see that." I feel terrible now. "I'm sorry. I had to, though."

"Had to?"

"Yes." Things are getting sticky here. I can't tell Shannon about Marissa's mom. Am I going to have to lie now? Before, I just omitted the truth. Now I may have to lob it out the window.

"Was it an assignment?"

I hesitate just long enough for her to frown.

"Yes," I say. "Kind of." I look away from her. "But not a school assignment."

"Not a school assignment," she repeats.

Suddenly I know what to do. I pull her close and say, "Look. For the last time, Marissa is a friend and that's all. I love *you.*"

. . . . .

Thursday afternoon Shannon has soccer practice and I don't feel like hanging out at Ottomans. Riley and I meander over to the soccer field to take a gander at the girls.

"You going to the homecoming dance?" I ask Riley.

He belches and shrugs. "I dunno. I haven't asked anyone."

"It's in, like, three weeks. Pick someone and ask." I indicate the field, ripe with prospects.

"What do you care?"

"Dog, I don't want to rot there alone!"

"Alone? Won't you be there with your pseudo-wife? Isn't that the point?"

"To rot and *fester* alone," I add.

"All right, all right."

"Rotting and festering and congealing."

"ALL RIGHT." He slugs me, not hard. "Who should I ask?"

I consider. Trying to keep a straight face, I say, "How about Dez Hayes?"

We howl, almost falling off the bleachers.

"Can you see it?" Riley gasps, trying to catch his breath. "'Um, Dez? I know you're the rockin'-est hottie in tenth grade, but how about going to the homecoming dance with me, a complete scrof?'"

"Scrof? Hey! Where did you hear that word? My brother calls me that."

"Heh. He calls me that, too."

We laugh our scrofulous asses off.

We decide he should ask Shannon's friend Kaylee to the dance. There. That's done.

Riley's brother Carter comes by, wearing a T-shirt that says STUPIDITY ISN'T A CRIME, SO YOU'RE FREE TO GO. Riley takes off with him, and I wave goodbye to Shannon, then mosey to the football field to wait for my brother to finish practice, so I can snag a ride home with him.

Finally the jocks lope off the field to the locker room and I gather my stuff. Garrett doesn't spend all day primping after practice, like some of these prima donnas.

As I approach the gym, I see the back door open, and Garrett comes out. I'm about to call out to him when I see his face undergo a transformation: it lights up, kind of like Shannon's does when she sees me.

Then I see a girl with blue streaks in her hair walking across the parking lot toward him.

CHAPTER NINETEEN

Number of times Salvador Dalí leapt into the air
for Philippe Halsman's famous photo: 28
Number of times people outside the shot had to throw water,
furniture, and three cats in the air while Dalí jumped: 28
Number of people happy that Photoshop was invented: 28,000,000

I so don't get the whole homecoming hullabaloo.

First off, Shannon goes into a tizzy when I tell her that Riley is going to ask Kaylee to the dance. She literally gasps. "Really?!"

"Um, yeah?"

"Did he say he liked her?" she asks.

"Uh—"

"Because don't tell him I told you this, but she totally likes him."

"Really? Okay."

"She says he has pretty lips." Shannon mashes both hands against her mouth. "Ohmygod, don't tell him I said that!"

"Ew!" I say. "I'm not going to *tell* him. I'll be too busy scrubbing that visual from my brain with a wire brush."

I have some fun making her beg before I reassure her that I have no intention of telling Riley and, in fact, probably won't even remember it. I have less fun listening to her talk about what she's going to wear to the dance, and what she wants me to wear, and what Kaylee might wear, and what Riley should wear if Kaylee wears what Shannon *thinks* she will wear.

I hold her while she talks, until words like "spaghetti straps" and "matching cummerbund" and "boutonniere" all run together in a soothing hum of foreign words.

. . . . .

This time Marissa has a huge bruise on her arm after Hurtle.

"Cool!" I yell.

"You're so bizarre," she says, shaking her head.

"You have to let me photograph it," I say.

"No! You're insane. It's bad enough I let you shoot my black eye."

"I'm insane? *I'm? Insane?*" I walk around in a circle, my hands and face raised to the sky. "Who is the person in this room who keeps aiming her bike down a death-wish hill? Anyone? Anyone? Bueller?" I point at Marissa. "Could it be . . . *you?* Why yes, I think it's you!"

"All right, shut up!"

I sit down next to her. "So what happened?" I say. "And seriously, maybe you should stop doing Hurtle."

"No, I wasn't even doing Hurtle when it happened. It was another totally random thing of being in the wrong place at the wrong time. It's embarrassing. If I'm going to get all wounded, at least there should be a good story, right?"

"So what is the story?"

She sighs. "I was standing next to my brother, and I see some girls I met there last time, and I'm like, 'hey howzit goin'?' and I start walking toward them, only I didn't see some idiot skater guy barreling down the hill doing a handstand on his board—"

"Doing a handstand?"

"I know! In a crowd of people! Jerk. So I'm about to walk over to these girls, and bam! He crashes right into me and I go flying."

"Ohhh-owww," I say, wincing.

She shows me the scrapes on her palms. "You should see my ass," she says.

Blink. Blink.

"My right leg and hip are one big bruise."

"Yikes. Okay. I'm fine with not shooting photos of your, um, ass. But could I please take a couple of shots of your arm?"

"Phhft. You're serious, aren't you?"

"Yes."

"Why?"

"I'm Gritty, you're Pretty, remember?"

She gives me a blank look.

Wow. This may very well be the strangest conversation we've ever had. First asses and then a line that sounds like flirting. Marissa knows I mean Mr. Malloy's nickname for us: the Pretty-Gritty Team. I can't exactly take it back without implying that she's

146

not pretty, which would be rude. And mean. And untrue. I settle for saying, "You know what I mean."

She nods. "Yes."

We sit there for a second.

"And yes, you can take a picture of my bruise," she adds. "This one." She points to her arm.

"Sweet!"

·····

Shannon's parents drive her over to our house the night of homecoming so they can take pictures of the two of us all dressed up in our fancy outfits. Shannon is wearing a green velvet dress with long black gloves. I'm wearing a suit with a cummerbund, which turns out to be a flap of useless shiny material that goes around your waist and matches the girl's dress. She looks gorgeous. I look like a farb.

I think I even see Shannon's mom wipe a tear away from her eye. *Groannnnn.*

My dad drives us to the dance and says to have a good time. Shannon's mom will bring us home afterward. We walk inside the gym, which is all decked out in balloons and streamers and stuff to make us think it's not a gym.

"Let's look for Kaylee and Riley," says Shannon. She grabs my arm and pulls me along.

There's Big Jake with Dez. Go, Big Jake! There's Aisha and Bald Jake and Lola and Guy We Don't Know. There's some girl with short, silvery-gold hair with that Stone guy. Cappie? Jeez. Halloween was *last* week. She looks like a dandelion.

I look around for Garrett. There he is with Willow at the cheerleader table. I watch him for a minute, and sure enough, his glance flicks over to Cappie with the regularity of a lighthouse beacon.

I wonder what's really going on: whether they're together and "hiding in plain sight," as Garrett calls it, or they're *not* together, but he can't keep his eyes off of her.

I don't see Marissa. I forgot to ask her if she was coming to the dance.

We dance. We sit. We dance some more. Shannon's hair is in a complicated pile on top of her head, and little strands start coming loose, framing her face. She looks so tasty. I really wish we could go somewhere alone after the dance. But her mom is coming to pick us up at ten thirty. Her dad is probably too tired and decrepit to stay up that late. I'm thinking her mom will not even stop the car at my house. She'll just slow down and throw my cummerbund-wearing ass to the curb. Sigh. Who can blame her? She can probably see the lust I have for her daughter blazing out of my eyes.

I can't wait to get my driver's license. Seven weeks from today I turn sixteen. Then I'll wow them at the DMV with my mad driving skills and celebrate by driving over to Shannon's house all by myself.

Kaylee and Riley started out overly polite and shy with each other, but they've warmed up and are laughing together now.

Shannon watches them, a big smile on her face. "Maybe we can double-date with Kaylee and Riley," she whispers to me.

"No," I whisper back.

"What?"

"No."

"Why not?"

"How can I get you naked with other people around?"

"Blake! You're so obsessed."

"You say that like it's a bad thing."

She cracks up; then—be still, my heart—she hunches over. She pulls her upper lip above her front teeth and twiddles her fingers together. She says, very quietly, just for me, "*Ex*-cellent, Smithers."

I feel a wobble in my heart. *I'm in.*

She let me in.

She drops the pose and giggles, blushing.

This girl slays me.

Shannon is everything I want. I thought she would be like the starter kit girlfriend for me, you know? After I figured out where things go and how they work, I would take my skills with me when I moved on to the next level.

But right now I can't imagine ever meeting anyone more perfect for me than this girl.

CHAPTER TWENTY

Do not attempt to load or unload film underwater.
—*Underwater camera manual, 1983*

"Hey, I didn't see you at homecoming Friday," I say to Marissa on Monday. "Did you go?"

"Naw."

"Naw?"

"I went to Hurtle."

"You went for a bike ride instead of the homecoming dance?"

"Blake, man, you should come with me again. It's so wild! And it's dark now at six o'clock."

I stare. "Wait a minute. Are you telling me you rode your bike down that stupid hill in the dark? Let's see it. Where's the new bruise?"

"It's not stupid. It was a total rush!"

"You're going to end up in a body cast," I say, shaking my head.

"Don't be such a wuss," she zings back.

Ow. That's gonna leave a mark.

"I'm not being a wuss. I just think you should have come to homecoming. It was fun."

She narrows her eyes, studying me. "Was it?"

"Well." I lift my hands. "*You* know. Fun enough. More fun than road rash."

"It helps to be invited," she says. "Besides, I was having a blast with these girls I know through Hurtle. Now, *they* are fun."

"Whatever."

We turn our attention to Mr. Malloy, who writes on the chalkboard: "Perspective and texture. Rockaway Beach. November 15."

People start buzzing.

Mr. Malloy ambles around the classroom handing out permission slips. "It's one week away, people. Get a parent to sign this, and bring it back to me. The beach is an excellent location for studies in texture. Great for perspective, too. Lots of opportunities for shooting the horizon. Which, of course, no one in this class will place smack in the middle of the frame, will they? I'm looking forward to seeing some innovative shots . . . worthy of the photo contest in March." He peers around at us, his beret cocked at a rakish angle. "And dress for cold weather. No swimsuits this time of year."

"Dang," I say. "And I wanted to wear my banana hammock!"

Chuckles.

One point!

• • • • •

"Guess what I heard!" says Shannon as we hunch over a tiny table in Ottomans. Someone has commandeered our soccer beanbag. From now on I will *reserve* that beanbag.

"What?"

She glances over at the table of cheerleaders, one of whom is Ellie, Mr. Hamilton's daughter. "I heard," she whispers, "that Ellie and Manny are, you know, doing it."

Ahhh. *It.*

"Oh," I say. Should I express my admiration? My envy? Or is she waiting for me to make a joke? "Um, mazel tov to the happy couple?"

She leans her head against my shoulder. "You're so funny."

"No, no," I say. "I'm about as serious as a seizure right now. Are we falling behind? Are we winging out of the loop? Are we *losers?* Because you know, much as I'm against it, I would be willing to—" I heave a big, fake sigh. "*Do* it if we had to. But only if it meant getting our ratings back up."

Blushing, she turns her face into my neck. "Blake."

"Shannon," I continue. "This is serious! You say the word and I will step up to the plate."

Her giggle warms my ear.

"No, really, I don't mind," I add. "We can cash in our V-cards this weekend if we have to."

She laughs harder. "V-cards?"

"V for virgin," I whisper.

"Blake, stop!"

"Okay." I don't want to push her. I'm still having flashbacks from my dad's "No means no!" tirade.

Shannon says softly, "I'm not ready yet." She looks me in the eye. "Okay?"

"Okay." I got it.

We sit in silence for a minute, with me stroking her arm. Then I say, "How about now?"

She laughs.

"You know I'm messing with you," I say.

She nods. "I don't mind," she says. "And who knows?"

I can't answer; I can hardly breathe. *Who knows.*

This feeling in my chest must be that thing with wings we read about in English: hope.

·····

This time, Cappie is sitting at the kitchen table and Garrett is bustling around the kitchen like a waiter. Apparently she failed to render him unconscious on this visit, because he's very busy scooping chocolate chip ice cream into the blender and measuring out milk as if it's the priceless elixir of life.

"Why, hello there!" she greets me, as if we're long-lost buddies.

I stand and glare at her. I'm not sure what I want to say to Chick Trickster, but the words "shut" and "up" come to mind.

She cocks her head at me. "Peace?"

"Phhft. Right."

"Don't start with me, honey. I'm in a good mood. But if you want to try me, I will rain down a hail of invective on your ass."

Invect-a-wha—?

Not sure what that means, but I get it. Raining down anything on my ass = not good.

Garrett cracks up and flips the switch on the blender, no doubt eager to make an offering to the Goddess of Threats and Hunger.

"Not too whippy," yells Cappie over the noise of the blender.

"You got it, babe," Garrett yells back.

Oh, the humanity! He's like a neutered barista.

"Hey, can you make me one, too?" I ask.

"Make your own," he says.

Whew. The real Garrett is still in there somewhere. I shrug and walk out of the kitchen.

"Oh, come on," says Cappie. "Don't go away mad, Blake. Just go away. No, I'm kidding. Blake! Hey!"

I step back in. "What?"

"I'll fix you a shake," she says, smiling.

I study her. Very few of her teeth are showing, which reassures me. "Really?"

"Sure. How hard can it be?"

Garrett pours his concoction into two glasses, he and Cappie clink, and they each take sips.

"Ahh, perfect," says Cappie. "Now I'll make one for your brother, and we can break bread, or dairy products, together like civilized people."

She steps over to the blender and examines it as if it's a NASA control panel. Picking up the ice cream scoop from the counter, she plunges it into the carton of chocolate chip ice cream and digs around inside. She pulls the scoop back out a little too forcefully, and a huge glob of ice cream goes flying across the room.

The Dog Formerly Known as Prince, who has been lurking under the table all casual-like, makes his move. He snarfs up the ice cream, shuddering a little at the cold.

"Cappie, Blake can make his own," says Garrett. "Don't even bother."

"No, no. I want to do it. It can be a peace offering. I've been cranky with him."

Garrett and I watch her slop around in the melting ice cream, getting it all over her hands and even a little on her face. Then she dumps way too much milk into the blender and reaches for the switch.

"Wait!" yells Garrett, but he's too late. Cappie flips the switch, *forgetting the lid,* and ice creamy liquid shoots out of the blender like a scene from a movie. She bangs off the switch.

The counter, the floor, and Cappie are coated in milk and flecks of chocolate.

The Dog Formerly Known as Prince wags his tail and makes his way over to her, all helpful.

I laugh so hard I fall on the floor.

．．．．．

The beach is cold.

Not just cold like, *Brr, wish I'd worn my heavy coat.*

Cold like, *Ohmygod where's my hat and gloves, oh that's right, I'm* wearing *them, but they're drenched from the rain! And the coat feels more like a T-shirt because the wind is knifing through it.*

That kind of cold.

We take turns holding umbrellas over one another so we can point our cameras without getting them wet. And forget about trying to get shots of the horizon because . . . where *is* it? All we can see is a solid wall of dark gray meeting medium gray topped with light gray.

I've never gone to the beach before and had exactly zero percent fun. Today is that day. I'm sure most of our shots will be blurry from us shivering as we tried to focus. A couple of people go to the trouble of setting up tripods in the sand. Maybe they'll have better luck.

Marissa even attempts to build a sandcastle.

"Dude, it's getting washed away by the rain even as you build it," I comment.

"No, it's not," she says. "I totally love castles, don't you? I'm going to travel all over Europe after high school and see lots of castles. Think of the photo ops!"

I grunt. "The only castle I've ever seen was the one at Disneyland."

She laughs. "You can come to Europe with me." She sticks a tiny piece of driftwood on top of the mound of sand, like a flag. "There. Finished." She stands up, the knees of her jeans soaked. "Take a picture of me with my castle, please? My hands are sandy. I don't want to get any on my camera."

I try to stop shivering long enough to shoot a couple of photos of her and the blobby castle.

After an hour of sandy slogging, Mr. Malloy herds us back to the bus and makes the driver stop at a Coffee Jones, where he buys every single one of us a hot chocolate. That's pretty cool of him. And I'll say this for Beret Boy: he didn't bitch once about the weather. He held umbrellas, he offered encouragement, and he pointed out angles that we were too busy being wet and cold to even notice.

We drape our wet coats over the seats at the back of the bus and put our wet shoes in a circle near the heating vent. We warm our hands on our hot chocolates and giggle together like people who've survived a brush with the elements.

The bus warms up on the drive back. Mr. Malloy banned electronics on the trip, which seems totally power mad. Come on, an hour and a half without iPods or Game Boys?

A few people skulk to the back so they can text furtively on their cells. Others play cards, but most of us gather around Nate, who brought his guitar. It's all very Woodstock, only we're covered in sand instead of mud.

Marissa finishes her hot chocolate and sighs with satisfaction. A slight smile curves her lips as she listens to Nate play the guitar. After a few minutes she wanders off to a seat by herself. She wipes the fog off her window and stares out at the passing scenery.

I listen to Nate pluck out another song, then I join Marissa.

"How ya doin'?" I ask.

"Good." She smiles lazily at me. "Isn't it pretty out there?" She indicates the trees. "I wish I had a camcorder. I would let it run for the whole drive. Then I could watch the trees and the fields and cows and stuff go blurring by anytime I wanted." She slides down in the seat and closes her eyes. "But I'm so sleepy. I'm going to close my eyes for a minute. My mom and I were up late last night. She's not ready for bed when she gets off work, so I stay up and talk to her."

"What's your mom's job?"

"She's working downtown, cleaning office buildings at night after everyone leaves."

"Huh. Good for her."

"She hates it," mumbles Marissa, yawning.

I feel kind of sleepy, too. I think about moving to a different seat, but I'm too lazy to even do that. I slide down and close my eyes. A few minutes later Marissa's head drops against my shoulder.

We wake up when the drone of the motor stops. Our day of perspective and texture is over.

CHAPTER TWENTY-ONE

Owning a fancy camera doesn't make you a photographer.
It just makes you the owner of a fancy camera.
   —*Spike McLernon's Laws of Photography*

"Happy, slappy, toe-tappy Friday to you, people. The weekend is anon. That's a word meaning 'soon,' according to my ever-present and effervescent advisor, Mr. Hamilton." There's a muffled voice in the background, and Cappie adds, "From the Middle English." Then she cracks up, and a male voice joins in her laughter.

"Is that Mr. Hamilton?" asks Shannon.

"Where?"

"On the radio. In the background," says Shannon. "It sounds like him."

"I don't know."

We're eating lunch with Riley and Kaylee—West Park High's newest BF-GF couple. Jasmine stopped by at the beginning of lunch, but she left after a few minutes. Probably feels like a fifth wheel. That must suck.

Cappie's voice rings out again. "I've got a giftie for you nifty listeners. From 1993, when you were still a dream, just a gleam in your parents' eyes, here's 'Laid,' by James."

We listen for a minute. I've never heard this song before, but it shreds! The guy is wailing about his bed being on fire with passionate love, and his girlfriend only coming when she's on top; then he starts doing this wild "eeeeeee" kind of yodel. Cappie may be a freak, but she knows her music.

Shannon lowers her voice. "Do you think there's something going on with them?"

"Who?"

"Cappie and Mr. Hamilton."

"What?"

"She always seems very cozy with him."

"He's a *teacher*."

"He's a *hot* teacher."

"Shannon!"

"I'm just saying."

"She acts cozy with a lot of guys," I say. I haven't told anyone about Cappie and Garrett, because, well, I'm pretty sure she's capable of removing my entrails through my rectum, and I don't need that.

Riley and Kaylee aren't paying any attention—they're in their own little world at the moment, their heads close together as they share an iPod and a cup of pudding. We eat lunch in companionable silence for a minute; then Shannon says, "My grandma is in the hospital again."

"Oh, no. Is she going to be okay?"

"Yes," she says firmly. "We Gold women are tough."

"Gold? Your last name isn't Gold."

"No. It's my grandma's name. Before she married my grandpa. Anyway, we come from a long line of tough women. Grandma's been in the hospital before, and she always gets better."

"Oh. Well, good." I hold her hand. "I always knew you were gold."

Shannon has a faraway look in her eyes. "My great-grandma came over to America from Ireland. Did I ever tell you that?"

"No." Maybe I should try that "gold" line again. I don't think she heard it.

"She came over here when she was seventeen—can you imagine? She worked as a maid in a big New York hotel."

"Huh."

"She married a Jew, Harold Gold, which is where we got the name. It was scandalous back then."

"Of course."

"So don't mess with me!" she says all of a sudden, mock-ferocious. "The blood of the Gold women runs in my veins!"

"Ugh. Blood," I say, turning over her hand to study the veins in her wrist. "Look! It's right there." I point to the veins. "I can see it!"

"You'll never believe what happened at the ME's office today," says Garrett.

"Shut up, I'm busy," I say. I'm the current high scorer in Splattercrash 3—Gore Galore.

"No, listen, you'll love this," he says.

My dad always thinks we're going to love his gross stories, too.

"So Dad's working on this guy. The dirty guy, we call him."

Sigh. I can't drive this virtual ambulance when Garrett is yammering. I hit pause.

"He's all filthy and greasy-haired. He's got hollow teeth, even! And the ones that aren't hollow are just black stubs."

I make a face, rubbing my mouth.

"Anyway, he doesn't have any track marks, so he doesn't seem to be a junkie. Dad's gotta figure out why he kicked off. But first he notices this bump on the guy's face, looks like a bruise or something. Dad's thinking, Huh, wonder what this is? and he scrapes at it with his knife, and blam! All this gray pus starts splurting out."

"Aauugggh!" I scream.

Garrett cracks up. "It's the first time I've ever seen Dad grossed out. He does this little squeamed-out dance, his arms all—" Garrett demonstrates a thoroughly icked-out Medical Examiner Move. Something you don't see very often, I'm guessing.

"Garrett?" I say.

"Yes."

"I don't need to hear that shit. In fact, I could have gone the rest of my life without hearing the story of *the dirty guy.* Okay?"

"Come on, it's funny! Can't you picture Dad?" He demonstrates the grossed-out jig again.

This time I do laugh. I can't help it. I'm a Hewson.

$$\cdots\cdots$$

The aroma of roasting turkey floats upstairs, where I'm on the phone with Shannon. "I wish you were here," I say, sprawling on my bed.

"Me, too," she sighs.

Even though she's miles away from me, the sound of her breath in my ear gives me wood. "Let's do something tomorrow," I say. "Go to a movie or something."

"I can't."

"Why not?"

"I'm getting up early to go Christmas shopping. It's a family tradition. The day after Thanksgiving is when they have the best sales." She pauses and says with a little catch in her voice, "I can't believe Grandma won't be able to go this year. She loves the sales. And she always buys us hot chocolate and we sit and watch the ice skaters in the Meriwether Mall."

"Aw. Sorry, babe."

She sniffs. "We're going to take her some Thanksgiving dinner in the hospital."

"That's nice."

We're quiet for a moment.

"Hey, Blake? I was talking to Ellie the other day. About . . . things. She was very, um, helpful."

"Things?"

I hear someone calling her in the background.

"Oh! I've got to go," she says. "The cousins are here."

"Wait! What about Ellie? What things?"

"Nothing. Never mind."

Synapses are firing in my hot little brain. Talking about *things* with Ellie. Ellie who is allegedly *doing it* with her boyfriend. "No, don't go yet! WHAT THINGS?!"

She snickers. "I can't say right now. Hi, Lainie!"

"Call me later, then!"

"I will."

Small silence.

"Bye," she says.

"Bye."

I hang up, noticing the silent *I love yous* suspended in midair.

· · · · ·

The traditional Thanksgiving gluttony is over and we're all lying around like tranquilized rhinos.

Mom is on the phone with Nonna. "Me, too, Ma. I can't wait. Kiss Poppy for me. I'll call you next week."

We're going to New York for Christmas break to visit the grandparents. Mom's so happy that I can't help but feel happy, too, even though this means missing Christmas *and* my birthday with Shannon.

That's right. I have the stupidest birthday ever invented: December 26. What day of the year do people least want to give someone a present? Correct! The day after Christmas. I can't tell you how many combo-presents I've gotten over the years. And! To add insult to injury, this means I will turn sixteen three thousand miles away from my sweetness.

I've been harboring a secret fantasy that Shannon's Christmas present to me will be . . . Shannon. And I could give her every inch o' my love, in the immortal words of Led Zep.

Ever since her casual "who knows?" comment, and now *especially* after she's had her talk with Ellie about "things," Houston and I have been on high alert, all systems go, waiting for the countdown to blastoff.

Dang. I guess I'd better buy her a real gift.

CHAPTER TWENTY-TWO

When attaching accessory lenses, be sure to attach securely.
If the lens becomes loose and falls off, it may crack,
and the shards of glass may cause cuts.
—*Mitsu ProShot I.S. 5.3 camera guide, 2007*

I hate to contribute to the swelling of Garrett's head. He already thinks he's an expert on women. But Christmas is coming up fast, and I still have no idea what to get for Shannon.

Finally I break down and ask him. "Man, what do girls want?"

He looks up from the book he's reading. "Huh?"

"For presents. What do girls want?"

"Oh," he says, putting down his book. "For a second, I thought you meant something more profound. In which case, my answer would have been: no one knows. And also: no one will ever know. And finally: don't even try to figure it out."

"Garrett," I say with a pained look. "Buddy. Leave the comedy to me, okay? You're gonna sprain something. Seriously. That looked like it hurt. You okay, man?"

He narrows his eyes and goes back to his book. Maybe I should have let him have his "joke."

Because now I'm on my own again for gift ideas.

. . . . .

"Mom, what should I get Shannon for Christmas?"

Mom is lying on the floor in corpse pose. Not that she's pretending to be a corpse; that's what they call it in yoga.

"Blake, I'm in *savasana*."

"I know. Corpse pose." It's like I'm the only one in this family not obsessed with corpses.

"That means I'm trying to be completely still and achieve mental balance."

"Right!"

"So can it wait?"

"Sure." I sit down on the couch.

After a minute Mom opens one eye and looks at me.

"Are you almost balanced?" I whisper.

She closes the eye again. "Blake!" Then she sighs and says, "Think about what Shannon likes to do."

Hmm. I ponder. What *does* Shannon like to do? She plays soccer, but soccer is finished now. She likes to read, but buying her a book seems boring. She does something musical . . . piano, maybe? "I think she plays piano."

"You think she does, or she does?"

"Um."

Mom opens her eyes and sits up.

"Are you balanced?" I ask hopefully. Maybe she can give me some ideas now.

"I'm as balanced as I'll ever be. Blake, you know Shannon better than I do. Better than most people, probably. Think of what she likes to do—not what you think she likes to do—then go to the mall and see if you get any ideas."

"But I hate shopping!"

"Then don't get her anything," she says impatiently. She gets to her feet and rolls up her yoga mat.

Strike two.

• • • • •

"Hey, Dad?"

"Yeah, bud."

"What do girls like?"

He looks bewildered for a moment. "Uh . . ."

"For presents. I'm trying to think of a Christmas present for Shannon."

"Oh!" The relief on his face would be funny if not for what he says next: "Go ask your mom. I have no idea."

• • • • •

"Mrs. DeWinter?" Truly: I am *that* desperate.

"Yes?"

"Hi, it's Blake."

Silence.

"Shannon's b—. . . uh, friend."

"Yes."

Nothing. She gives me nothing! No "Hi," no "How are you?" not even a "What the hell do you want?"

"I wondered if I could, um, ask you something."

"Yes?"

Ohmygod, she has said only one word so far. Three times.

"I was wondering if you . . . what you think, um . . . what Shannon might like for Christmas."

Silence.

"From me, I mean." I wipe my hand across my forehead. This is a first: a phone call making me sweat.

"Oh. From you." Her voice is as flat as a pane of glass.

"Yeah. For Christmas." *Oh, please,* I think. *Have a heart. Help me out here.*

"There is something," Mrs. DeWinter says reluctantly. "Her father and I were going to get it for her." She pauses. "But maybe . . . yes, maybe it would be nice coming from you."

I wait, holding my breath.

"There's a necklace she saw in the mall."

"Oh?" Now we're getting somewhere!

"Do you know that jewelry store in the mall? Metals?"

"I can find it."

"She saw a necklace in the window that she liked."

"Great! Which one?"

"Oh, you'll know it when you see it," says Mrs. DeWinter. Is she smiling? Her voice sounds like she's smiling.

"I will?"

"Yes. If you know Shannon, you'll know immediately which necklace she likes."

"Heh-heh. Okay, thanks. Thanks, Mrs. DeWinter."

Either she's screwing with me or she really believes I'll take one look at a necklace in a store window and know that it's meant for Shannon.

· · · · ·

I cannot tell you how happy I am that Metals has only! one! window!

Houston and I concentrate all available brainpower on analyzing the selection of necklaces.

Gah! There are a million of them. I'm in Necklace Hell! Gold . . . silver . . . is that bronze? Some with blue stones, some with red stones, some with little diamonds. Real diamonds? Surely Shannon's mom doesn't think I can afford to buy her daughter a diamond necklace. But which one is the one I'm supposed to "know immediately" that she'd like? My eyes jump around in a panic. I start to hyperventilate, fogging up the window.

When I lean my forehead against the glass in despair, I see a necklace near the front corner.

And she's right. Psycho-Mother is right. I look at it, and somehow I know immediately that it will look amazing on Shannon.

It's silver, and it looks gypsyish. Or maybe belly dancer–ish. Tiny silver disks cascading down in links that end in blue teardrop jewels. I can't describe it very well. But I can picture her wearing it, with her blue eyes picking up the color in the jewels.

I cup my hands around my eyes, trying to make out a price. Crap. It's the kind of necklace that doesn't have a price tag on it!

I straighten up. Oh well. *At least I found it,* I think, heading into the store.

I am the best boyfriend ever.

· · · · ·

Shannon and I arrange to give each other our presents the night before I'm supposed to leave town. It won't be a full-blown date, more like half an hour at her house, but at least we'll have some time together. Since it's going to be such a short visit, my mom will hang out with the DeWinters while Shannon and I exchange gifts. I can't wait to see her face when she opens my present.

Mom lets me drive the car over to the DeWinters'. She only gasps once on the way. Really, pedestrians should not wander around in the dark without reflective gear.

Shannon opens the door and smiles, inviting us inside. We walk in, and I can smell cinnamon and some other holiday-type spices. Mrs. DeWinter gives me a smile that is less pained than usual; it's on the verge of looking natural. Mr. DeWinter creaks out of his chair for the sole purpose of greeting my mother. I almost expect to see some kind of hydraulic lift maneuver him out of the chair. Then he sinks back down and resumes watching ESPN.

The two moms head off to the kitchen, talking about "mulled wine" or something, and Shannon and I escape to her room.

We crash into each other as soon as we're safe inside her room, staggering in our tight embrace.

"I'm going to miss you so much!" says Shannon.

"Me, too," I say, covering her mouth with mine.

"Blake," she gasps.

"Mm."

"The door." We're pressed against Shannon's closed door.

"Oh, right," I say. With one hand I fumble at the doorknob, locking it.

She giggles into my neck. "Blake. You *know* my mom will be up in a hot second if I don't open the door."

"Let her try to get in," I say, maneuvering Shannon over to the bed.

She giggles some more, even after I throw her—gently—down on the bed.

"Blake, come onnn."

"As you wish." I lay down on top of her, bracing myself on my arms.

She's not giggling anymore. She's not smiling, either, but the expression on her face is not fear. If I thought she was scared, I would stop. Her eyes bore into mine.

I can feel her heartbeat flutter against my chest. *Someday,* I think. *Someday we won't stop.*

After a long moment I move to stand up.

Shannon grabs me and pulls me close. "I love you," she whispers.

"I love you, too," I say. What better time to say it?

There's some kissing, and then I drag myself away from her warm softness with a stifled groan. "Sucks to be fifteen," I grumble, opening her bedroom door.

I pick up her present, which ended up on the floor. "Here. Merry Christmas."

She claps her hands and takes the box from me. "Wait! You first. I'm so excited." She reaches for a flat gift-wrapped present on her desk and hands it to me. "I hope you like it."

It's got to be a book. I hold it up and shake it, pretending to listen for a rattle. "It's not a puzzle," I say. "It's not a chess set. What could it be? A bar of solid gold?" Shannon waits tensely while I tear off the paper.

It *is* a book. About us. There's a photo of Shannon and me on the front, taken at Ottomans that day we were goofing around with the camera. We look so smiley and cute. I turn the pages slowly. Shannon *made* this book. She put in pictures of us, and ticket stubs from a movie we went to, and some preserved petals from the corsage I gave her for the homecoming dance, and all kinds of other stuff that is special to us. There are stickers of shooting stars and hearts and captions on all the pages.

"Wow!" I say.

"It's a scrapbook," she says. "Do you like it? Is it lame? Am I such a *girl?*"

"Shannon," I say, "it's great! I love it. And yes, you're such a girl. That's the thing I like best about you. Now your turn." I point to the present, still in her hand.

She wiggles happily and peels off the wrapping paper. She looks up at me when she sees the velvet jewelry box. "Oooh," she breathes. She opens the box, and I wait for her to shriek and cover me with kisses.

"Ohh!" she says. "How pretty." She lifts the necklace out of the box. "It's beautiful, Blake! Thank you." She kisses me. "Put it on me."

I take the necklace from her, my heart sinking. She didn't react like I thought she would. "Don't you recognize it?"

"What?"

Stupid little ant-size links! I struggle with the clasp, sweat popping out on my forehead. "From Metals? Don't you recognize it?"

"Metals? Oh, that's where I've seen it! I thought it looked familiar."

"Isn't it—?" *It's the wrong one,* I think. "Never mind." I give up trying to fasten it around her neck. "I can't get this hooked."

"Let's go show my parents!"

"Er!" I jump up, wanting to stop her.

She turns back curiously. Of course she wants to show her parents. I can't hide in here forever.

I got her the wrong damn necklace.

She likes it, but it's not The One. The one I would *know immediately* was meant for Shannon.

If I knew Shannon.

She skips to the living room to show the parents.

While Mrs. DeWinter fastens the necklace around Shannon's neck, she looks right at me. In her cold eyes I read the judgment, *I was right. You don't really know my girl.*

I am the worst boyfriend ever.

CHAPTER TWENTY-THREE

Your first ten thousand photographs are your worst.
—*Henri Cartier-Bresson, French photographer (1908–2004)*

I feel like punching something.

Or *someone*.

It takes all of my concentration to sit politely in the DeWinters'
living room and squeeze out words that are not curses. I can't look
at Shannon's mom again, or I will shriek, "Bitch! How could you
do this to me? Why didn't you just *tell* me which necklace to buy?"

Maybe she really thought I would know. Maybe she thought
I *might* know, and she wanted to test me. How sick is that?

Well, I hope she's happy now. I fucking failed.

Shannon doesn't know the difference; she's smiling and putting her hand up to touch the necklace every couple of minutes.

But *I* know the difference.

It's the difference between giving your girlfriend a nice gift—
"pretty," she called it—and giving your girlfriend something that
would take her breath away and maybe make her so happy that

she would remember getting the gift for the rest of her life, because it was something she wanted and *you knew!*

After a few minutes Shannon notices my silence and takes my hand. In front of her parents! Take that, Mrs. DeBitch!

There's more chitchat: flying to New York tomorrow ... Grandma's health issues ... blah blah blah ... do we think it will snow? ... what's the forecast in New York ... blah blah blah ...

I zone out and focus on caressing Shannon's hand.

When it's time to go, I say goodbye to the Evils, I mean the DeWinters, as quick as I can. I just want to be away from these people.

Then all three parents stare at Shannon and me, waiting to see whether or not we will kiss in front of them.

I move in close and put my arms around my girl and give her a smacking kiss.

Take that, olds!

I stomp down the driveway to the car. I turn back and wave goodbye to Shannon. As soon as she closes the front door, I slap both hands down on the hood of the car as hard as I can. It hurts. I'd like to leave dents.

My mom raises her eyebrows as she approaches. She clicks the remote to unlock the car. "I was going to ask if you wanted to drive home," she says, "but as your father likes to say, 'Don't drive angry.' And you, my friend, seem a little angry."

"You think?" I snarl.

She doesn't react. Of course she doesn't. She's the goddamn expert in tact.

I hurl myself into the car and slam the door. She walks around to the driver's side. I'm shaking by the time she starts the car.

"Drive down the block," I say, and it enrages me even more to hear my voice crack.

I love my mom; she puts the car in gear and drives down the block. She sees an empty spot and pulls over to the curb. She puts the car in park and looks at me.

I slam open the car door and stomp up and down the sidewalk, yelling every curse word I know through my hands, which are clamped over my mouth. I know Mom hears me. But I can't stop. I don't think I've ever felt this mad before.

I kick the tires of the car. I slap my hands down on the hood a few more times, and it hurts every time, and I'm glad. Finally I sink down on my knees in the grass on the parking strip. It's wet and cold, but it feels good. I need to feel the ground so I can come down. I need to feel cold so I can cool down.

My cheeks are wet when I get back in the car.

At some point my mom must have turned off the motor, because it's dark and quiet inside. She waits.

"Sorry," I mumble.

"It's okay, honey," she says.

And I start bawling.

. . . . .

You will never believe this in a million years, so I'll just say it: Marissa and her mom are walking up to our house when we get home.

"Jesus!" I yell, and this time Mom speaks up. "That's just about enough, Blake."

"Sorry."

"That's your friend Marissa, isn't it?"

"Yes. And her mother."

"Ahh." My mom lifts her hand to acknowledge them. "Looks like they came to pay us a holiday call," she says.

"Effing great," I say.

"I see that you weren't expecting visitors," she says. "But please pull yourself together. I expect my family to be gracious hosts. Always."

"I know."

"Okay. Take a couple of breaths and let's go."

She gets out of the car and heads for the front door, where Marissa and her mom have stopped.

I rub a hand across my face roughly. I hope it doesn't look like I've been crying. I open the car door and head for the house.

My mom is smiling and shaking Marissa's mom's hand. "So nice to meet you, Anne. And it's nice to see you again, Marissa.

Please come in." She opens the front door and ushers them inside.

"We shouldn't have come," says Marissa's mom, shrinking inside her coat. "We should have called first. I'm sorry."

"Mom," mutters Marissa. She's holding a wrapped gift.

"No, no. This is perfect timing," says my mom. "We just got back from another visit. I'm so glad you came by tonight. Tomorrow you would have missed us. We're going out of town to visit my parents."

My mom keeps up a soothing flow of words. "Here, let me have your coats. Please make yourselves at home. Isn't it cold out? I wonder if it will snow. Anne, do you like tea or coffee? I have both. Blake, would you find your father and tell him we have visitors?"

"No!" says Marissa's mom.

We all freeze.

"I mean, no, you don't have to find your father," continues Marissa's mom. She flutters a hand up to her mouth. "Sorry. We can't stay. We just came to drop off a present." She pulls her coat closer around her and looks at the floor.

Marissa's face is bright red. "*Mom,*" she says, mortified.

"Oh, dear. Are you sure?" asks my mom.

My heart thumps with pride at my mom's kindness. She pretends that someone yelling no! after an invitation to have tea is perfectly normal. She always makes everyone feel welcome, no matter how strange they are

"It's really no trouble at all, Anne," continues Mom. "I don't want to keep you if you're on your way somewhere else, but we'd love to visit with you for a few minutes."

Marissa's mom shuffles her feet, still looking at the floor, as if she doesn't know what to say or do.

"Thank you, Mrs. Hewson," says Marissa. "That's really nice of you. We'll just stay for a minute." She takes her mother's arm and steers her into the living room. "Mom," she hisses. "Take off your coat."

Marissa's mom jerks her arm away from Marissa.

I glance at my mom, who is watching them. She doesn't react, except to turn to me and say quietly, "Please go fill the teakettle with water and put it on to boil. Then come back here. You don't have to wait for it to boil."

"Okay." I hurry to the kitchen. As I pick up the shiny kettle, I examine my face in its reflection, looking for signs of my earlier freak-out. My normal face looks back. Maybe a little more stressed than usual. I fill the kettle with water and adjust the gas flame under it. I wonder who the present's for. Me? But why? I didn't get a present for Marissa.

Marissa is smiling and chatting with my mom when I enter the living room. Marissa's mother hunches into the couch cushions, plucking at her hair. Without her coat, she looks frail and cold.

"Here." Marissa hands me the package, which is heavy and flat.

I take the present and hold it uncertainly. "Should I unwrap it now?"

"Yes!"

I pull off the wrapping paper and find a book titled *Earth from Above*. It's got tons of amazing full-color photos of Earth. From above. "Wow, thanks!" I say. I turn to Marissa's mom and repeat, "Thank you."

"You're welcome," she says. Her eyes flick to the door, almost as if she's thinking, *Now can we go?*

"Oh, how thoughtful," says my mom. "What a great book." She stands up. "Anne, would you like to help me with the tea while the kids talk photography?"

Marissa's mom stiffens and looks at Marissa.

Marissa nods and kind of cocks her head, like, *Go on.*

I've never seen anyone act so nervous around my mother. How much more can she do to make this twitchy woman feel welcome?

Marissa's mom exhales loudly, and I get a whiff of her breath. Ugh. Someone should really give her a case of breath mints for Christmas. She stands up and follows my mom into the kitchen.

"Thanks again," I say to Marissa.

"You're welcome. My mom and I just wanted to say thanks again. We owe you a lot."

"Stop it, you don't," I say, embarrassed.

We sit there for a minute.

"How's Shannon?" asks Marissa.

Ohhhh, I groan silently. A visual of Mrs. DeWinter flashes into my mind.

"Fine," I say.

Long pause.

"We just came from there, actually. Shannon's house. I took her a present," I say.

"Oh yeah? How'd she like it?"

"Good, good." I nod. My face hurts from all the fake smiling. What am I *doing*? I drop my head in my hands. This is Marissa; she's my friend. I don't have to pretend with her.

"Actually," I say, "it sucked reallyreallyreally bad."

"What?"

It's such a relief to tell Marissa everything . . . about asking people for ideas . . . finally asking Shannon's mother for help . . . buying the perfect necklace, or so I thought . . . and finding out tonight that it was not the right necklace, it was, in fact, the *opposite* of the right necklace.

Somewhere along the way I realize Marissa is giggling. I've managed to turn this traumatic event into a funny story. How did I do that?

I'm not sure, but I feel much better.

"You know what?" I say to Marissa.

"What."

"As my man Groucho Marx would say, 'I've had a perfectly lovely evening. But this wasn't it.'"

She laughs.

CHAPTER TWENTY-FOUR

After its opening at the Museum of Modern Art in New York in 1955, the Family of Man exhibit traveled around the world. The selection process took three years, starting with two million photos. It was winnowed to ten thousand, with the final 503 shots coming from 273 photographers and 68 countries.

I am so done with New York.

"What's a four-letter word for Mongolian desert?" yells Poppy from the living room. He's a crossword puzzle hound.

"Gobi," yells my brother.

How sad is it that we're reduced to doing crossword puzzles with the grandparents for fun? In *New York*. The Big Apple, the City That Never Sleeps, the hub of . . . something. But you know what? We've already done the Empire State Building, the Statue of Liberty, the museums, and a Broadway show. Garrett and I even got to go to a Mad Montoya concert for my birthday.

I would have gladly exchanged Mad Montoya for a birthday party with Shannon. You know, a *private* party? Where she could have given me a very special, once-in-a-lifetime present for my sixteenth birthday?

Well.

It *could* have happened.

But instead I'm chillin' with the olds.

Plane ticket to New York—four hundred dollars. Combo Christmas/birthday presents for your sixteenth birthday—two hundred and fifty dollars. Missing birthday sex while you hang out with your grandparents—priceless.

"Russ, get in here and wash your breakfast dishes," yells my mom from the kitchen.

Coming," yells my dad from the living room, where he's lazing on the couch watching CNN and telling Poppy medical examiner horror stories.

"You stay right where you are, Russell," yells Nonna from the kitchen.

Welcome to the East Coast grandparents' house. Nonna and Poppy weren't born in Italy, but they embrace the whole waving-your-hands-around-and-yelling part of their heritage.

And my mom! It's hilarious to watch her regress to being, like, their *kid* as soon as she walks through the door of their house. The woman has master's degrees in theology and psychology, but as soon as she gets inside the Bossy New Yorker Zone, she turns into Yellen McYellalot.

My dad loves visiting the in-laws; he gets to sit around and talk shit with Poppy while eating one huge meal after another. Nonna won't let him help with the cooking or the dishes, either, no matter how much my mom protests.

"Ma, why do you do this?" my mom always yells when we first get here. "At home the boys all do their share. They don't sit around and expect me to wait on them hand and foot."

"Yeah? Well, you're in *my* house now."

My mom always ends up rolling her eyes like a teenager and saying, "How can you be such a throwback? You've only been to Italy twice!" Then she hugs my Nonna and cries, and they sit around drinking coffee and eating homemade biscotti and gossiping about the rest of the family.

After about twenty-four hours, my mom joins in with the lazing around and eating. She tends to let Garrett and me goof off, too. I think it's kind of a vacation from responsibility for her. If Garrett or I do something really out of line, Nonna or Poppy yells at us.

We've been here a whole week now. I need to get back to my peeps. Especially my Princess of Peeps. We've been texting and calling each other on our cells, but I need to feel Shannon in the flesh again. The longer I'm away from her, the more she seems like a dream, like I'll go home and she'll look at me politely and say, "Who are you again? My boyfriend? I don't *think* so."

"What's a nine-letter word for rapidly ascending or descending musical notes?" yells Poppy.

"Glissando," yells Nonna without even pausing. She used to teach piano lessons.

"I should have known that," mutters Poppy. "Can you believe this goddamn market?" He's talking about the stock market. He used to be some kind of financial guy, took the train into the city every day for forty years. He's, like, seventy now, but he's still got a full head of hair, silver with black streaks in it, all cool and *Sopranos*-looking. I've noticed other old ladies checking him out when we're with him. I definitely inherited my Italian Stallion magic from him.

Poppy divides his attention between his crossword puzzle and the TV, where stock quotes are scrolling across the bottom of the screen.

"So this headless corpse comes in," says my dad.

Errggh.

Poppy looks up, delighted.

"Male, about forty; killed by a shotgun blast to the chest. Filled with bird shot. But then the killer decided to burn the body," says my dad.

Guhh. I feel my breakfast threatening to come back out for a visit.

"Jesus," says Poppy.

"We figured the killer wanted to disfigure the corpse, hence the missing head and the burning. If there are no dentals and no prints, it's hard to identify the guy, right?"

"Right." Poppy could listen to these tales of atrocity all day.

"Only problem is," says Dad, "the body was burned mostly on the front, not the back."

"Yes?"

"And the guy had his name tattooed on the back of his calves. Jorge on the left calf, Rios on the right."

Poppy and Garrett crack up. Even I smile faintly.

Murderers. Will they ever learn?

"His head came in a couple of days later," adds my dad.

·····

It's New Year's Eve. Garrett and I had planned to take the bus into the city and celebrate in Times Square.

"No," says Poppy.

I widen my eyes and look at my parents. They both shrug New Yorkishly, like, *Hey, whaddaya gonna do?*

"That's insane," adds Nonna for good measure.

"Why not?" asks Garrett.

"It's a mob scene like you wouldn't believe," says Poppy. "Trust me, you don't wanna go there. Stay home and watch it on TV in comfort with us."

Garrett and I look at each other.

"Besides, it's a scene tailor-made for the terrorists," adds Nonna. "Think about it: a gathering of thousands of people in one spot, waiting around like sheep for the slaughter. For hours."

Oh. The terrorists. Of course. They screw everything up. And way to freak me out, Nonna!

"Come on," I say. "Don't make us stay home. We're in New York!"

"Did you hear your grandmother?" asks Poppy, his eyes flashing. He's got these piercing black eyes; he looks like he's about to jab his finger at me and say, "Drop it, or you'll sleep with the fishes!"

"But—" I try one last time.

"Put a sock in it, Blake!" he yells. Heh. Somehow I don't feel *yelled at* when Poppy yells at me.

Sure enough, this New Year's Eve finds Garrett and me decaying in front of the TV, watching other people party in one of the most famous landmarks in the world. I don't know about Garrett, but I'm all anxious now, expecting bombs to go off at any moment. When the lighted ball finally drops and no one explodes, I can actually feel my body relax.

We all cheer and drink our champagne. I've never drunk cat piss before, but I feel certain it is similar to champagne. The olds kiss one another, then insist on kissing Garrett and me. I think about Shannon. I hope she's not kissing anyone. Except her frigid mother and her living-dead father.

And tomorrow we fly home!

· · · · ·

"Calm it down, Studly," says Garrett, wheeling into the parking lot of school.

"What?"

It's the first day back from winter break. I seem to have brought back the Zit That Ate Manhattan on my chin. I keep staring at it in the passenger mirror, aghast.

"You're like a puppy," continues Garrett. "You're practically leaving nose prints on the window. Calm it down or you're going to bark like a dog when you see your girlfriend." He eases the car into a space and sets the parking brake but doesn't shut off the engine.

I wait for him to continue his insult/advice, but he's silent now, listening to the radio.

Ah. Cappie is announcing.

"Good morning, freaks and geeks. That was 'Wake Up' by Arcade Fire on KWST. How are you this sludgy Monday? Feeling like you've been bludgeoned?"

"Yes, we're back. Back and slack after two weeks of jack," says Cappie. "Did you miss me? It's cold and dark without the light, isn't it? Don't worry, babies, Chick Trickster is here. I'll be gentle with you. Here's Early Mo with a little ditty called 'Five A.M.' This is 88.1—KWST."

There's a small smile on Garrett's face. I almost call him on it. I'm about to say something like, "Speaking of puppy love," but I don't. We're both happy to get back to our girls; at least mine lets me acknowledge her in public.

When I see Shannon across the hall, I feel like I've had all the air in my lungs vacuumed out.

When you haven't seen someone you love—there, I said it—for almost two weeks, it's not exactly that you forget what they look like, but their image starts to get blurry in your mind. Here's my girl, in all her three-dimensional, succulent glory, right in front of me.

A wave of shyness hits me. I force myself not to put my hand up to my chin, where the giant zit laughs at me. I hope she doesn't take one look at it and think, Eww. Pimple Boy does *not* think he's going to kiss me with that *pustule* so near his lips?

"Hi," I say. I stare at Shannon, soaking up all the things I missed while we were apart: her hair is so shiny and soft—I want to touch it. Her eyes are so blue they make me think of summer. Her lips are so perfect, I need to taste them.

Two weeks ago I would have walked up to her and put my arms around her. Now I feel . . . not exactly afraid, but unsure. She looks too good for me.

"Hi," says Shannon.

"Hey, Blake," says Kaylee. "Have you seen Riley?"

"No," I say. "I just got here." I barely glance at Kaylee; I'm busy with my detailed inspection of my girl. It's good that she's wearing a bulky winter coat, because otherwise I might start to slobber. In general I don't love winter, when girls have everything covered up with lots of clothes.

"How are you?" Shannon asks. She seems shy with me, too.

"Good. Great." I nod like a bobblehead. *"Now."*

She smiles and looks down.

"See you," says Kaylee, and leaves.

"I missed you," I say in a low voice.

She looks up at me, not smiling now, and moves closer. I can smell her flowers-and-rain scent, and I kind of shiver when she takes my hand. "I missed you, too."

She reaches into the collar of her coat and pulls something out to show me. Is she wearing the necklace I got her? Aw. My girl.

Wait. That's *not* the necklace I got her.

"Look what my parents got me for Christmas," she says.

I lean closer. It's a black velvet ribbon with a jeweled piano attached to it—the black keys on the piano are made out of something dark and sparkling, and the white keys are made out of something pearly, I think it's called mother-of-pearl. "Wow," I say.

"Isn't it gorgeous?" she says, peering down at it.

I open my mouth to agree, but nothing comes out. I swallow.

Shannon looks up at me and a change comes over her face. "I was going to wear your necklace," she says quickly. "But it really looks better with low-cut tops. And it's winter right now, so it's cold."

I nod.

"I'll be able to wear it all the time when it gets warmer," she adds.

I force a smile onto my face, hoping it doesn't look as painful as it feels. My hand creeps up to the disfiguring zit on my chin.

CHAPTER TWENTY-FIVE

Two words to live by: Flip it. As soon as you get your shot horizontally,
flip the camera and take it vertically.
—*Spike McLernon's Laws of Photography*

"Welcome back, my tenth grade tormentors," calls out Mr.
Hamilton. He is practically bouncing off the walls. "I hope everyone had fantastic holidays!"

Could he cheer down once in a while? We, the captive audience, are in a fragile, post-vacation state.

Marissa is not in class today. I'll call her later. Maybe she and
her fractured family all glued themselves together for such a festi-
val of merrymaking that she's burnt. I wonder if they go visit the
dad in jail. But I doubt it. She wouldn't tell me what he did to end
up in prison, just that "some things can't be fixed, no matter how
sorry you are."

Every time I glance over at Shannon, her necklace leers at me.
It seems to be saying with a glint, "This is the one you should
have known *immediately* was perfect for her. Loser."

By lunchtime Shannon has tucked the offending item away

under her sweater. Maybe she could feel me dying a little every time I looked at it.

Kaylee and Riley join us for lunch, and now I'm irritated by them. Do we have to be this tight little foursome all the time?

I perk up talking about New York, feeling like a jet setter among the country bumpkins.

"Too bad your gramps wouldn't let you go to Times Square for New Year's," says Riley. "That would've been cool. You could've called us on your cell from the crowd, and we could've looked for you on TV."

"That *would* have been cool," I mutter.

"Yeah, too bad," echoes Kaylee. "Because what if you never go there on New Year's again?"

My mood falls to the ground.

Shannon slips her hand into mine and squeezes.

And just like that, I feel better. She's some kind of wonderful. Like the song says.

· · · · ·

Marissa is absent again today. Huh. Now that I think of it, I didn't hear from her over the break, either. Not that we e-mail or call on a regular basis, but before she and her mom left our house that night, we did say to each other, "Talk to you over the break."

I hate this sinking sensation I get in my gut when I think of

Marissa and her mom. Why can't everything be okay for them now? Her mom finished rehab, she's got a job, Marissa is happy. Maybe her mom can save up for an apartment and they can live together, and maybe someday even Gus, the brother, will forgive the mom for whatever it was she did to him when he was a kid.

I picture all of these hopeful fantasies for Marissa's life; then I watch them smoke and curl up around the edges and crumble into ash.

Mr. Hamilton is poking through our journals this morning.

I riffle through the pages of mine. I did write *some* stuff. Not much, though. I don't know a lot of guys who *journal*. I was bored on the plane ride back from New York, so I wrote about the trip. And I wanted to write about Shannon, but I was too embarrassed. Don't tell anyone, but I, er, copied some of my photo homework into the journal. *Shhh.*

"Good work, Shannon," he says. "Very prolific, Aisha. Let's see, Riley. Nothing? Nothing? It's January, you'd better get to work. Okay, Blake, hand it over."

I hold up my journal and say, "I trust you'll find this is all in order," like I'm on some old-fashioned TV show.

The corners of his mouth twitch, and he pages through my journal, pausing to read something. I panic: Is it obvious that I used some of my photo homework to pad the journal?

He hands it back to me, saying, "Very eclectic. But you'll need to write a lot more before the year is over."

After he walks away, I turn a quizzical look on Shannon and

she whispers, "It means varied. Um, diverse. It's actually a very good word for you." She reaches for my notebook. "Let's see."

I pull it out of reach.

She widens her eyes. "Blake! Come on."

"Not unless you let me read yours."

She lowers her chin and looks at me from under her lashes. With a slow smile, she hands it over.

I snatch it out of her hands before she can change her mind. She reaches for mine, and I hold it out of reach again.

"Damn it, Smithers," she says in a crabby old man voice. "Don't *make* me come over there!"

Okay, Mr. Burns gets me. I hand it to her.

We both settle down and start reading.

Oh, she's addressed her entries to Mr. Hamilton. He's her epistle-er. Heh. Here's an entry about me. She wrote about the homecoming dance and said I looked about as comfortable in my tux as a four-year-old in a wedding.

I flip through some more pages. Here's some stuff about a fight with her mom. Evil minion of Satan. And some deep thoughts on music. Haha! She doesn't like Cappie very much. More about me. Sweet.

Oh, here's an entry about our first fight. Aw. She felt really bad afterward. "How could I be such an insecure shrew?" she wrote. Hmm. Shrew. I almost ask Shannon what a shrew is, but I've got the gist. She's deep into my journal, anyway.

I keep reading the entry about our first fight:

I hope he knows how much I like him. Maybe even love *him.
Not that I would tell him that! (Don't you tell him, either,
Mr. H.!) I mean we just started dating a month ago—it's too
soon to use the L-word. I remember our first kiss . . . I saw
stars. No, really. It was in August, during the Perseids star
showers. He was so cute. He was worried that this older guy,
Andrew, was going to hook up with me.*

I nod at the memory. I was! Big, hairy Andrew.

*But I wasn't attracted to Andrew. For one thing, he was
really boring. And Blake is so funny! He was making up all
these crazy names for the constellations that night, like Little
Bo Peep Tripping over Her Sheep and the Sprawling Giraffe.
Hee! And when he called the Little Dipper the "espresso
cup to the stars," I was hooked. I've been crazy about him
ever since.*

I glance over at Shannon to say something mushy, but she's
paging rapidly through my journal now.

I flip through some more pages of Shannon's journal. I'm all
over the place in here!

Oh.

No.

And now I know what she's looking for in my journal: some
mention of *her.*

I close my eyes. *Insert headsmack here,* I think. How could I be so stupid? I barely wrote anything about her. At most, I reported boring stuff like, "Shannon and I went to the movies and saw XYZ."

I breathe in and out, wanting to grab my notebook and say, *It doesn't mean anything! Just because I didn't write about you doesn't mean I'm not crazy about you, too.* But I sit and wait.

Finally she closes the notebook and sets it on my desk without looking at me. "Eclectic," she says.

CHAPTER TWENTY-SIX

Depth of field:
Where things are in the shot, and how they're related to each other.
—*Blake Hewson, homework, Photo II*

Mr. Malloy looks distracted today. And my God! He's not wearing his beret. What is happening? Is the world collapsing in on itself? I really wish Marissa were here so we could laugh about it.

"Today is—" he starts. He looks down at his desk. He walks over to the bookcase and makes a sweeping arm gesture by the books. "Today is free study day. Please work alone or in small groups, and uh, peruse some of the masters of photography. Make a list of at least three critically acclaimed photographers. Your homework will be to, to . . . emulate their style."

"How long do we have for the homework?" asks someone.

"Uh," says Mr. Malloy. "Two weeks." You can tell he just made this whole thing up on the spot. He sits down at his desk and shuffles some papers around. The man's got something on his mind. Probably wishes we would all go away.

I carry *The Abrams Encyclopedia of Photography* back to my desk, wishing we had a Moody Corner in here so I could curl up in a big, comfy chair while I look at the pictures. There's a full-page black-and-white photo of some guy's penis—shot by Mapplethorpe, of course—which I'm thinking the school would not be thrilled to know is in our classroom. If Principal Ito knew that Mr. Malloy had basically just given us an assignment to stare at some guy's baloney pony, I'm thinking he might not be very supportive.

There are lots of other nude photos in the book, too. I really love one by Manuel Alvarez Bravo called "The Good Reputation, Sleeping." It's a female nude. She just looks so peaceful and relaxed, stretched out on the terrace. And you wonder why she's got wrappings or bandages or something around her feet. Maybe she's a ballerina? She looks so beautiful. I wonder if I'll ever get to take nude photos. How do you shoot them without being embarrassed? Or worse, sporting a boner?

I don't hear from Marissa the rest of the day.

Or the next.

·····

Marissa's grandmother sounds, I don't know, really *old* when she answers the phone. "Hello?"

"Mrs. Stanmore?"

"Yes."

"Hi, this is Blake. Marissa's friend. Is she there?"

Mrs. Stanmore doesn't answer for a long time. Maybe she's losing her hearing.

"Mrs. Stanmore?" I say a little louder.

"Yes, Blake. I'm here."

"Is Marissa okay?" I ask, my heart thumping.

There's a wavering sound in Mrs. Stanmore's voice as she says, "Marissa isn't here right now, honey."

"Oh. But is she okay?"

Silence.

"What's going on?" I say, a little sharply.

"I don't . . . Marissa is—"

"What?"

"She's looking for her mom. She hasn't been home since yesterday."

"What?!" I say. "Where is her mom? Did you call the police?"

Mrs. Stanmore's voice breaks a little, and she sounds so tired when she says, "No. I haven't called the police. I can't. They won't do anything. Anne has a history of drug abuse, so they won't look for her. And Marissa told me she was going to look for her mom, so she's not really missing."

"But what happened?"

Mrs. Stanmore doesn't answer for so long that I think she's not going to. When she does, she doesn't sound tired anymore. She sounds mad. "The same damn thing that's been happening for ten years. I'm sick to death of it. I have to go now."

And she hangs up.

I click off the phone and stare into space. My first impulse is to head for Old Town.

Then I sit down, suddenly tired. Is it really my responsibility to go looking for Marissa? And why would she do that, anyway? Why would she stay out all night and worry poor Grandma to death?

I can see how Mrs. Stanmore would get sick of this crap.

• • • • •

"Mom?"

"Mm-hm."

"What do you do when someone's got a messed-up family?"

My mom puts down her book and gazes at me. "Marissa?" she says.

I nod.

"Depends. What's going on?"

I hesitate. But my mom's a professional. It's not like telling Shannon or Riley. It's her job to keep things confidential.

"Marissa's mom is a meth addict," I say.

"I see."

"And her father is in jail."

"Okay."

"She lives with her grandma."

"Mm-hm."

"And her mom was gone for almost a year, but then she came back. She . . . I took this picture . . ." I throw my hands up. "Oh, it's a long story! But the bottom line is that Marissa's mom came back from wherever she was and went into rehab, and she got better, right? Then she got a job and she's been living with Marissa and her mom, Marissa's grandma, right? But now . . . she's gone again!"

"Marissa's mother is missing?"

"Right."

"And where is Marissa?"

"She went to look for her."

My mom sits up straighter. "Where would she go to look for her mother?"

I take a deep breath. "I think she probably went to Old Town."

My mom looks out the window into the darkness. "Get your coat," she says.

·····

My mom wears her clerical collar when we go to Old Town. She hardly ever wears it outside the hospital. "It might help," she explains. "Sometimes people in crisis are more willing to share information with someone from a religious vocation."

Not to mention that they probably won't try to sell you drugs, I think.

203

We park downtown and start walking. My mom is calm and friendly. She smiles at people and even talks to them. People that I would cross the street to avoid. People who can barely get their words out, they're so drunk. Hard-eyed gutter punks who look like they'd just as soon slice you up as share the sidewalk with you. Glassy-eyed girls who stare down at the ground in shame when my mom approaches.

Some people melt into the shadows as we get near them, slipping down side streets where the lighting is dim. Some people huddle under blankets on doorsteps. The smell of urine and vomit rushes out at us from a scary alleyway.

No one knows Anne. Or they claim they don't. No one has seen Marissa. Or they claim they haven't.

Mom and I head back to the car. "One more place," she says. "It's a couple of blocks away, closer to the bridge."

I grit my teeth and follow, wishing we could just leave. It's clear that we're not going to find Marissa. My whole body feels cold and rock hard with tension.

She stops across the street from Pioneer Park. "Let's check the park before we go," she says.

"What? Mom!" I say. "No way!"

She looks at me.

"Mo-om! People get murdered over there!" I protest. "Dad would flip if he knew you wanted to go into Pioneer Park. At *night*."

"Blake."

"No. No way."

"Blake, take it easy. You can wait here."

"*What?* Mom, no."

"I'll only be a minute. It's possible that Marissa has gone there to look for her mother. It's a well-known spot to buy drugs."

"Mom, I *know!*" I practically yell. "Please don't go over there. I'm not kidding. Those people are serious. They will not care that you're a . . . a religious vocational person. MOM!"

She's walking across the street.

I run after her.

And you will not believe this.

That's where we find Marissa.

CHAPTER TWENTY-SEVEN

If I could tell a story in words, I wouldn't need to lug around a camera.
—*Lewis Hine, American photographer (1874–1940)*

Marissa's teeth are still chattering.

She's sitting at our kitchen table with her hands wrapped around a mug of hot tea that my mom made for her. But she's still cold.

Not just cold. I think she's so far beyond upset that it's a speck in the distance.

She stayed out all night last night, she told us on the drive home. Walking around town. When it got to be the dead of night, like three a.m., she went into the Pioneer Mission chapel and sat there, trying to stay warm while she waited for morning.

"Why didn't you call your grandma?" I ask.

"At three in the morning?" she snaps.

"Yes!" I snap back. "Don't you think she was awake worrying about you anyway?"

Marissa's lips tremble, and all of a sudden tears come spilling down her cheeks. "I know," she whispers. "I suck. I should have called."

My mom stays by the stove, heating up some soup. "Blake, give Marissa the phone," she says. "She can call her grandma now."

Marissa cries harder. "What am I going to tell her?" she moans. "I didn't find Mom!"

"That's a secondary issue at the moment," says my mom. "First let's relieve your grandmother's worry about *you*."

Marissa dials her grandma's number. "Hi," she says in a voice barely above a whisper. She squeezes her eyes shut. "I know. I know, Gramma. I'm sorry." A pause. "I'm at Blake's. He and his mom came looking for me." Another pause. "I know. I will. Okay." Marissa looks up at my mom. "Should she come get me?"

"No, honey," says my mom. "I'll take you home. But first have some soup."

"Okay." Marissa speaks into the phone again. "Blake's mom will bring me home. She made some soup, so I'm going to eat first." Pause. "No. Not since yesterday. I know, Gramma. Please don't cry. I'll be home in a little while. I love you, too."

Marissa hangs up and hands the phone back to me. She raises the cup of tea to her lips with shaking hands. I almost lean across the table to hold the cup steady for her. Instead I flatten my hands on the table, because they're shaking a little, too.

My mom places a bowl of soup in front of Marissa and one in front of me, too. I look at her questioningly, and she tilts her head at Marissa, as if to say, *Don't make her eat alone.*

I pick up a spoon. The Dog Formerly Known as Prince pads under the table and lies down by Marissa's feet. Maybe he senses that she could use some extra comfort. Or maybe he just smells chicken.

Marissa and I eat in silence while my mom putters around the kitchen. By the time we finish, Marissa has stopped shaking. Her eyelids look heavy and her shoulders sag with exhaustion.

My mom comes over to the table and tilts her head at me again, indicating I should give her my seat. I carry my bowl to the sink while Mom slides into my chair and folds her hands together on the table in front of her.

"Marissa."

"Yes."

Marissa sets down her spoon and looks at my mom's hands. She can't seem to look my mom in the eye.

"You won't do this again," says my mom.

A blast of silence hits the room.

I wait. Marissa doesn't look up.

"It's inconsiderate and destructive," adds my mom. "You could get into real trouble wandering around those potentially volatile settings. And it's not fair to your grandmother. It's time to show her some consideration."

"Okay," says Marissa. Another tear slides down her face.

"Let's get you home. It's late."

I glance at the clock as we stand up. It's almost midnight! And we have school tomorrow. It feels like we've been in a time warp.

"Thank you," Marissa says to my mom.

Mom pulls her gently into an embrace. "Sweetheart," she says. "It's time to let go."

Marissa buries her face in my mom's shoulder and cries and cries, like something big is falling away from her.

·····

The next morning, I shiver inside Monty, waiting for the car to warm up while Garrett scrapes ice off the windshield. It got down to freezing last night. What if we hadn't found Marissa?

I unwrap a cereal bar and take a bite. If Garrett catches me eating in his car, he will punish me. Probably with his meaty fists. But I'm starving. I didn't have time for breakfast. Uck. It tastes like sawdust and paste. Why can't Mom ever buy Pop-Tarts?

Garrett moves toward the driver's side door and I hide the yuck-bar in my pocket.

He drives in silence for a few minutes, cranking up the defroster to clear the condensation from the interior windows. Finally he says, "What the hell, man?"

I jump. "What."

"What the hell went on last night?"

"Huh?"

"You and Mom were gone for hours; then you came home with that girl Marissa. I could hear you guys."

"If you could hear us, then you know what was going on."

Pause. "Dad made me go back in my room."

"Oh. Well." I'd rather eat ten sawdust bars than talk about this. "It's a long story, and I don't feel like going there right now."

Garrett doesn't answer, just glances at me and keeps driving. When we get into KWST range, he flips on the radio. It's Carter this morning, yammering about the new skate park. Garrett turns off the radio. If it's not Cappie announcing, he doesn't care enough to listen.

"Dog," he says.

"What."

"Are you in trouble?"

"Huh?" So tired.

"Did you get your girlfriend . . . your *friend*—"

"What are you talking about?"

"Did you get that Marissa girl in trouble?"

"What? No. *What?*"

"Pregnant, man! Did you forget to put a hood on the anaconda?"

"Oh my God!" I'm ice-down-the-back awake now. "No!" I look at him. "Why would you think that? And how many times do I have to say it? She's. Just. A. Friend!"

"Okay, okay," he says, doing a shushing hand motion in my direction. "I get it."

I fume. He drives.

"But listen."

"Just leave me alone, all right?" I'm pissed now.

"Dog. Listen. I'm sorry. I just want to say one more thing."

I scowl out the window.

"*Always* wrap it before you tap it. Maybe you should start carrying a condom around. Just in case."

"Maybe *you* should . . . shut up," I finish lamely.

· · · · ·

"Hey," I greet Marissa in photo later that day. I didn't have a chance to talk to her in English. "How are you, um, feeling?"

"Good," she says. Her eyes look clear and *un*-heartbroken. "Much better. My grandma and I talked last night. Not too long, because it was so late. She's going to get me a cell phone. She doesn't ever want me to be out of touch again."

"Finally!"

"And I'm going to do what your mom said." She looks down at her hands. "I'm going to let go. I can't fix my mom. I hope she's okay, but I can't make her come home or stay straight." She swallows, and her eyes get shiny. She shakes her head impatiently and takes a deep breath. "*Any*way! I need to focus on school and getting my driver's license and normal stuff like that. Ever since my mom came back to town, my life has been . . . well, it's just not how I thought it would be."

I nod.

"I hope she's okay," she says. "But things were better when she wasn't around."

I nod harder.

"So what did I miss this week?"

I take out my notes and tell her about choosing three photographers that we're supposed to try to emulate.

"Who did you choose?" she asks.

"Walker Evans, Henri Cartier-Bresson, and Manuel Alvarez Bravo."

"I know the first two. Who's the third guy?"

Mr. Malloy isn't in the room yet, so I go to his bookcase and pull out *The Abrams Encyclopedia of Photography.* I open the book to the pages about Manuel Alvarez Bravo and hand it to Marissa.

She reads the text. "Look, he lived to be one hundred," she says, pointing to the dates of his birth and death. "Maybe photography keeps you healthy." She studies the photos next. "Wow," she breathes. "Look at how pretty that shot is." She's looking at the girl, nude, stretched out on the terrace.

"I know!" I say. "I like that one, too!"

"But I love this shot even more." She points to his famous "Optic Parable," a photo of an optician's shop, with lots of eyes and reflections of eyes in it. "I wish I could take pictures like that."

It strikes me as interesting that she doesn't comment on the photo on the opposite page, "Striking Worker, Assassinated." It's just what it sounds like: a dead guy, blood pouring from his head and pooling on the ground next to him. The thing that gets me every time I look at that photo is how young and handsome the guy is. He's wearing nice clothes and a fancy-looking belt. When he got dressed that morning, he just thought he was going to a protest about workers' rights. He had no way of knowing it was the last time he would go anywhere.

Marissa turns the page and says, "I'm thinking of entering my series of flowers in the photo contest."

"Me, too," I deadpan. "I have so many flower shots to choose from. How will I ever decide?"

"Don't disrespect my flowers." She laughs. "Why don't you go ahead and enter your string-cheese series?"

"Me? I don't do the cheese, girl! I don't do heartstrings. I am all about bikers and empty streets and snakes!"

She guffaws. "Stuffed snakes, yes!" She pulls my portfolio in front of her and flips through the images. "Ooh, you have lots to choose from. I like this. And this one. Jeez, look at all these shots of my bruise. You're so stunted. Oh!"

I glance over. She's staring down at the photos of her mom that day in her backyard.

Shit. Why did I put those in my portfolio?

"Sorry," I say.

"It's okay." She flips through the photos, her face impassive. "Too bad about the flash burnout on this one."

I look over at the shot she's indicating. "The what?"

"The flash burnout. You got too close to the subject. So the flash overexposed her. Well, *me*, I mean."

It's the last shot I took at Marissa's house. It's the only one I took of Marissa and her mom together. I was in such a hurry to leave that I didn't take enough time to frame them. I was too close, and the flash overexposed Marissa's face, turning it bright and blurry.

"Yeah, it would have been a good shot otherwise," I agree.

Marissa slams my portfolio shut, and I jump.

"Sorry," she says. "Sorry." She touches my hand quickly.

I look down at my hand in surprise.

She jerks her hand back and fumbles with my portfolio, pushing it toward me. "Here."

"Thanks." I reach out for the portfolio, and our hands brush again as I take it from her.

A gigantic silence opens up between us.

It's not until class is over that we speak again.

"Blake?"

"Yeah?"

"Do you think I could, um—"

I wait.

"I feel weird asking, but would it be okay if I use your laptop to edit my photos?"

I hesitate.

"It's okay, you can say no! It's just that I don't have Photoshop on my grandma's old computer. I could do it at school, but . . . in fact, you know what? That's what I'll do. I can go to the computer lab after school—"

"It's okay," I interrupt. "When do you want to come over?"

"Really?"

"Sure. How about this weekend? You can come for dinner."

Marissa beams. "That would be great!"

"Okay, I'll let you know."

It's not until I'm walking down the hall that I think of Shannon.

CHAPTER TWENTY-EIGHT

Dragging the shutter will liberate your ambient light.
—*Spike McLernon's Laws of Photography*

This time I'm smart enough to tell Shannon, even though I reallyreallyreally don't want to.

This time she doesn't pout or compare the number of times she's been to my house versus Marissa. She *thinks* it—I can see it in her calculating expression—but she says out loud, "Is she coming over on Saturday?"

In a rush of relief I say, "No! No, it doesn't have to be Saturday. I'll tell her to come over Friday, and that way you and I can get together Saturday. Okay?" *Buddy? Pal? Sweetheart?*

Shannon nods. "Okay. I've got a piano recital at four that day. Do you want to come? We can go out after."

Bobble bobble. "Yes! Sure!"

.....

"Don't forget the Rule of Lug Nuts," calls Garrett.

"The what?" I'm a nervous wreck. Mom and I are heading out the door for my driving test at the DMV.

"Let's go, honey," says Mom, hurrying to the car.

Garrett comes galloping into the living room. "Don't tell me you don't know the Rule of Lug Nuts!"

I seriously think I might stroke out. "What? I don't know what that is!"

"Oh my God, have you been studying the wrong handbook?"

I scrabble in my backpack. "I don't know!"

"Maybe they gave you an out-of-date handbook. Oh, you are so screwed."

"Blake!" calls my mom.

"What is it?" I think I might cry. "Just tell me what it is." I grab my DMV handbook and peer at it frantically. "This is the one they gave me!"

"Okay." He puts a hand on my shoulder. "Listen carefully. The Rule of Lug Nuts is . . . whoever has the most lug nuts *rules* the road." He claps me on the shoulder and walks away, calling, "Good luck!"

. . . . .

Mom lets me drive home, my brand-new state-issued temporary driver's license resting in my wallet.

Except for turning too wide around a corner where some construction workers were tearing up the road with jackhammers, then swerving a little to avoid oncoming traffic . . . I think it went well. Hey, I passed the test. Who cares about the score?

I stop at the grocery store, and Mom buys a chocolate cake, to celebrate.

When we get home, she makes chicken curry for dinner, with lots of side dishes in case Marissa doesn't like it.

But Marissa has a second helping during dinner, saying shyly, "This is really good. What kind of food did you say this was again?"

"Thanks, honey. It's called curry. Indian food. The rice is called biryani."

"Mm."

Garrett is sitting across from Marissa, looking bored. He's always kind of lost on Friday nights once football season ends. I haven't seen Cappie around here lately, either.

The phone rings and Dad glances at the caller ID. "Work," he says, going into the other room with the phone.

Garrett looks after him. "Dad's on call this weekend?"

"Yes," says Mom. "Do you want more carrots, Marissa?"

"No, thanks."

Dad walks back into the room. He hangs up the phone and sits down.

Garrett watches him.

"You're up, big guy," says Dad.

"YES!" Garrett actually jumps out of his chair and pumps his fist in the air. "When? Tonight?"

"No. It's getting kind of late in the day. We'll go in tomorrow."

"Man! I can't wait! Are you sure we can't go in tonight?"

It's hard to believe that these two are talking about cutting up a body; it sounds more like a movie premiere.

"You'll be fresher if you get some sleep tonight."

"How am I going to sleep?"

My dad beams: the proud papa of his cadaver-craving first-born. "You know what? I'll have you go in early tomorrow to get started, just like I would with any other *diener*. I'll join you after you've had time to take some tissue samples."

Marissa looks from Garrett to my dad in puzzlement.

"Really?" Garrett may have to be sedated. "What have we got?"

My dad glances at Marissa and my mom.

"Russ," says my mom. "We don't need to hear—"

"They're talking about my dad's job," I explain to Marissa. "He's a medical examiner."

"Oh, right," she says. "It's okay. You can talk about it. I mean, you don't have to act different just because I'm here."

"Sure, Dad, go ahead," I say. "Why should we have normal dinner conversation just because we have *company?*"

My sarcasm flies right over his bushy head, and he says matter-of-factly, "It's a female gunshot victim."

"Errrgh," I groan.

"Wow!" says Garrett. You would think my dad just said, "It's a Ford GT 40, and it's all yours."

"Yep. Very similar to a case I had not long ago. The police, uh, delivered the fatal bullets. She was a transient. Probably a tweaker. They're claiming she threatened them and that they thought she was reaching for a weapon. Turned out to be a cell phone." My dad sighs and rubs his face. "Oh, and Marissa? This is confidential information."

I can hardly bring myself to look at her. My mind has crashed into that one word.

Tweaker.

I risk a glance. Marissa nods and sets down her fork. Her gaze moves to the window and her hands twist in her lap.

I widen my eyes at my mom. She looks distressed, too.

"Let's change the subject," she says. She must not have told my dad about Marissa's mom, or he wouldn't be talking about dead tweakers.

• • • • •

After dinner I load the dishes in the dishwasher while Marissa sits at the kitchen table working on my laptop. I can see that she's cropping photos and fixing stuff like color levels and sharpness.

"I'll be back in a minute," I say. I call Shannon from my room, and we chat for a little while. She's out with Dez and Ellie, but I think she likes the fact that I called, even though Marissa is here.

"My recital is at Sylvan Music tomorrow," she says. "Are you still coming?"

"What time does it start, again?"

"Four."

"I'll be there. Well, unless my parents make me go somewhere with them."

"Okay. If I don't see you, I'll call you when it's over."

"Okay, babe. Bye."

"Bye."

I wander back to the kitchen and find Marissa staring out the window again.

"How's it going?" I ask.

She turns to look at me, but she doesn't act like she sees me. "What?"

"I said how's it going?"

"Good." She focuses on the laptop again. A photo of flowers in buckets at the farmers' market fills the screen. It's not my kind of subject, but even I can see that it's beautiful; the colors are really rich, and the way some of the flowers are lit by the sun and others are in shade make it a nice layered shot. Marissa edits out someone's leg at the edge of the frame and says, "Blake?"

"Mm-hm?"

"How would someone find out, like a member of the public . . .

how would someone find out about that woman your dad was talking about?"

"Marissa!"

"Blake," she says, her shoulders slumping. "I'm freaking out."

"It's not her."

"How do you know? Is there a way we can find out?"

I raise my hands up. "Mariss! Stop. It's not her. You *are* freaking out."

"Just tell me! Is there a way we can find out? Like, look at the name on the chart or something?"

"What, go down to the office and start looking through their files? Right! My dad said she was a transient. If she didn't have any ID, then she's a Jane Doe."

We frown at each other.

"Besides," I add, "your mom doesn't even have a cell phone, does she?"

"I don't know," she says, her voice barely above a whisper. "I have no idea. But it's possible."

And that's the thing. It is possible.

∙ ∙ ∙ ∙ ∙

Even after my mom drives Marissa home, I can't stop thinking about what she said. She's infected me with her insanity.

It's not her, I think. *Don't be stupid. There must be hundreds of homeless tweakers roaming the streets. What are the odds that it would be Marissa's mom?*

I lie down on the bed to read. We're studying *Huck Finn* now. I open the book and read a few pages before I realize I'm not taking in any of the story.

She's gone missing before, I think. *She must be able to take care of herself or she would have been dead a long time ago.*

Shit. Maybe I should go with Garrett and Dad tomorrow.

I toss my book across the room and sit up. And then what? Say, "Guys! Do you mind if I check out this corpse before you cut her up? Thanks!"

Yeah. *That* would work.

Dad didn't say how old the victim was; for all we know, she's twenty years old. Or sixty!

Maybe we should call Marissa's grandmother.

No! I punch my pillow. I have to stop thinking like this. Just because Marissa is flipping her pixels doesn't mean we have to drag Grandma Mary into it.

I pull my blanket up over my shoulders. The dead woman in the cold room won't get out of my head.

•••••

"Garrett."

"Studly."

"Can I ask you something?"

He's so buzzed he's practically making honey. "Shoot." He's folding a shirt and setting it on top of a pair of jeans on his dresser. Ohmygod, he's picking out clothes for tomorrow, as if he's got a date.

"Is there a way—"

"No."

"No?"

"No, you can't borrow my car."

"What? No! I don't want to borrow your *car*. God! Not everything is about your car, Garrett."

"Good. Now that you've got your license, I'm just heading you off at the pass, pardner. There won't be any borrowing my car. So what do you want?" He tosses a pair of socks on top of the shirt.

I scowl at him. All of this heading me off at the pass has messed with my concentration. "I was *trying* to ask," I say, "If there's a way to find out how old someone is? Someone who's been brought into the morgue."

He adds a pair of underwear to the stack of clothes. "What do you mean? We determine the age during the exam."

I get a visual of rings on a tree stump, and shake my head. "No, I mean *before*."

"Before what?"

"Before the exam."

"Scrof, what the hell are you talking about?"

I exhale and say, "All right, look. That woman that Dad was talking about? The one that's your case tomorrow?"

"Yeah?"

"Is there a way to find out how old she is? Like, before you do anything to her?"

He stares at me.

"Because Marissa thinks—" I scrub both hands through my hair in frustration. "This is completely crazy, okay? But she thinks it might be—"

Garrett raises his eyebrows.

"Her mom."

Garrett squints at me, as if trying to judge whether or not I'm testing a new joke on him. After a long minute, he must be satisfied that I'm as serious as a heart attack, because he says, "Why would she think that?"

"Because her mom's a nut job. I mean, she has problems. Drug problems."

"Ah."

Wow, Garrett sounds just like Mom when he says that one syllable.

"Also, she's missing."

"Missing as in a missing person?"

"Well, yeah. But the police won't file a formal report, because of her history. She's disappeared before for, like, long periods of time."

I have Garrett's full attention now. "What's her poison?"

"Huh? Oh. Meth."

"How long has she been missing?" Now Garrett looks clinical, like Dad, asking questions in that matter-of-fact tone.

"I don't know. A few days? A week?"

"I see. And you want to find out how old the woman is so you can rule out Marissa's mother?"

"Yes."

He nods. "And what if she's the right age?"

I sit down on his bed.

"Anyway, it can't be done. After we do the exam, we'll know more about the case. And if Marissa has valid reasons for think- ing it's her mom, she'll have to contact the police."

"Garrett, man."

"What?" he says, an edge to his voice.

"She's my friend! And she's so scared it's her stupid mom."

"Yeah, I get it. But what else can she do?"

I don't want to say it.

But I say it. "Maybe I should look at her."

His eyes bug out. "Who? The *case?*"

I can't say anything else. I can't even nod.

"Get out," he says, and opens the door to his room.

· · · · ·

I feel bad for killing my brother's happy *diener* buzz.

I'm in my room, and I can hear him stomping around next door in his room.

It was a stupid idea. I don't want to look at a dead body, anyway! I probably wouldn't even recognize if it *was* Marissa's mother. Do faces collapse and get weird in death? I can't picture Marissa's mom right now. All I can remember about her is her bilge breath and her tattoos.

Wait. Her tattoos. I would remember those, wouldn't I? Didn't she have something on her neck? I think about scrolling through my photos, but then I remember all her tats were covered up when I took her picture at Marissa's. And what if she's gotten new tattoos over the old ones? Do people do that?

Why did Marissa have to come over tonight? I think. *Why can't my dad talk about current events during dinner?*

My bedroom door bangs open.

"So are you saying you want to come with me tomorrow?"

I shake my head. "Nope. Never mind."

"Good." Garrett walks a few steps away and comes back to the doorway. "Because people can't just waltz into the state medical examiner's office and ogle the cadavers."

"I said never mind!"

He clomps downstairs.

I locate *Huck Finn* on the floor and decide the floor looks good enough for me. I flop down on my back and open the book. I manage to read a whole chapter before Garrett comes back.

"Dad would never let you."

"Jesus, I said *never mind*."

"It's the kind of thing we'd have to sneak in to do."

I close the book.

We lock eyes, Garrett staring down at me with a tight look on his face, me goggling up at him.

Finally I break the silence. "When?"

He paces. "You can't come with me tomorrow. Dad would find out and I'd—" He shakes his head and says, almost to himself, "I'd probably be banned from working at the ME's office."

"So then when would we—?"

"It would have to be tonight."

A weird little quiver starts in my legs and moves up my body. I sit up and cross my arms. "You know what? I really appreciate it, but you're probably right. We can't risk it."

"What? Now you don't *want* to?"

I shake my head. "I'm not sure I could positively ID her."

He throws up his hands. "Then why the hell did you bring it up in the first place?"

"I'm sorry."

"What about your friend being so worried? What are you going to tell her?"

"I don't know. I can't think." I put my head in my hands. "Marissa would know if it was her mom, but—"

"Whoa, whoa, whoa." Garrett pats the air in a STOP motion right above my head. "Stand on the brakes, man. Are you saying a third person would be involved?"

"No. Well, yes. If I can't ID her, then it would have to be

someone close to her. We can't ask her grandma. It would have to be Marissa."

"You're on crack," he says, and leaves.

He doesn't come back this time.

As I crawl into bed later, I'm ashamed to realize I'm glad he said no.

·····

"Blake."

Dark.

"Wake up, man." Someone is shaking my shoulder.

I jolt awake.

Garrett is standing next to my bed.

"What?" I mumble.

"Get up," he says, and the look on his face doesn't allow for questions.

I push back my covers and sit on the edge of the bed in my boxers, shivering. My mouth is gunky and dry. I need a drink of water.

"Get dressed. Meet me downstairs," he says, and leaves.

CHAPTER TWENTY-NINE

Make your peace with waking up early. The early bird gets the good light.
Of course, so does the late afternoon bird, but why limit yourself
to beautiful slanting light once a day?
—*Spike McLernon's Laws of Photography*

I throw on my jeans and a sweatshirt. I grab a pair of sneaks and tiptoe down the stairs. It's dark. I don't know if it's midnight or four a.m. Where is Garrett? There's no light on anywhere.

"Here, man."

I jump. I peer through the darkness and see Garrett standing by the front door.

"What time is it?" I ask.

"Five. Put your shoes on." He opens the front door. It's pitch-black outside, too, no porch light.

I stuff my feet into my shoes, and Garrett hands me my jacket.

"I put your cell in your pocket," he says.

"Okay." I step outside onto the porch, next to him, and he closes the door quietly.

"It's good that you're not asking a bunch of questions," he

says. "Because if I have to talk about this, I might change my mind."

I immediately want to ask a bunch of questions. *What about Mom and Dad? They're going to wonder where we are when they wake up. What about Marissa? Are we actually going to the morgue?*

Through some miracle I manage to clap a mental hand over my mouth and follow him out to the car.

He eases the car door open and indicates that I should get in. "Just crawl over to the passenger seat," he says. "I don't want to have to close more than one door. It'll be bad enough starting the engine. We just have to hope they don't hear it."

I do as he says.

He eases the door closed and turns the key in the ignition, wincing. The car starts, and he throws it into reverse and backs down the driveway. Usually he lets his baby warm up first.

"How do you get to your friend's house?"

"My friend's house? Oh! Marissa. Um, turn left at the corner."

I give Garrett directions. When we're halfway there, the predawn cold has woken me up enough to think, *What are we* doing? *Is he really going to get Marissa so we can take her to the morgue? This is crazy! Marissa infected me, and now I've infected Garrett with her insanity!* I plan my speech: "Garrett, man, never mind. I can't go through with it. Thanks, anyway. I don't know what I was thinking."

I stay silent. The mind-boggling stupidity of this idea is so obvious as we drive down the dark streets. But it's too late to stop now.

What I wouldn't give for a glass of water. And a TARDIS. I would go back in time and *shut up* about the possible identity of gunshot victims.

Garrett turns down Marissa's street and I point out the house. He drives past it and parks at the end of the street.

"Go get her," he says.

I sit there staring at him. "Go get her?" I repeat.

"I am not playing, Blake." Garrett using my given name gets me moving. He *must* be serious.

I get out of the car and walk down the street toward Marissa's house, trying to figure out what the hell I'm going to do when I get there.

Wait. Maybe I should pretend I couldn't get her. Like, she didn't hear me calling her, or she's not there or something. Then I could tell Garrett we can abandon this deranged idea.

Next thing I know, I'm standing in front of the house trying to remember where Marissa's bedroom is. Upstairs, right? She's mentioned it's upstairs. But is it the bedroom in the front or the back? And how am I supposed to get to her? Break into the house? Throw pebbles at her window like some kind of Romeo? I put my hands on my hips, frowning.

I feel exposed standing out on the sidewalk in front of her house. What if a neighbor sees me, some random guy stalking the house?

What if a cop car comes by on patrol? I walk down the driveway and slip through the gate to the backyard.

Okay. I'm standing on the patio looking up at what I hope is Marissa's bedroom window.

I picture Garrett waiting in the car, getting more and more impatient. I can't think of anything else: I bend down and try to see if there are any pebbles lying around. As I bend down, my cell phone shifts and almost falls out of my pocket. Duh!

I take out my cell and scroll through the names, looking for Marissa's. How happy am I that her grandma finally, *finally* got her a cell phone! But what if her cell isn't on? What if her grandma hears the phone?

Shit.

Okay, I don't have time for this head-stuck-up-my-ass thinking. It's getting later by the second.

I punch the button for Marissa's number and wait while it rings. I can feel my heart beating in my throat.

"Hello?" comes a groggy voice, and I could faint with relief. It's Marissa.

"Mariss," I say.

"Yeah?"

"It's Blake."

"Blake?" Rustling sounds. "What time is it?"

"It's crazy early," I say. "Listen. I need you to wake up. Do you hear me? Marissa?"

"I hear you. What's going on?"

"I'm at your house."

"What?" Her voice is sharper now.

"I don't have time to explain. You have to trust me. I'm at your house, and I'm waiting outside. I'm in the backyard. Is your room the one in the back?"

"Yes." There's more rustling, and I look up at her window. She pulls up the shade, and her dim silhouette appears in the frame. "Blake, what are you doing?"

I can't see her expression. "Please, Marissa. You have to trust me. Get dressed and come down. Leave a note for your grandma."

"I don't understand. What time is it?"

I close my eyes and sigh. "This is never going to work," I mutter, more to myself than to her.

"What's never going to work? Why do I need to leave a note? Are we going somewhere?"

"Yes, we're going somewhere. I *so* don't have time to explain, Marissa. My brother is waiting in his car, and he's going to fucking freak if we don't get back to him, like, now. Get dressed and meet me out front. I promise I'll tell you everything then."

"Okay!" She hangs up and closes her shade.

I run around to the front of the house and down the street to the car. Garrett looks up at me as I lean down to his window. "She's coming," I say. Then I run back to meet her.

•••••

Garrett parks down the street from the medical examiner's office. "There's a surveillance camera on the parking lot," he explains.

Marissa is silent in the back seat, her eyes wide and scared. We told her what we're going to do. It took a while to make her understand. When we first started talking about going into the morgue, she must have thought she was still asleep, having a nightmare. I'm sure when she asked me how to find out who the victim was, she never imagined she'd have to look at the body herself.

Once she understood, though, she didn't refuse. She didn't cry.

She's not going to chicken out. I can see it in her face. She really wants to know if it's her mom who died.

"Here's what's going to happen," says Garrett, turning around in his seat so he can see both of us. "We're going to walk over to the back door of the morgue. You guys are going to wait outside while I go in and make sure no one is there."

"Who would be there?" I ask.

He narrows his eyes. "I told you I am not playing, Blake. Get your head in the—" He stops. I can tell he was about to say "in the game." "Just use your head," he fumes. "Anyone could be there. People get killed in the middle of the night, you know what I'm saying? There could even be cops. Now, do you want to keep talking about it? Or do this?"

"Do this," whispers Marissa.

Garrett glances at her, and his expression softens. "Okay. So I'm going to check things out, make sure no one else is there. If it's clear, I'll come get you. The cold room is near the back door, thank God." He runs a hand across his forehead. "Marissa."

"Yes." She answers quickly, like an attentive student.

"You will—" he says, and stops.

The three of us sit there in a moment of surreal silence.

"You will come in and look. They're just—" But the words get stuck in his throat again.

The three of us get out of the car. We're a block away from the building, and with every step I want to say, *Wait. Let's not do this.*

Then we're standing at the back door, and I'm still speechless.

Garrett pulls a credit card–size passkey out of his back pocket. I can see his hand trembling. He swipes it through the reader, but the little red light stays red. Locked.

"Shit," he says.

I moan.

"Wait, wait," he says, swiping it again. "Why won't it work?"

Red.

Garrett looks at me, his eyes dark with panic. Then his face relaxes. "Ohhhh," he breathes. "It's after hours! I need the alarm code." He closes his eyes for a moment. "Let's see. I think it's—"

He *thinks?* What if he's wrong? Is a siren going to go off and floodlights and . . . and the alarm system will auto-dial the cops?

"Okay," he says after a second, and punches in four numbers. The keypad makes a mocking little beep, and the light stays red.

Our three hearts collectively sink. Full disclosure: mine does a blip of relief, too.

"Okay, wait," says Garrett.

"*Damn,* Garrett!" I burst out.

"Shut," he says through gritted teeth, *"up."* He hovers his trembling fingers over the keypad, and I wonder what will happen if he's wrong a fourth time. Will it be like a secure website that locks you out and you have to call tech support?

He punches in four numbers, and with a cheery chirp the light turns green. Garrett grabs the handle and opens the door. "Wait here," he says. He steps inside, and the door whooshes shut behind him.

I look at Marissa. She hasn't said a word this entire time. Her face is blank and white. She looks like a wax statue.

"Don't worry," I say. It's the single most stupid thing I've ever said. *Ass-wipe!* I rage at myself.

Garrett opens the back door, his face white, beads of sweat glistening on his forehead. He motions us inside. "No one's here," he whispers.

I have an urge to say, *Then why are we whispering?* I conquer it.

The bright lights inside are like a scream. They make us cringe and scurry.

The smell is the second thing to hit us. It's not horrible, it's just very definitely *there.* A raw, gassy odor.

"Over here," says Garrett, taking Marissa's elbow gently.

All of a sudden, watching my brother lead my friend across the cold tiled floor to see if her mother has ended up here dead, I feel a lump in my throat. I blink furiously and clench my fists hard. *No. Goddamn it, no! Don't you dare.*

Garrett pushes the big button that opens the sliding glass doors of the cold room, like some entrance to a mall in hell. The lights come on automatically. There's only one *case* in there.

Marissa stops walking. Garrett looks back at me desperately and I move forward to help. Then she takes another step forward and another one, approaching the covered figure.

Garrett hurries over to the gurney and starts to unzip the bag. "You can do this," he says, and his voice is ragged. "It's almost over, baby."

The kindness in his voice almost does me in again.

Garrett pulls the cover back from the head of the figure and Marissa moves closer.

I hold my breath.

··········CHAPTER THIRTY··········

Photophobia: fear of light.

Marissa leans closer to the body to take a good look. Garrett hovers nearby.

I wait, a few steps away.

Marissa's hands fly to her mouth and her face crumples. I rush over to her.

Garrett drops the cover back over the face of the—*ohmygod, her mom?*—and pushes Marissa into my arms.

He looks at me and says in a low voice, "Get her out of here. I need to zip up the—" He goes back to the corpse.

Marissa is crying but making a terrible effort to be quiet. I hustle her out the back door as she's whisper-sobbing, "I'm sorry, I'm sorry."

We make it out the back door, and Garrett stops to set the alarm, then closes the door and locks it, his hands trembling. I put my arm around Marissa's shoulders to help her to the car; she's shaking like she's standing in an icy river.

I hold her tighter and walk her to the car. It seems so far away. Garrett runs ahead of us, unlocking the car. I help Marissa into the back seat and climb in after her.

"I'm sorry, I'm sorry," she cries.

"It's okay," I say automatically. What should I *do?*

She lies down on the back seat and curls up in a ball, shaking and shaking.

I look at Garrett, who has opened the driver's side door. "Get in!" he snaps. "Do something. Help her."

I climb in the back and perch on the edge of the bench seat, closing the door carefully.

Garrett starts the car, puts it in gear, and drives away from the scene of our nightmare come true.

Marissa is shuddering and crying. I balance on my corner of the seat, looking down at her. She is illuminated each time we pass a streetlamp; then her huddled figure is hidden in the shadows again. Light. Dark. Chiaroscuro.

I can't think of anything else to do. I lie down and curl up next to her, like spoons, and put my arm around her.

Garrett drives. I don't know where he's going, but he keeps driving for a long time. We're not going back to our house or Marissa's house. We would have been there by now.

Marissa stops crying after a while, but I stay where I am. She's holding on to my arm. "Blake," she says suddenly. "It wasn't her."

"WHAT?!"

"I'm sorry I didn't say it right away. I was so scared in there, in that horrible room, and I felt like I was going to faint, and then even though it wasn't her, I couldn't stop crying," she says. "I was so sure it was going to be her that it was almost like it *was*. Does that make sense?"

"Oh my God," I say.

"Did she just say that *wasn't* her mom?" asks Garrett.

"Yes."

"Oh my God!"

One more time she says, "I'm sorry."

We breathe.

"Okay," says Garrett. "That's good. I'm glad."

A few minutes later he stops the car and Marissa and I disentangle our arms. We sit up, not looking at each other.

We're parked outside of a Coffee Jones, which looks bright and bustling and caffeinated. People are going on with their lives . . . their normal lives. I study them as they come and go. How many of them have done unimaginable things? How many of them are carrying around some horror in their hearts?

"I need something," says Garrett. "Coffee. Jack Daniels. Something. You guys coming?"

Marissa shakes her head. "I'll wait here."

I was about to get out of the car, but I sit back down again. "Man, could you get me something?" I ask. "A caramel mocha thing? Only if they don't have Jack Daniel's."

My first joke. Post-nightmare. Maybe I'll be all right.

"Sure. You, Marissa?"

"That sounds good."

Garrett nods and walks into the Coffee Jones.

Marissa and I look out our respective windows. "I hate her," she whispers.

I slide over next to her. Without a word she lays her head on my chest.

"I hate her!" she says in a louder voice. Her fist punches the seat. "She was normal once. Why can't she just be normal again? When I was little, she was like any other mom. By the time Children's Services came to get us, she wasn't even feeding us. My grandma even got me a little refrigerator for my bedroom—I was always sneaking food when I came to live with her. I was afraid she would stop feeding me, too."

I listen. I stroke her hair. I want to go back in time and take care of that little girl.

When Garrett comes back, he gets into the car holding a cardboard tray with three cups.

"Garrett, man," I say. "Thank you."

"No problem," he says. He holds out a cup.

I take it from him and pass it to Marissa. "No. I mean thank you for the other thing. I know you took a huge risk doing this."

He sighs and shakes his head, holding out the second cup.

"Last night I kept thinking, What if it was *my* mom?" He makes a choked sound and turns away.

My throat gets tight again.

After a minute he says, "I knew it had to be this morning or never. I still can't believe—" He runs his hands over his head as if to massage some sense back into it.

"I really appreciate it," says Marissa.

"Do you?" He turns back, looking searchingly at her. "Or do you wish we'd never gotten you into this?"

"I appreciate it," she says again.

We sip our drinks in silence.

After a minute Marissa says in a low voice, "And."

We wait.

"It wasn't my mom. But it might as well have been. She's dead to me now."

She starts crying again, holding her cup awkwardly. I take the cup from her, and then *I* hold it awkwardly. Garrett reaches for both cups in my hands, setting them in his cup holder. I move toward Marissa, patting her shoulder. But that seems lame.

I put my arms around her again, and she holds on to me. This is starting to feel natural. An image of Shannon flits through my mind and keeps going. I'm not doing anything wrong. I'm comforting my friend.

Garrett turns on the car and starts driving again. Marissa and I sink down onto the seat, and eventually she falls asleep. I scrunch up next to her, watching the view through the back windshield: dark sky, trees, lit-up billboards, dark sky, telephone lines, trees . . .

When the tears start coming out of my eyes, they slide down my nose and into Marissa's hair.

•••••

"Where do you want me to take you guys?" asks Garrett.

I sit up, yawning. I must have fallen asleep, too. My arm is sore and numb. Marissa sits up, rubbing her eyes in a cute girly way.

"What time is it?" I ask.

"It's almost eight o'clock," says Garrett.

Marissa is shivering. I take off my coat and hand it to her.

"I need to go to work," says Garrett. He does not say "work at the morgue," I'm relieved to note.

Ohmygod. He's got to go back there and cut up that woman now.

"Sorry, but I have to drop you somewhere," he says. "Marissa, do you want me to take you home?"

Marissa pulls my coat over her like a blanket, still shivering.

I don't want to leave her alone.

"Mariss," I say. "Do you want to hang with me today?"

She stares at me, as if about to say something, then nods.

"Um, Garrett? Just take us to—" *Where?* "I don't know where."

"You don't want to go home?"

"No."

"Mom and Dad won't care if Marissa is with you."

"I want to go to the movies," says Marissa suddenly.

"Um, okay."

"I just want to shut off my mind. I want different pictures inside my head. Okay?" She looks fierce.

"Okay. But movies aren't open yet."

"I don't care. We can sit outside the mall until it opens." She turns her face to the window.

Garrett and I exchange a look. He drives to a coffee shop near Meriwether Mall and parks. He opens his wallet and takes out all the money he has, handing it to me. "Listen. Go have breakfast. Take your time. Get a newspaper, and you know, loiter. Like you're clueless. The mall will be open in a couple of hours. And tip the waitress big, for the loitering. Got me?"

"Yes."

Marissa and I get out of the car, and I lean down to say goodbye. "Thank you, Garrett."

"No problem, man." His face is pale. "Call me if you need me."

"Good luck today," I say quietly.

Marissa stands with my jacket clutched around her. We go into Shari's Shoppe and sit down and order breakfast. We read the paper, just like Garrett suggested. We read bits out loud to each other, like my parents do sometimes.

I don't know about Marissa, but I'm finally starting to feel better. It's warm and cheery inside, full of the smell of coffee and bacon and maple syrup. There are families and truckers and little old ladies. Marissa and I talk about wishing we had a camera with us. We snag some extra paper menus and draw pictures.

At some point I realize Marissa has taken off my jacket and started smiling again. Maybe she'll be okay.

"Want some pie?" I ask.

"Pie?"

"Or cake," I add. The waitress has already put the check down on the table, but I don't care.

"We just had breakfast."

"I know. But now I want pie."

She giggles. "All right. And I want cake."

I order a piece of apple pie and Marissa orders a slice of banana cake, much to the chagrin of our waitress, who probably figures we're going to leave her a dollar tip. We devour every crumb, like we're starving.

It's finally late enough to leave the coffee shop and walk over to the mall. I buy a couple of cookies for the road and give them to Marissa. She takes the little white paper bag and slides it into her pocket.

On the way, my cell phone rings. It's the Shannon ringtone. The sound jolts me out of this pretend vacation day we're having.

"I'll wait over here," says Marissa, walking away.

I hold the ringing phone in my hand until the call goes to message. Then I turn off the phone and join Marissa.

........CHAPTER THIRTY-ONE........

To avoid damage to the equipment and to prevent personal injury, never place the camera on an unstable stand or tripod. Mount only on a stable tripod.
—*Mitsu ProShot I.S. 5.3 camera guide, 2007*

We pick a comedy, of course, and it's a relief that the filmmakers don't sneak in any tearjerker moments. As we're walking out of the theater, I see Dez and Aisha from school. Marissa is laughing about one of the scenes in the movie, so I just ignore the other girls and hope they don't see us.

We're hungry again, so we go to the food court and eat lunch. Marissa scarfs down a sub sandwich and I eat two corn dogs. Now what? We look at each other, and that question hangs in the air.

"I guess I should go home," she says. Her smile has vanished.

"I guess," I say.

"Um, can you lend me bus fare? I didn't bring any money." She looks away.

"What did you say in the note you left your grandma?" I ask.

"Oh. I said I woke up early and couldn't sleep, so I was going to walk around downtown looking for—" Her words cut off again.

"Won't she be worried?"

Marissa sighs. "Yes. But truthfully? I think my grandma has been so worried for so long about, well, everything, that she's almost numb to it. The worrying. She used to boss me around a lot more than she does lately. I think she's really tired." She stands up suddenly. "I should call her."

"You should."

She reaches in her pocket. "I left my cell at home. I was half asleep when I walked out the door."

"Here." I turn on my cell phone and hand it to her.

She takes the phone and sits back down, dialing the number. After a minute she says, "It's the machine," then leaves her message: "Hi, Gramma, it's me. Sorry I didn't call earlier. I went, um, downtown this morning, and now I'm at the movies. I'll be home soon." She hits the off button and hands it back to me.

I study the call log: three calls and two texts from Shannon, one from Riley, and two calls from my parents. I forgot to ask Garrett what he was going to tell them. Too late to worry about it now. It's one o'clock in the afternoon.

Marissa and I walk to the bus stop. She hugs herself, hunching into her coat.

"You don't have to wait with me," she says. "You can call your brother to pick you up, if you want."

"Don't be a farb," I say. "I'm coming with you." This is a test.

Marissa smiles. "Really? To my house?"

248

Test results: yes, she would like some company. "You can't get rid of me just like that. What kind of date do you think I am?"

Uh-oh. Her cheeks go pink and I realize I've just announced we're on a date. That wasn't exactly what I meant. I was just trying to keep it light. I wanted to take her mind off our grisly mission this morning.

"Do you have any pie at your house?" I ask.

She laughs. "No. Well, maybe. My grandma bakes sometimes. Or *we* could make a pie."

This kind of silly conversation gets us through the bus ride and most of the walk home to her house. As we get closer, though, she falls silent. Half a block away, she stops.

I stop, too. "What?" I say.

"I don't want to go home," she says, so quiet I almost can't hear.

"You don't?"

She shakes her head. Then she looks up. "I'm really sorry, Blake. You must think I'm losing it. I just feel so—" She lifts her hands and lets them fall.

"I know." I give her arm a nudge. "I really know."

We stand there for a second, and I look back down the sidewalk the way we came.

"Come on," I say.

She doesn't ask me where we're going; she just walks with me, relieved.

We take the bus to my house.

"Hellooo," I call as we walk in. I'm ready for the shit to hit me square in the face. My mom must be out of her mind with worry.

The Dog Formerly Known as Prince comes running from the kitchen, one of my mom's shoes in his mouth. He wags and wails and dances with happiness while I pet him. Marissa gives him a few tentative pats.

"Maybe no one's home," I say. I know my dad and Garrett are at work, but where's my mom?

Marissa and I walk into the kitchen; sure enough, there's a note:

Blake—

Dad and Garrett are at work. They should be home in time for dinner, so you won't have to eat alone. But I'm not happy with you and your brother at the moment. You may not disappear from the house in the middle of the night without repercussions. Actions have consequences. [I groan loudly.] *I'm going out for a bike ride and then a movie. Finish your homework.*

Love, Mom.

P.S. Shannon called for you, wondering if your cell phone was off. She wants you to call her.

Who knows what Garrett told them?

"Everyone's gone," I say. "Par-tay!"

Marissa giggles.

We stand there for a second.

"Hey," I say.

"What."

"Want me to get my camera? We can take turns shooting photos."

She considers. "Um, not really. I think I wouldn't take very good shots today." She spins around. "This is stupid. I'm really sorry, Blake. You probably have homework or other stuff to do. Shannon's looking for you. I shouldn't have come." She takes a step toward the door.

"Marissa."

She stops moving and takes a deep breath, exhaling heavily.

I touch her hand. "You don't have to keep saying that you're sorry. I don't have anything else I have to do. Or anyone I have to call. Okay?"

She stares at me.

Our eyes lock, and for once, we don't look away. We don't make sure to keep things friendly and simple.

We don't look away.

We don't look away.

Her lips quiver. Is she going to start crying again? I don't want her to cry anymore. I move closer, and without even thinking about it, I kiss her.

CHAPTER THIRTY-TWO

Design is all about lines. Nature is all about curves.
—*Spike McLernon's Laws of Photography*

People say, "One thing led to another."

It's true.

People say, "We got carried away."

Not true.

There's always a point when you can stop. More than one point, as a matter of fact. Think about it: with each piece of clothing that comes off, you can choose to stop. When it's time to take "precautions" (a buzz-kill if there ever was one), you can choose to stop.

So when people say, "We got carried away," what they mean is, "I didn't want to stop."

Your heart and mind might protest a couple of times. Weakly. *This isn't Shannon. This should be Shannon. I should stop.*

Then your mind goes blank. *It doesn't matter who it is. I just want this to go on and on and never stop.*

Your body wants what bodies have wanted since the beginning of time. *I don't care, I don't care.*

And eventually it's over. That's when you have to explain it to yourself.

Because you have to explain it to yourself before you can explain it to others. *One thing led to another. We got carried away.*

·····

When I wake up, Marissa is lying on her side with her back to me. I'm kind of afraid to move. Either she's asleep, and I don't want to wake her, or she's awake and doesn't want to look at me.

I turn my head very carefully to see the clock radio on my desk. It's three thirty. We should get up.

Was it really just this morning that we snuck into the morgue? This day wins the grand prize for random. It started off so bad, so reallyreallyreally bad. But now I'm lying in bed with a naked girl next to me. I'm a sex machine. Like the song says.

How can that be bad?

Er, well, except for the fact that she's not my girlfriend.

I can't think about that right now. It will kill my, what do people call it? My afterglow.

Finally I really have to pee, so I sit up more slowly than a human being has ever sat up before, praying not to wake or disturb Marissa. I venture a peek over her shoulder; her eyes are closed.

Okay. I stand up and grab my boxers from the floor, then tiptoe out of the room and across the hall to the bathroom.

When I come back, she hasn't moved. Should I lie back down next to her? Put my arm around her? Put my clothes on? Wake her? What? I wish I could quickly Google some FAQs about what to do after you've had sex for the first time.

I'm getting cold, so I grab my shirt and slip it over my head. My gaze falls on my camera sitting on the desk. I pick it up and focus on Marissa's smooth shoulder. So pretty. One photo won't hurt. And I'll show it to her. If she wants me to delete it, I will.

I've shot about ten photos of Marissa from different angles and shutter speeds when she wakes up and rolls over. She sees me with the camera, and God love her, she laughs.

"You are such a goof, Blake," she says.

And just like that, we're okay. I thought we would be weird with each other. But she's still Marissa. My friend. Even though she's, um, lying in my bed without any clothes on.

I kneel down next to her. "Here, you can look at the shots. I'll delete them all if you want."

She scrolls through the shots on my camera, commenting, "That's a great angle. Ugh, could you have made my ass look any bigger? Oh, I like that. It's so close up you can hardly tell it's skin."

She hands the camera back to me and sits up, holding the sheet in front of her. "Do you want me to pose for you?"

Uh.

"I could be your first nude model."

Gulp.

"I mean, not *really* nude," she says. "I'm not crazy. Just a few tasteful shots."

I can't answer, so I just nod.

She turns around and fluffs the pillows, then switches on my bedside lamp and adjusts the lighting. Marissa is so businesslike about it that I stop feeling like a perv and look through the lens, deciding how I want to shoot her.

She sits cross-legged, holding the sheet in front of her, then lets it drop just low enough that her breasts are barely covered. It's an awesome pose, with her looking straight at the camera, her head lowered slightly. She looks shy, as if she's waiting, like a bride or something.

"God, Mariss, that looks great," I say.

"Let me see!" She bounces up and down, and I move closer to show her the shots. "Wow, those *are* good. You do good work, Blake."

I stand up and perform a little swagger, then act like I'm tipping my cap to her. "Why thank yew, ma'am."

She giggles. Then she lies down on the bed and drapes the sheet across her body artfully, so that her arms and legs are exposed, but the area between her belly and her thighs is covered. She pretends to be asleep while I shoot; then she rolls over and I shoot the length of her bare back, with her ass covered up. I remind her about that famous photo by Bill Brandt of the woman on the beach with her ass filling up most of the frame, but Marissa refuses to go there.

"We could do one like the Manuel Alvarez Bravo shot," she says.

"Okay. But you'd have to be on the floor, I guess," I say. "Unless you want to go outside!"

She laughs and gets down on the floor, pulling my bedsheet with her. She stretches out long, like the girl in the photo, then covers her, um, private bits with the sheet, leaving the rest of her body exposed. "Her arms were up, right?" she says.

"Uh-huh." I step back as far as I can to get her framed right. She looks lovely. Not as peaceful as the girl in the photo, because I think that girl was really asleep, but Marissa brings her own self to the pose.

"Great, Marissa."

"Let's see!" She sits up, and I kneel down next to her. "Ohh," she breathes. "I *do* look like her."

I nod.

"What are you going to do with them?"

"Huh?"

"Don't leave them on the camera! I don't want to end up 'The *Bad* Reputation, Sleeping.'"

We chuckle nervously.

"I won't," I say. *Note to self: hide a new folder on the laptop.*

Marissa stands up and climbs back into my bed.

Hmm. I thought she would get dressed now. I glance at the clock. Four fifteen.

My heart gives a lurch. Shannon's recital. *Okay, but I didn't say I would definitely be there,* I think.

Any minute, though, someone is going to come home.

"Mariss, we should get dressed," I say.

"Oh." She sighs and lets go of the sheet, preparing to get out of bed. I can't resist; I click one more picture. She's so naked and sad.

"Blake," she says. "Enough."

"Okay." I set down the camera, and we get dressed in silence.

Then we stand staring at each other. We'll probably never look at each other this way again. We're wearing clothes, but our feelings are naked. Our affection nude.

What do we say? There are about a million unspoken words floating around us.

"I won't tell anyone," she says finally. "I know you've got a girlfriend."

What the hell do I say to that? *Good?*

"Okay," I say. "But I don't know, I mean, yeah, I've got a girlfriend, but . . ."

She touches my arm. "It'll be okay, Blake. You'll be okay. And we're fine." She lifts her hands up. "I'm not going to act weird around you. And you'd better not act weird with me, either." She shoves her hands in her pockets. "Today was just—"

I nod.

She puts her arms around me, and we give each other one last hard hug. Then we go downstairs.

When my mom gets home, Marissa and I are working our way through a bowl of caramel-cheese popcorn and watching *This Is Spinal Tap.*

"Hey, Mom! How was the movie? Who'd you go with? Did you buy anything? Can I borrow the car?" I say really fast, hoping to stun her with my speedy words.

"Blake," she says, narrowing her eyes at me. But she won't punish me in front of Marissa. My mom is cool that way. "You're not supposed to drive anyone alone yet."

"Please, Mom?"

"Not to mention that you are extremely grounded," she adds.

I slump.

She looks at Marissa. "Blake is not allowed to drive anyone under twenty years old yet, with his provisional license. I'll take you home. Are you ready to go?"

Marissa looks at me and nods. "I'm ready."

There's no chance to say anything private before she leaves, but I think it's okay. We're back to normal. "See you Monday," I say as they walk out the door.

Marissa smiles. When she reaches the car, I open the back door and call out, "Mariss!"

"What?" She turns around.

"Did you like *Spinal Tap*?"

She shrugs. "It was pretty good." Then she climbs into the car.

Pretty good? I shake my head. Poor thing.

It's almost six o'clock. Shannon's recital must be over. I should call her.

And say *what?* I think I'll take a shower first.

Grabbing a bag of Chex mix, I head upstairs and turn on the water.

I stand there munching chips and nuts while the day replays in my mind. Not the bad part. I've stashed the bad part in a steel vault. I replay the good part. The part with skin and sighs.

I step into the shower and let the hot water pelt me, washing away the last traces of Marissa.

"Blake, phone," yells my dad.

"What?" Who would be calling me on my parents' line? "I'll call them back."

A few seconds later my dad opens the bathroom door and walks over to the shower. He slides open the door and says quietly, "It's Shannon. She sounds upset. You'd better come talk to her." He holds out a towel while I turn off the water.

My heart thuds. Upset? What could have happened? Marissa just left, so there's no way she could, well, *know*.

"Where's the phone?"

My dad takes the phone off the counter and holds it out to me. Then he leaves the room, closing the door behind him.

"Shannon?"

"Blake!" she says, her voice high and tremulous.

I stare into the mirror, shivering in my towel. "What's going on?" My eyes are guilty. I've never seen myself look that way before.

"Blake," she says again, this time with a sob.

There's a red mark on my shoulder. I lean closer to the mirror. Teeth marks. I turn my back on the mirror, the phone shaking in my hand. "Shan, I'm sorry I didn't go to your recital."

"Didn't you get any of my messages? I called you, like, fifty times!"

"You did?"

"No! Well, not fifty. But a lot."

I open my mouth, but what can I say?

"My grandma died," she cries out.

"Ohhhh," I moan. Relief and sympathy flood my brain, and I have to sit down before my knees buckle. I perch on the edge of the tub. "Oh, Shan, I'm so sorry."

She cries and mumbles things about her grandma for a while.

I keep telling her I'm sorry.

Finally she remembers her frustration. "Where *were* you today? Why didn't you call me back?"

"Oh, I'm really sorry," I say again, stalling. What the hell do I say? *Well, the first thing I did today was go to the morgue, and then I went to the movies, and later on I did it with Marissa.* "I, um, had to help someone out."

"Who?"

Okay. I suck at lying. Every lie I've ever told has come back to bite me in the ass. I could lie to Shannon right now, but I already know that it won't work. I take a deep breath and say, "Marissa."

I listen to the absolute silence.

I wait. I have an urge to keep talking, to try to explain, to babble excuses. I squeeze my eyes shut and force myself not to speak.

After, literally, about ninety seconds, Shannon says in a flat voice, "Why?"

"Um." I should have been thinking during those seconds of silence. I should have been thinking of what to say next.

Now it's Shannon's turn to wait me out.

"It's really complicated," I say.

Huge silence.

"Her home life is really messed up. You wouldn't even believe how messed up."

"Try me."

"Her mom—" I sigh. "I'm sorry, Shannon. I can't tell you. It's about Marissa's mother, and it's private."

"Private." She pauses. "Between you and Marissa."

"Yes."

"Fine." She's crying again. "I got it." And she hangs up.

......CHAPTER THIRTY-THREE......

Do not leave the camera in places where it may be subject to
temperatures of extreme heat or cold.
—*Mitsu ProShot I.S. 5.3 camera guide, 2007*

I'm really tired and fried.

This is the strangest day of my life, and *it won't end.*

I get dressed and go downstairs to beg my mom to let me drive over to Shannon's, even though I'm grounded, even though I'm provisional, but before I can open my mouth, she says, "What happened today, Blake?"

"What?"

She waits. My mom is better than anyone else at that waiting thing.

"Nothing." Less than thirty seconds later, I crack. "Marissa had a really bad day. Um, really *terrible,* in fact. But it's okay now."

"It's okay now," she repeats.

"Yes."

Long silence.

Then I add, "Well. Not *okay,* but better."

My mom waits me out some more, but this time I don't

break. Finally she says, "I hope so, honey. Because you know how vulnerable that girl is. She needs people she can count on in her life."

"I know. She can count on me." I draw myself up when I say this.

"I'm glad to hear that."

"Mom, um, not to change the subject, but I kind of had plans with Shannon tonight. She's having a bad day, too."

My mom closes her eyes and shakes her head, but I barrel on. "Her grandma died."

"What? Oh no. Poor Shannon."

The phone rings, interrupting my plan to wear my mother down until she hands me the car keys.

"Hello?" she says. "Yes. Yes. All right. I'll be there soon." She hangs up. "I've got to go to the hospital. One of my kids."

She doesn't say anything else. I know she means that one of the children at the hospital is near death. She pulls me close for a hug. "The gates of heaven are crowded today."

I'm so sick of death right now I could die.

After my mom changes clothes, she offers to drive me to Shannon's. Rather than admit that Shannon may very well throw a flowerpot down on my head while I'm knocking on her door, I accept.

"I'll see you later, honey," she says when we pull up at the house. "Please give my condolences to the DeWinters. Tell them to call me if they need anything."

"I will." I wave as she drives away; then I pull out my cell and dial Shannon. To my surprise, she answers.

"What."

"Shannon."

"What."

"I'm outside your house. Please let me come in. I'm so sorry about your grandma. I just want to hug you."

Crying. She's crying again, and I'm also so sick of crying people I could weep. For a split second, I can imagine clicking off the phone and just walking away.

But no. I can't do that. She's my girl.

I will not worry about all the other stuff that happened today. For now I will try to fix this one problem.

Eventually she comes to the door and lets me in.

I don't even have to make nice with Mrs. D., because it's *her* mother who died, so she's in her bedroom.

Shannon takes me to her room, and we sit close together, arms around each other. I apologize again that I wasn't there for her when she needed me, and she, amazingly, says it's okay, that she understands, she's just upset about her grandma.

Wow. I feel like a steaming pile of fertilizer. How could I cheat on this perfect girl?

She talks about her grandma. I'm so very, very tired that I don't even try to feel her up.

Finally she walks me downstairs and asks her dad to drive me home. He reluctantly levers himself out of the Chair of Stagnation and jingles his car keys at the door.

"Aren't you coming?" I say.

"No. I don't want to leave my mom," she says. "I'll talk to you tomorrow." She kisses me goodbye in front of her dad, and I trudge out the door after him. Then I stop and turn back.

"Shannon."

"Yes?"

"I love you."

· · · · ·

"Your eyes are not veiled, they will give you away without fail."

Cappie's voice rings out over the air, and I stop munching my burrito to listen.

"School yourself while you fool yourself. Oh, my friends, it's not too late, there's still time for fate." She lowers her voice dramatically. "Now pay attention to the song because the song is never wrong."

"Sympathy for the Devil" drifts across the airwaves.

I swallow my mouthful of food, which now feels lumpy. *School yourself while you fool yourself.*

I glance over at Shannon, who is sitting a few feet away in a sunny spot with Kaylee and Jasmine. Her grandma's funeral was last week. She's back at school now, cheering up little by little. Sometimes when she laughs at something, I see a look cross her face like, *How can I laugh when my grandma just died?* But people die. All the damn time. We have to grieve and then keep living.

She looks so gorgeous sitting there, her hair shining in the sun, her lips curved in a small smile, that I want to get up and go over to her right now and kiss her in front of everyone. But she might taste the bitterness of guilt on my lips, so I stay put.

I hate being a cheater.

I clearly suck at it, since I find myself on the verge of confessing to Shannon at least twice a day. But then I imagine the look on her face. She hasn't even recovered from her grandma's death. No way am I going to slap her with some "it just happened" story.

God! I'm scum.

But no matter how loathsome and low I feel, I still can't bring myself to wish it never happened.

I don't know how that can be.

It just is.

Marissa and I went right back to the way we always were.

Mostly.

I haven't forgotten a single moment of that day. Not a sound, not a touch. I know she hasn't, either. If things were different, maybe we would be together.

But I want to be with Shannon. I love her. I'm smitten. Smited? And I think Marissa needs someone who is, I don't know, bigger than I am. Someone who will hurtle down hills with her.

It's like the Shannon and Marissa parts of my life are all jumbled up inside me and I can't separate them without breaking something.

CHAPTER THIRTY-FOUR

A photograph is a secret about a secret.
The more it tells you the less you know.
—*Diane Arbus, American photographer (1923–1971)*

Shannon hasn't been to my house in ages, what with the whole funeral/visiting family/staying close to Mom period. Then she was busy getting caught up with school and piano and stuff.

I missed her. For the first time, I realized how much I would rather be with her than almost anyone else.

And today she's here. It's Saturday, so we can hang out all day. She's in a good mood, too, goofing around in my room, laughing at all my jokes. Things are finally getting back to normal.

She strikes a pose in front of the Rose Tyler poster. "Hey, big fella," she says in a suggestive voice. "*Now* who's your girl?"

"You are, sugar lips." I look around for my camera. "Hold that pose."

I look for the camera.

Oh.

Shit.

Oh *shit.*

I never deleted those photos of Marissa.

As I stand there in shock, Shannon darts past me and grabs the camera.

"Don't," I say, trying to grab the camera back.

"Ha!" Shannon yells, and jumps out of reach.

"Shannon, come on." I step toward her, my hand out.

She dances away, laughing. "Ha ha! It's time, once again, to turn the camera on the camera*man*." She thumbs the on button, and my heart almost stops.

"Not right now," I say. "I don't want to."

"No?" she teases. "Too bad. Right now *I* am the photographer, and *you* are the subject! We'll call this the I Don't Want To series." She aims and shoots, hardly taking the time to focus.

"Shannon, stop," I say, reaching for the camera.

She twists out of my grasp and leaps up onto the bed, laughing.

"Fine," I say. "Fine. All right? Go ahead." I stand with my arms out. If she takes enough photos, the shots will be far away from the Marissa photos.

Breathless, she takes a few more pictures, giggling at my obvious irritation.

"Okay, that's good, that's enough," I say. Inspiration! "Here. Give me the camera, and I'll take some of you."

"No, no, no. Not today, young Spielberg," she says. "Today *I* am the director. Oh! Let's do that mini-movie thing! Stand over there and do something in slo-mo. Pretend you're throwing a ball or something."

My heart is pounding crazily. If I can just get the camera away from her, I will smash it to pieces if I have to. Okay, I'm going to do what she wants until I can figure out how to get it away from her. I could kick myself for showing her the mini-movie thing!

I act out pretending to pitch a baseball.

She takes about a dozen shots of me doing that. "Cool! Let's see how it turned out." She sits down on the bed and pushes the review button.

"No!"

"Jeez, Blake, chill." She frowns up at me, then bends her head to the screen, holding the review button down so that it scrolls through the shots really fast.

"Sorry. Sorry. I didn't mean to yell. Just give me the camera and we'll load those onto the computer and make a little movie, if you want."

"I will. Just a second. Look how great this looks! You really do look like you're pitching a ball." She's still clicking back through the shots in review mode. "Oh, look, there you are, looking mad. You're all, 'come on, give me the camera!'"

"Shannon, *stop!*" I shout. Maybe if I act mad, she'll quit messing around. I don't even care if we get into a fight at this point, I just want to get the camera. *Out.* Of her *hands*.

Shannon goes rigid.

No.

Oh God.

She doesn't move. She just stares.

I know exactly what she's looking at.

Marissa. Getting out of my bed. Naked. With an expression that is almost sad.

Without raising her head, Shannon clicks the review button again. And again. Faster. Her breathing speeds up.

I get my hand on the camera, but she wrenches it away from me.

When she looks up, a cry comes out of her throat. "Aauuww! How many?"

I stare at her, my heart crashing into my gut.

"How many times?"

I shake my head.

"How many, Blake?!"

I'm not sure what's she's asking, but I answer the question I *think* she's asking. "Just once."

Her face is stunned. She must have thought I would say something like, "We were just goofing around with the camera. Nothing happened. Just taking pictures."

She almost can't believe it. "You did?"

I sink down on the bed.

Silence.

"When?"

I stare down at the floor.

"When?" she screams.

Ohmygod she's going to bring my parents running. "It was three weeks ago."

"Three weeks ago," she whispers, counting back. "No." Her hands fly to her cheeks. "*No*. Not *that* day."

I hold my head in my hands.

Her voice is almost pleading. "Not *that* day? The day that my grandma died? And I was calling you and calling you." Her voice chokes, and she drops the camera, spinning for the door.

I jump up and grab her around the shoulders, trying to hold on to her.

"You lied to me! You kept telling me she was just your friend! *Bastard.* I hate you!" she screams, and slaps me with every ounce of rage and strength she has.

She clatters down the stairs.

I don't move for a second, because I'm seeing stars. She dusted me good.

I close my eyes and hold on to the doorway, waiting for the stars to subside. I don't mind. I deserve this.

Then I stumble downstairs.

"Blake, what on earth?" says my mom. The front door is standing open.

I tear out the door after her, but Shannon is an athlete. I'll never be able to catch her on foot. She's already at the end of the block.

"Mom," I pant, running back to the house. "I need the car."

"What?"

"Shannon is . . . We had a fight. I need to go after her."

My mom hesitates, then shakes her head. "No."

"What?"

"*No,* Blake. What on earth is going on? You've got a big red handprint on your face, and Shannon ran out of here crying."

"I know. We . . . She's . . . come *on,* Mom!"

"I'm sorry, but I'm not letting you get behind the wheel when you're in a state like this."

"But I . . . Oh forget it!" I tear out the door again.

I run all over the place.

No Shannon.

How could she have gotten so far away? Is she *hiding* somewhere?

Not only do I feel horrible for hurting her—no, let's face it, for *breaking her heart*—now I'm worried that she might get hurt. Hurt even worse than what I did to her. What if she runs out in front of a car? Does she have any money to call home? Did she grab her purse on the way out?

I head back home. *How many times how many times how many times* rings through my head.

CHAPTER THIRTY-FIVE

Always back up your images. It's not a question of *if*
you'll lose important photos, but *when*.
—*Spike McLernon's Laws of Photography*

I stay in my room the rest of the day. I spend the whole time trying to write a letter to Shannon. There must be some way to explain. Some combination of words that will make her understand
that sometimes things just happen, and that I really love her and
will do whatever I have to to prove it.

So far I haven't figured out the right combination.

I try to listen to some tunes on my iPod, but I can't. I have
never felt so bad that I couldn't listen to music. I've reached a
new low.

My mom comes to the door after a couple of hours and
knocks. "Honey?"

"I don't want to talk," I say.

When I go to take a leak later, I see that's she's left a bottle of
Coke and a plastic container with a sandwich outside my door.
The Dog Formerly Known as Prince is lying nearby. He sits up,
wagging his tail as if to say, *I can haz sammich?*

I pee, wash my hands, then come back and pick up the food.

Garrett's door is open. I find myself walking over to it without even meaning to.

"Hey," I mumble.

"Hey, Blake."

Great. If he's being all sensitive and not calling me Studly, he must know what happened.

I stand there for a minute, shuffling my feet.

"Want to come in?" he asks.

I almost never go into Garrett's room, because of the smell. And because, well, he's forbidden me to. I step through the door, taking a tentative sniff. I don't smell farts or sweat, just a faint whiff of dog.

Garrett gestures to a beanbag chair on the floor, and I collapse into it, thinking, *I'll never get to share the soccer beanbag with Shannon again.*

We sit there in silence. It's a relief. I don't feel like talking, and I appreciate that Garrett isn't questioning me.

He's IMing and studying. I can't concentrate on two things at one time like that, but he does it all the time.

I eat my sandwich and drink my Coke, belching a couple of times. When I'm finished, Garrett glances over at me and says, "You okay, man?"

I don't know what to say. Finally I shrug.

He studies me a second, then stands up. "Be right back," he says.

I stretch, then burrow deeper into the beanbag, feeling the tiniest bit better.

Garrett comes back into the room carrying a stack of DVD box sets. He hands them to me.

It's the first two seasons of *Doctor Who*. He knows they're my favorite, because Rose Tyler is in them.

"Want to watch in here?" he asks.

"Really?"

"Sure. I haven't seen those episodes in a long time."

"Thanks." I crawl out of the beanbag and put Season One, Disc One, in his DVD player.

When I become aware of the room again, Garrett is zonked out on his bed. It's four thirty. I've been watching Rose and the Doctor for three episodes. I crawl out of the beanbag and stretch, feeling my joints creak from not moving for so long.

Garrett starts up, blinking and disoriented. "What time is it?"

"Four thirty."

"Oh." He sinks back down on his pillow. "Man. I was sleeping hard. Having the weirdest dreams." He yawns.

"About what?"

"Wolves and forests and shit. Looking for something."

"Huh."

"I've got to snap out of it, though." He sits up groggily. "I've got a date tonight."

"With Cappie?"

"Nah." He sees me looking at him and shrugs. "Not tonight. I'm going out with Aracely."

"Really?" I'm impressed. That girl is hotter than Dez Hayes. "The homecoming queen?"

"That's the one."

"Damn," I say.

He chuckles. "She's really nice." He looks closer at me. "How you doin'?"

I blink. Oh yeah. For a while I forgot that my life was wrecked. "Fine."

"No. For reals."

I don't answer. It's all crashing back into me now: shame and guilt and sadness.

"Garrett?"

"Yes."

"I can't be like you."

He looks at me.

"I can't be with more than one person at a time."

"Ohhhh." He seems to understand now. "But you always said that Marissa was just a friend."

"She is!" I say automatically. "I mean she was. But then something happened. That day. *You* know."

He raises his eyebrows. He knows which day. "Ahh."

"But it was just one time!"

He nods, even though we both know that just one time might as well be just fifty times.

"And Shannon found out today."

He shakes his head. "Brutal."

"I still don't even know how it happened," I say.

He nods.

"I mean, I never thought about, you know, doing it with Marissa. Really. I thought Shannon and I would—" I put my head in my hands. "I'm serious as a car crash, man. I still don't even know how it happened. It had something to do with all that other stuff. You know." I glance at the door and lower my voice. "That stuff at the morgue."

Garrett looks down at his hands. "Maybe—"

"Maybe what."

"It's something I've been thinking about lately."

"*What?*"

"Sex as medicine."

Blink. Blink. My brother is freakishly wise.

Just like that, I kind of understand. And I feel a glimmer of relief that someone else understands.

Not that it helps.

I'm still a loser who cheated on his girlfriend. But now I feel like a sliver in my soul has worked its way to the surface and I can throw it away.

. . . . .

I'm hungry again, but if I go downstairs, I'll see my parents, and I don't feel like talking. I hear Garrett leave for his date around six o'clock. I'm back in my room, curled up on my bed, letting Doctor Who take me on adventures.

I'm in the middle of Episode Four, where the Slitheen family have taken over the bodies of portly politicians so they can fit their alien bodies inside. It reminds me of the time Shannon was so bitchy I imagined her unzipping her forehead to reveal an alien inside. She never once farted in my presence, now that I think of it . . . unlike the Slitheen.

There's a knock on my door.

I almost call out, "I don't want to talk," but figure I have to face them sometime, so I say, "Come in."

It's my dad. "You okay, bud?" he asks.

I shrug.

"What happened?"

I don't answer.

He sits down on my desk chair. "Mom told me Shannon ran out of here really upset."

I stare down at the floor.

"Blake, you didn't, uh, you didn't forget our little talk, did you?"

"What?" Confused.

"About no meaning no?"

"Ohhh," I groan. "No, *Da*-ad! How could I ever forget our little talk? I'm still trying to stop convulsing."

He laughs. "Good. Hey, you made a joke. You must be going to live."

I find myself grinning a little. "I did, didn't I? And you laughed. One point." I score an invisible point in the air. Then I remember that I broke my girlfriend's heart today and I slam back into self-loathing. "She hates me," I mutter.

"Nooo." He leans over and rubs my arm. "How could she hate you?"

"She does." I feel tears squirt into my eyes. "She should."

My dad wants to help.

But the truth is, I *am* a lying, cheating bastard. I deserve to feel horrible.

After my dad leaves, I load the last disc in Season Two, and I select the final episode, "Doomsday."

The one where Rose and the Doctor part ways.

........CHAPTER THIRTY-SIX........

Unauthorized substitution of parts could result in fire,
electrical shock, or other hazards.
—*Mitsu ProShot I.S. 5.3 camera guide, 2007*

I can't drop out of school. I can't run away from home. I can't join the Witness Protection Program.

But how am I going to face Shannon in public?

I've thought about calling her, oh, a hundred thousand times, probably. But I can't believe that she would talk to me. I've also thought about e-mailing her, oh, two hundred thousand times, at least. But what the hell would I say besides a bunch of empty sentences? *I'm sorry. I didn't mean to hurt you.*

Even I can hear how stupid they sound. *Sure, sorry you got caught, right. And if you didn't mean to hurt me, then why did you do it?*

I lie awake in the dark as all of the day's terribleness hammers away at me. The image that stabs me over and over is Shannon's face when she realized the full extent of my betrayal.

When I wake up in the morning, I'm surprised to find that I ever fell asleep.

A letter, my brain commands. Write a letter. Yes, it will suck, but you have to do *something*.

But first: breakfast.

The house is quiet when I go downstairs. Everyone is still asleep. The Dog Formerly Known as Prince is still in Garrett's room, so I make myself a lonely bowl of cereal and take it back to my room.

I spend an hour sweating over a letter to Shannon, trying to explain. It feels like trying to translate a book written in Blake-ish into the language of Shannon, which I don't speak very fluently. But I have to try.

After approximately sixty-five drafts, I have a letter:

Dear Shannon,

Please believe that I wish I could go back in time and do things over. I would say "I love you" every day. I would tell you everything about Marissa's mother, and all the messed-up things she's done, and how that led me to get involved in Marissa's home life. Most of all, I would remember that I wanted you and only you before I did something in a moment of weakness.

I hope someday you can forgive me. I know this is hard to believe, but I never wanted to hurt you.

Blake

I seal the letter in an envelope and set it on my desk. Now what?

I hear the door to Mom and Dad's room open, and a minute later there's a knock on my door.

"Come in," I say.

The door opens, and both of them stand there in the doorway with tentative smiles.

"Morning," says Dad.

"How are you?" says Mom.

I stare at them for a minute. Do they even know how lucky they are? I wonder if I'll ever fall in love again. Maybe I'll end up living here with Mom and Dad forever, a forty-year-old man whacking off alone for all eternity in his childhood bedroom. Oh well. Like Woody Allen says, "Don't knock masturbation. It's sex with someone I love."

"Honey?" prods Mom.

"Fine," I say.

"Want some breakfast?"

"Maybe. I had some cereal before."

"Okay. Come down and join us, if you like." My mom's glance falls on the envelope sitting on my desk with Shannon's name on it. She doesn't comment.

"I'm going to—" I say, and stop.

"Yes?"

"I'm going to go to Shannon's later."

Now that I've said it out loud, I realize the thought has been stewing in the back of my brain like medicine you don't want to swallow.

"Did you talk to her?"

"No."

"No?"

"I don't think she'd talk to me if I call."

"I see. Do you want a ride over there?" asks my mom.

"Um, no." To my horror, yet another set of tears bubbles to the surface! Whatever brain filter I have that keeps me from dissolving into babyhood every five minutes seems to be ripped. This time it's the thought of standing at Shannon's door and my parents witnessing it being slammed in my face.

My parents exchange glances. "Let's talk about this later," says my dad. "We'll see you downstairs."

I look up a minute later when Garrett comes into my room. He sets the keys to the Marauder on my desk and walks out.

· · · · ·

It's ten a.m. I pace my room, trying to rehearse what to say to Shannon.

There must be some way to make her understand. It can't really be over, can it? Just like that?

My cell rings, and I jump on it, looking at the caller's number. Not Shannon. Marissa.

Oh shit!

"Hey," I say.

"Blake, what happened?" asks Marissa without even a hello.

"What?"

"Shannon just called me."

"What?!"

"I'm freaking out. All she said was, 'You can have him. I don't want him anymore.' Then she hung up."

My knees give out, and I sink down on my bed. *You can have him. I don't want him anymore. I don't want him.*

Marissa says impatiently, "Helllllooo? Blake, what's going on?"

"She knows," I say.

Big bang of silence.

"She picked up my camera and was goofing around with it," I add. "She saw those pictures I took of you."

More gaping silence.

Then: "How could you be so stupid?"

"I know," I say.

"I told you not to leave those photos on your camera!"

"I know."

"I totally CANNOT BELIEVE YOU."

"I know."

We sit together on the phone, not speaking. Just breathing.

"If I could kick my own ass, I would," I say after a long time.

We laugh a little, then stop, appalled. How can we laugh?

"Are you going to talk to her?" asks Marissa.

"Well, I have to. I can't drop out of school." Funny how I keep fantasizing about this.

"Oh no," she whispers. "School. How can we show our faces there ever again?"

"Maybe she won't tell everyone," I offer.

"Right."

"I'm sorry," I say.

"You are?"

Do I hear a tiny inflection of hurt?

"Not for . . . you know. I'm not sorry about that." I examine my feelings quickly. It's true. I'm still not sorry about that. Even though my life is ruined.

"I'm sorry, too, Blake. But not for that, either. I'm just sorry things are messed up now."

Could this whole thing be any more complicated? I remember when my biggest screwup was buying the wrong necklace.

I miss those days.

•••••

I'm sitting in Garrett's car outside Shannon's house. I hate to turn off its comforting rumble.

I really don't want to do this.

I would rather sleep on a bed of nails for the next month. I would rather shave my entire body and bathe in orange juice. I would rather drink muddy water. Like the song says.

But I cannot show up at school tomorrow without trying to see Shannon.

I shut off the car and walk up to the front door. Before I can change my mind, I knock.

Mrs. DeWinter opens the door. She doesn't even make an effort to disguise her look of revulsion. "What."

"Can I talk to Shannon, Mrs. DeWinter?" *Be nice,* I remind myself. *Someday Shannon might forgive you; then you'll have to see this woman again.*

"No."

I feel feral. My fists clench. "Please."

"No," she says. Her voice is not calm now. "What did you do to her? She came home crying yesterday and says she never wants to see you again. What did you do?"

What did you do what did you do what did you do?

So Shannon didn't tell her mom. Maybe that means she won't tell anyone. Maybe it's too embarrassing.

"I don't . . . I don't want to say," I stutter. "It's between Shannon and me."

Mrs. DeWinter comes out of the house and gets in my personal space, shutting the door behind her. "You listen to me," she hisses. *"Nothing* is between you and Shannon, do you understand me?"

I inch back.

"If you did something to hurt her, so help me I will—"

"I didn't!" I protest. "Not like that! I would *never* hurt her. I mean, I did hurt her. Her feelings. But I didn't do anything to hurt her physically."

Mrs. DeWinter gives me a long, crazy-woman stare to see whether or not I'm telling the truth. After a minute she appears satisfied, because she backs up and opens the door. "Good. Because I will not hesitate to contact the authorities, Blake, if I hear differently." She steps inside and gets ready to close the door.

"Wait!" I move toward her, holding the envelope out. "At least give her this. Please!"

She regards the envelope as she might regard a handful of dog shit.

"Please," I say one last time.

Her lip curling, Mrs. DeWinter grabs the letter out of my hand and slams the door.

I drive down to the end of the block and pull over to the curb. I don't get out of the car and pound on the hood or scream obscenities. I just sit there with my whole body twitching like a broken toy.

I am so glad my parents didn't have to see that. The look of disgust on her face! I feel like a worm.

My mom has been saying these three words to me my whole life, but I think today is the first day I really feel their meaning in my bones:

Actions have consequences.

When I get home, an e-mail from Shannon is waiting in my in-box: *Please don't call or write to me anymore.*

CHAPTER THIRTY-SEVEN

> Don't forget negative space in your composition—
> use it to convey loneliness or isolation.
> —*Spike McLernon's Laws of Photography*

We're on our way to school. It's the worst Monday in the history of my entire life.

Garrett keeps the radio off. Out of respect for my catatonic state, I guess. I do feel like I'm made of very thin glass, like one of those easily breakable Christmas ornaments. One clumsy step and I'll shatter into a million pieces.

Garrett parks and leaves the car running for a minute. He seems as worried about my day as I am. "You ready, man?" he says.

I want to say, *No. Please drive me back home.* But I nod my crystal head and ease my fragile arms and legs out of the car.

Garrett even walks next to me!

Shannon is nowhere in sight. She is always there ahead of me, hanging out on the quad with her peeps. I see Kaylee and Jasmine, but no Shannon. The two of them see me and scowl.

"Uhhnnnn," I moan.

"Easy, big fella," says Garrett.

"Don't," I say.

"Don't what?"

"Don't call me big fella. *She* used to call me that sometimes."

"Dog. Dog, I'm so sorry. I didn't know." Garrett raises his hand as if to pat my shoulder, then drops it, remembering that we're at school and he's got a reputation to protect. "I've got to go to class now, okay?"

Ohgod, this is just excruciating. I can't bear his concern.

"Go. I'm fine," I say through my brittle lips. "See you later."

I manage to stiff-leg my way to biology and survive the hour, even though every time I think about walking into English class, my heart starts slamming around in my chest.

Finally the bell rings. The bell of doom.

I stop at the drinking fountain to quench my thirst. I've got serious dry mouth.

It's time.

I walk into class.

"Hi, Blake," Mr. Hamilton says, then cocks his head at me. I must look as bad as I feel.

Shannon is not there.

Oh. Thank. God.

I feel really bad, of course. And it's only prolonging my agony, but I am just so glad I don't have to face her yet.

Marissa is at her desk, writing in her journal. As I ease my body gingerly into my chair, she glances over at me. I give her a fractional nod, and we look away from each other. I know she's got to be glad Shannon is absent, too.

·····

I must have been high to think that just because Shannon isn't here today, word wouldn't get around.

By lunchtime the girl network has effectively spread the Top Story of the Day. I fully expect to hear Cappie talking about it on the radio any minute: "In other news: Blake slept with Marissa even though he said he loved Shannon and now Shannon has broken up with him and we all hate Blake and Marissa because Shannon is really nice and they are horrible. This is 88.1, KWST."

But the news must not have reached Cappie yet, because the airwaves remain free of our sad scandal.

Riley sidles up to me, his eyes round. "Flake, is it true? What Kaylee said? Did you and Marissa . . . ?"

I just slump, and he whispers, "No way!"

"It's not like that," I say.

"Kaylee is so mad, man. I shouldn't even be talking to you, know what I'm sayin'?"

"Yeah."

"Later."

He leaves, and I decide I can't face the lunch crowd alone. For the first time, I walk off campus without permission. I head over to Ottomans, checking out the customers while I stand in line. I don't see anyone I know; maybe I'll be safe here. I buy a meatball sub and eat it at a kid-size plastic picnic table. The meatballs don't seem to have any flavor.

No one is sitting in the soccer beanbag. I keep glancing over at it, even though I don't want to. After I finish eating, I snap a photo of my crumpled-up sandwich wrapper in the middle of the beanbag.

· · · · ·

"The deadline for the photo contest is coming up," says Mr. Malloy. "And remember, everyone who enters the contest will have his or her photos on display at school for a month. At the end of the month I will announce the winner, and that person's photos will be hung in the Third Thursday Gallery."

Mr. Malloy looks less distracted today than he has lately. His beret is back in place and his glasses are glinting. "I hope everyone will enter," he adds with a smile. "Now! Who's ready to talk about portraiture with me?"

I glance over at Marissa, who is scribbling something that looks like a list: "blue jay and bushtits, pink roses, Japanese garden shots, Grandma's cobbler."

Must be her contest entries. All pretty. I should enter some *gritty* to keep the judges from going into a diabetic coma.

The door swings open, and we all turn to look.

Marissa's mother stands jittering in the doorway.

"Um?" she says.

My eyes almost pop out of my head and roll across the desk. I whip around to look at Marissa. Her face is a mask of shock.

I didn't actually see the corpse in the cold room that day, but I can't imagine that she looked worse than Marissa's mother looks right now.

"Can I help you?" Mr. Malloy frowns.

Marissa jumps up and rushes to the door, mumbling, "Sorry." She steps into the hall. "Mom!" she says, closing the door behind her.

We all stare at the door, and I *know* we're still seeing in our minds that skin-and-bones, stringy-haired waif that Marissa just called Mom.

"Okay," says Mr. Malloy. "Where were we? Portraiture. Nate. Talk to me about the use of flash in shooting a portrait."

"Um, well, you would want to bounce the flash off the ceiling, if you can. It—"

"—told you it's just for food! It's not like I'm asking for a hundred bucks!" comes the raised voice from behind the door.

We hear Marissa's murmur, then the other voice even louder. "Come *on,* Marissa! Don't be such a bitch!"

Mr. Malloy moves toward the door.

"Fine!" comes a shriek.

I feel myself boil with hatred for that horror show of a human being; I wish she *had* been the corpse in the cold room.

I should get up. I should see if Marissa needs help.

But I do not move. It took everything I had to bring my body to school today and propel it from class to class. I got nothin'.

The door opens and Marissa steps back inside the classroom, her face red and contorted with pain. She stumbles to her desk and grabs her backpack.

"Sorry," she says again to Mr. Malloy, and she leaves.

Disbelief jolts my whole body.

And something inside of me slams shut.

•••••

If possible, Tuesday is worse.

Shannon is back at school, and her face, her sweet face, is so *crushed* that I want to throw myself at her feet and beg her forgiveness. I would do it in front of everyone—schoolwide assembly!—if I thought it would help.

But somehow, besides being crushed, the look on her face is *finished*. As if I'm no one special. Just some guy she used to work with at the community center.

I see her stony expression, and I remember her saying, "The Gold women are tough. So don't mess with me!"

Marissa doesn't show up in English. That's one more day without the three of us being in the same room together. Thank you, God.

People are still talking about us. A few guys make crude comments to me about Marissa. Some people look away when they see me coming down the hall; others shoot me looks full of loathing.

Cappie spares me further public humiliation by not mentioning Shannon and me during her Love Gone Wrong broadcast.

When I get to photo, I don't expect to see Marissa.

To my surprise, though, she's there. "Hi," she says.

"Hey." I take my stuff out of my backpack.

I know I should ask what happened with her mom, but I really don't care. I don't want to waste a single breath talking about her. I'm glad to see Mariss, I just don't feel like rehashing another drama. I'm still hip-deep in my own drama; I have no energy for anyone else's.

Marissa doesn't bring it up, either. After a minute she leans over and says, "Anything new with Shannon? Is she talking to you yet?"

I make a bitter sound. "No. That ship is sunk."

She makes a sympathetic face.

"I'm sure I'd feel much worse if I weren't so heavily sedated," I add.

A small smile lifts the corners of her mouth. "*Spinal Tap*?"

I feel a similar lifting at the corners of my mouth. I nod.

"I got called a slut today," she announces.

Ow! My smile slides off.

Marissa shrugs and says, "It's worse for girls. No one is calling you a slut, are they?"

No.

The next day is bitterly the same.

A crushed-looking Shannon. Twittery girls and scowly faces. Riley banished from my presence. Marissa gray and silent, sagging under the weight of gossip. By the end of the day, she's in tears. Apparently her friend Bree got into some kind of shoving match with another girl who called Marissa a word much worse than "slut."

I see her rushing away from school as I leave to catch the bus. I feel a tired kind of sadness. But I'm all out of wanting to help.

CHAPTER THIRTY-EIGHT

If memory card is accidentally swallowed, contact a doctor immediately.
—*Mitsu ProShot I.S. 5.3 camera guide, 2007*

"Look, it's time to stop this," says Cappie.

My heart smacks against my rib cage. Holy crap! When did she get here? Why is she always suddenly appearing out of nowhere like some special ops agent?

"Time to stop what?" I say, pressing a hand to my chest to keep my heart attack from going systemwide. I sit up from where I've been lying on the couch watching *Abbott and Costello Meet the Mummy*.

She narrows her eyes, pacing back and forth in front of me. "Time to get over yourself. Let the healing begin, my brutha!"

I don't speak crazy, so I don't answer.

"I made you a playlist," she says. "Actually, two."

She hands me her iPod. "You can borrow it for a couple of days. Go to the playlists called 'Blake's Broken Heart 1 and 2.' I didn't know if you were mad-sad or sad-sad, so I prescribed music for both conditions."

"Mad-sad? What are you—"

"Do you feel like crying or breaking stuff?"

"I—"

"Never mind, just listen to both," she says. You think you invented heartbreak? Check out my man Hank Williams, brother Sam Cooke, Roy Orbison. And you want tragedy? Remind me to tell you about Patsy Cline."

"I've never—" I say.

"Exactly!" She stops and points at me. "You've never heard of those people. But they've already said it all, and they said it decades ago. I mixed in some modern stuff, too, because I was afraid you might choke on the classics. But you listen as long as it takes until you realize that you're not feeling anything new. Okay? I'm tired of your pitiful face. Now where's Caveman? We're going bungee jumping."

I almost crack a smile. "Heh. Good one."

"We are." She heads out of the room. "Don't worry, you're not invited. No one expects *you* to do anything risky."

· · · · ·

Since it appears that I will not be allowed to drop out of school, no matter how heinous my social crimes, I should probably do some homework.

Biology . . . *hate*. History . . . yeah, yeah, Ms. B. (Borden? Barden?) said there's a test next week, I should study. Why aren't there any *funny* historical people? That would make it more interesting. English . . . I'm way behind on the reading and the journal entries. Not to mention that I'm a little late for writing about things that really matter.

I take out my photo stuff.

I don't have any ideas for what to enter in the photo contest. In fact, all of my work looks like crap right now. Crap photos taken by a craptastic human being.

Looking through my portfolio makes me remember something. I go out to the backyard and stand beneath the tree where Marissa found the bird's nest. It's still there.

I go into the garage and struggle with the ladder, banging my legs as I carry it outside and set it up under the tree. I climb the first two steps of the ladder, and I can see the whole nest. And there's the ceramic angel that Marissa placed in the nest, still sitting there. Waiting all this time for someone to remember it. One of its wings is chipped. Some of the paint has worn off. And the nest is a shambles: the twigs and stuff are drooping and falling apart, so that it's a miracle the angel is still in place.

I go back into the house and get my camera.

• • • • •

Cappie walks into the house stiffly. Garrett bounces in after her, looking like he just took a turn on the Tilt-a-Whirl. He's radiating adrenaline and immortality.

"What's up, little bro?" he shouts out, all loud and proud.

"Um, *nothing*," I yell back. "Jeez. Why are you so pumped? And what's wrong with her?"

Cappie is easing herself down onto the couch. "Ice," she groans.

"You got it, baby," says Garrett, bounding into the kitchen.

I sit down across from Cappie.

"Your brother," she says.

"Yes?"

"Is more than just a pretty face."

"Really." I stand up. "That's *so* fascinating, but you know, I've really got to be going." I tap an imaginary watch on my wrist and start to leave the room.

"He did it," she says, almost like she's talking to herself. "I thought for sure he would chicken out."

I stop. What the hell.

"Did what?" I ask.

"Jumped off the bridge."

Blink. Blink. "Huh?"

Garrett enters the room with a flexible ice pack and places it carefully on Cappie's shoulder. "I'm thinking you hurt your rotator cuff when you threw your arms back like that," he says.

"Like what?" I say. "What is she talking about? What bridge? She said you jumped off a bridge."

Garrett smiles. "You told him? Oh, man. The little scrof will tell my parents for sure." But he's still grinning, practically bursting with glee.

"Caveman," says Cappie, clutching the ice pack, "you're fearless. I had no idea."

"That's right. Check me out," says Garrett, laughing.

"Will someone please tell me what you're talking about?"

"We did a base jump off Blue Jay Bridge," says Garrett. "Well. *I* did."

"What?" I say. "Why?"

"Cappie and I were going to do it together. But she—"

"Ohmygod, did you get hurt when you jumped?" I say, staring at her. She *looks* like she's all in one piece.

Garrett takes the ice pack and moves it to her other shoulder. "She freaked at the last second. When she threw her arms back to keep from going over, she must have wrenched some ligaments in her rotator cuffs."

I start laughing, and I can't stop.

Thank you, Chick Trickster. I needed that.

· · · · ·

The Blake-is-a-Cheating-Bastard story has legs.

It won't die.

It's Monday again, an entire week later, and people are still shooting me dirty looks.

Read the newspaper, I feel like telling them. *There are a lot better candidates for hatred out there. I may be a terrible boyfriend, but I'm not blowing people up or chopping down rainforests.*

At lunchtime I take my sad sandwich to the cafeteria and look for a place to sit. Riley and Kaylee are together as usual. I don't see Shannon. She's been eating lunch somewhere else ever since the Incident. Maybe in the music room.

I settle at a table and pull out a comic book so I have something to do while I eat.

"Blake?"

I jump and cough, and Coke actually flies out of my mouth, dribbling down my chin. It's Shannon.

I hurry to swallow. Ohmygodohmygod, is she going to talk to me? Is she going to forgive me? Will I get my old life back?

A hush descends on the tables around us.

Shannon holds out her closed fist and says, "I can't keep this."

Automatically, I hold out my hand. She opens her fist and drops the necklace I gave her onto my palm and walks away.

I sit there like a schmo for a second, then stuff the necklace into my pocket. I glance over at Riley, who looks away, embarrassed for me.

I hear someone mutter, *"Burn."*

I go back to eating my sandwich, but each mouthful is like a wad of wet paper towels. The blood is beating in my ears so loud I can't hear anything else.

How could she do that? Why would she do that?

Why didn't she just put it in my locker or mail it to me if she didn't want it, instead of humiliating me in front of—

—the whole school.

Kind of like I humiliated her.

Wow. Who knew Shannon—sweet, kind Shannon—had a vengeful streak? Maybe I'm the first person who brought it out in her.

I would get up and leave, but I feel like I'm nailed to the seat. Quick: a joke. Defuse the drama. My brain chugs dully. Nothin'. I don't have one drop of funny in me right now.

I settle into seethe mode. She walked right up to me and held out her *fist*. Like she had a special treat inside. Then she said a total of four words and pretty much *shat* on my head. I can't believe her! I thought that maybe someday, not tomorrow or next week, but *someday* we might be able to look at each other like normal people. Maybe even say, "Hi, how's the family?"

Not that I give a fiddler's fart about her sloth father or her evil crone mother. Thinking about her mom gets my blood boiling even more. I guess Shannon is going to turn into a cruel witch, too. She was so sweet when I was with her, but what's that saying? The apple doesn't fall far from the tree.

I'm so caught up in my spiral of shame and rage that I don't even see Marissa walk up to my table.

"Blake, guess what?" she says, and I jump again.

She looks excited about something, but I can't see my friend Marissa in front of me. I only see the agent of my destruction.

"Can't you just leave me alone for once?" I burst out. I shove my lunch to the floor and slam away from the table. Even as I'm stomping away, I can't miss the expression of shock on Marissa's face.

.......CHAPTER THIRTY-NINE.......

Never subject batteries to strong shocks or continuous vibration.
—*Mitsu ProShot I.S. 5.3 camera guide, 2007*

First I think that she's just bailing on school. After all, that's the pattern.

But when Marissa is not there a second day, I text her:

M, where u at? Sorry I was a dick b4. Shan shamed me in front of the world. Plz call. Blakenator.

She doesn't call. She doesn't even text.

I think about the last time I saw her, and I want to dig a hole and crawl in. But I don't think the worms would even have me. They would form a special worm committee to inform me that I wasn't welcome in their neighborhood.

The next day, I finally get up the guts to call Marissa's cell, but it goes to voice mail.

By the fourth day that Marissa is not in school, I'm looking for her friend Bree, but every time I see her, she's all the way across the quad, or walking on the street while I'm on the bus, or something.

I text her a couple more times, and finally she answers:

B, got ur messages. busy w/ a buncha stuff now, but am fine. U don't have to keep saying sorry. bye 4 now, M.

Then a week goes by.

Mr. Malloy takes me aside and quietly asks me if I know where Marissa is. I guess even the school doesn't know what's going on with her. He tells me a local weekly newspaper wants to print some of her flower photos. He had mentioned their interest to Marissa before she disappeared.

That must be what she wanted to tell me the last time I saw her.

Two weeks go by. Two *whole* weeks.

I call and text a couple more times, but she never answers.

I even go to Pioneer Park to look for her. I make Riley come with me, because I'm not suicidal. He's a black belt in tae kwon do.

We go after school. We don't see Marissa, and in fact, there are only normal-looking people jogging by and feeding pigeons and chatting on park benches. The scary people don't show up till dark. But do I want to go back at night? Yes and no. Except for the yes part.

At school, the herd is slowly allowing me reentry. Riley hangs out with me at lunch most days, saying that if Kaylee doesn't like it, she can break up with him. Awesome. What a badass boy-friend. He's my new hero. Garrett deigns to speak to me in front of people, which goes a long way toward improving my ratings. I score an occasional point with a joke. Shannon and I keep a chilly buffer between us. I guess the whole "we can still be friends" thing doesn't apply to us; we don't even make eye contact.

But the public castigation—that word always makes me cringe a little, it's so close to "castration"—has tapered off.

On the third Monday that Marissa is not at school, I find Garrett at lunchtime and ask him for a ride to Marissa's house after school.

"Bite me," he says before I've even finished my sentence.

"Thanks for being a knob," I answer.

Ahh. Things are back to normal.

I stop at Ottomans for a smoothie after school. I see Ellie and Manny goofing around in the soccer ball beanbag and I feel my heart—I really do—I feel my heart *ache*.

I take the bus to Marissa's neighborhood and walk down the street to her house.

As I get closer, I see a Realtor's sign stuck in the lawn: FOR SALE. The hell?

I walk up to the front door and knock, but no one answers. I peer in the window and see big boxes strewn around the room, taped up and labeled in black marker: BOOKS, BOOKS, LIVING ROOM, DINING ROOM, LINENS, BREAKABLE, BREAKABLE.

·····

The next day, I text Marissa again:

Marissa, what is going on? R u moving? I tried calling your gram's number, but it's disconnected. Call
me!!!! Blake

Mariss Cell *is no longer in service.*

·····

The next Friday night finds me at the top of Tower Hill.

Milling around among the hurtlers without my bike makes me
feel kind of like I showed up at a concert without a ticket. I didn't
even take my camera with me.

I just need to find Gus. Maybe Marissa will be with him. If
not, at least he'll know where she is.

I make my way through the crowd of people and bikes. I don't
see Gus, although I do see the guy with the green spikes in his
hair. I check my watch. There are at least ten minutes before the
start . . . I should be able to find Gus before then.

There's a group of people who look like bike messengers.
Maybe they know him.

"Excuse me," I say to a woman with blond dreads pulled back
in a scarf.

She looks at me.

"Do you know a guy named Gus? He's a bike messenger, and he—"

"Gus Fairbairn?"

"Yeah! Do you know him?"

"Of course."

"Do you know where he is?"

The blond woman scans the crowd. "There he is."

I turn in the direction she's pointing. "Thanks," I say.

I don't know how I missed him before, he's so big. But now, seeing him in person, I hesitate. What if . . . what if Marissa told him? About us? Or what if she told him that because of me she's an outcast at school? What if he pounds me into ectoplasm?

I take a big breath.

No. I have to find out where she is. I can't worry about his brotherly wrath right now.

I weave my way through bikes and riders until I'm standing a few feet away from him. "Gus."

He glances at me, and his eyes widen. "You're my sister's friend."

"Yeah."

"Do you know where she is?"

Damn.

"No," I say, closing the distance between us. "I was hoping you did."

His shoulders sag. "She left."

"Left?"

His gaze slips past me, and he scowls. "With her."

Who? I almost say. But the clench of my gut tells me.

"And her cell is disconnected now," he says. "I can't get through to her."

"What about your grandma?"

He lifts a shoulder, lets it drop. "She's tired. She can't go through it all again. She sold her house and moved into a little retirement condo."

"But how could she leave Marissa?"

"She didn't. Marissa left her."

"No."

"She did."

"She wouldn't do that."

"She did. Gramma said my . . . my *mother* was no longer allowed at her house. So Marissa went with her."

"But where?" I plead.

"They've been crashing with different people. I told Marissa she could move in with me, but she wouldn't. She left some of her stuff with me, but she wouldn't stay. She was talking about going to Seattle."

I'm out of words.

Wait.

No, I'm not. "Who is Kat?"

The bulk and muscle of Gus shrink before my eyes. His expression becomes that of a haunted boy.

"Who is she?" I say again.

"Our sister."

"Is she . . . ?"

He nods. "She's an angel now."

Oh.

God.

Somewhere in a basement closet of my heart, I knew that. But I never opened that door.

"Is that why your father is in jail?" I say.

He swallows. Tries to speak. "She . . . Mariss and I were just kids. We didn't know—"

I wait.

"About dehydration and stuff. She was small. She was only two."

I feel like I'm falling, yet somehow I'm still standing.

Gus looks down at his right arm, where the inked memory of a little girl remains.

"What about your mom?" I say.

He shakes his head. "She wasn't around. She was in rehab."

Now I'm out of words.

Gus straightens up. "I gotta go. Call me if you hear from Marissa, okay? Here's my number."

I take out my phone and punch in the numbers he recites. "You call me if you hear, too." I tell him my number, and he adds it to his phone.

A roar erupts from the crowd, and I hurry to get out of the way of the wheels.

CHAPTER FORTY

Photography: Latin for "writing with light."

The week before the contest deadline I gather up my series and go to Mr. Malloy. I tell him everything. He takes off his beret and rubs his head absently while I talk.

"Do you have a signed release form?" he asks.

Oh. I never thought of that.

He sees the answer in my face. "We can't display them without her permission."

"Right. The thing is . . . can I just show them to you?"

"Yes," he says. "Please."

"Wait till I get them set up, okay? Don't look yet," I tell him, and he goes out of the room.

I lay out all of the photos in my series and then I call him back in.

He stands in front of the counter where I've laid out my shots.

The first photo is Marissa from last year, when we first met in the ninth grade. She's sitting in the grass with a shy smile on her face.

The second shot is Marissa's mother passed out in the street.

Mr. Malloy studies the shot, but he doesn't ask who it is.

"Marissa took this one," I say, pointing to the third photo. "I don't think she would mind if I use it." It's the ceramic angel sitting in the bird's nest, back in the fall when the leaves were just starting to change colors.

The fourth one is Marissa with a black eye.

There are several more of the black eye taken at different stages of healing and hue.

The next photo is Marissa at Hurtle, frowning at something in the distance, her expression a mixture of sadness and anger. I remember she was looking at that kid's mother, the jittery, jonesing woman.

The next one is a group shot of bikers taking off down the hill at Hurtle. Marissa is framed in the center of the shot, poised at the top of her bike pedals, her legs tense and the muscles of her arms standing out as she grasps the handlebars.

Then there's the photo of Marissa's mother standing next to the birdbath in their garden, looking like she's barely holding it together. And the shot of the two of them, Marissa's face shining white in the glare of the flash.

The next shot is Marissa's bruised arm. She's making a pretend stern face and holding her bruised arm bent in a "We Can Do It" pose, like that woman factory worker in the World War II poster.

I included a couple of photos from the day we went on the field trip to the beach, one with Marissa smiling next to her crumbling castle, and one where she's listening to Nate play his guitar on the bus. Something about that last one makes me wonder if she had a crush on Nate. I wonder if everything—*everything*—might have turned out differently if Nate had looked up and seen the expression on her face.

Only three photos left in the series.

One is in my room, with Marissa sitting up in my bed holding the sheet over her breasts, looking into the camera. The second to the last one is Marissa getting out of my bed. I cropped and enlarged the photo so that it's just a head shot, focusing on her forlorn face.

And the last photo is the ceramic angel sitting in the wreckage of a nest, as if unaware that it might plummet to earth at any moment. The branches are bare of leaves.

Mr. Malloy studies each photo thoroughly while I wait and watch.

He turns from the last one and walks back to me. He puts his hand on my shoulder.

"There's the heart," he says.

.... CHAPTER FORTY-ONE ....

Memory card full.
—*Display message on Mitsu ProShot I.S. 5.3*

Third Thursday Gallery has been around forever. Like fifty years. Every so often they show controversial art, and people walk around with picket signs outside the gallery downtown.

But this evening no one is picketing or indignant. I walk through the glass doors, my parents on either side of me, bursting with pride.

Mr. Malloy is already there. No beret! He looks cool, all dressed up in non-teacher clothes.

"Blake," he says warmly. "Good to see you."

"Hi, Mr. Malloy. These are my parents."

"A pleasure to meet you! And call me Connor, Blake. You don't have to be so formal when we're not in school." Smiling, he addresses my parents again. "Have you seen Blake's series?"

"No," says my dad. "He's been very mysterious about it."

"I can't wait," says my mom.

"Let's not keep you in suspense any longer," Mr. Malloy says, and leads them to a door marked STAFF ONLY.

"The owners of Third Thursday Gallery are friends of mine. They use this smaller gallery to display works that are under consideration by private collectors. In this case, they allowed me to hang Blake's series away from public viewing."

"That's very kind of them," says my mom.

"Well, they agreed with me that this series deserved to appear in a setting befitting its beauty and depth. Had the photos not included a model who"—he hesitates—"is unable to sign a release, we would have shown them to the public. As it is, however, at least you and Blake can view them in a proper gallery setting."

He opens the door and we step inside.

My photos, matted and framed, hang on three walls. A sign hangs above them, in the center. It reads HURTLE.

"I'll leave you to enjoy these," says Mr. Malloy. He closes the door behind him as he leaves.

My parents take a long time to study my series, and they both cry.

My dad cries at sad commercials, so that's no surprise. But my mom doesn't cry very often.

When we finish viewing the photos, we walk around the rest of the gallery, taking in the other displays. I'm really drawn to a series under a sign that reads BENTWOOD.

They are all black-and-white, and they have the same subject in each shot: a spindly-looking chair. Bentwood, I guess. Sometimes the chair is sitting in the middle of a field or stuck in the sand at the beach. Other times there's a guy sitting in the chair, or contorted underneath the chair. Always the same guy. He looks young in some shots, wearing a weird hat and grinning or trying to drag a big black dog up onto the chair with him. There's one shot of him, and he looks like he's forty or so, slumped in the chair with his eyes closed, halfway in shadow, halfway in sun. Chiaroscuro. In the last few photos, the guy looks thin and pale, even in black-and-white. It's clear that he's sick. The very last shot is shocking: he sits on the edge of the chair, wearing a robe, which has fallen open to reveal his ribs sticking out. His knees are just knobs jutting out of his skin. His hair has mostly fallen out and he has sores on his face. But he's looking at the camera with a small wry smile, as if to say, *Can you believe this shit?*

In some ways, this series reminds me of my series about Marissa. I look for the photographer's name.

Connor Malloy.

. . . . .

When I go down to breakfast, I'm greeted by an autopsy saw lying in the middle of the table. You would think my dad would at least have the courtesy to keep his disgusting tools at work, where they belong. It resembles a handheld kitchen appliance, except that it's got a wicked little double-edged saw on the end.

I decide to stand at the counter to eat my cereal, so I don't have to look at that thing or think about where it's been.

A snore floats out of the family room.

Mom comes into the kitchen, her hair wet. "Morning, honey." She cocks her head at me, as if wondering why I'm eating at the counter, then glances at the table. She sighs and reaches for the coffeepot. "You didn't touch it did you?"

"No! Eww!"

"It's too early for drama, Blake. I'm just saying you wouldn't want to touch your dad's work tools without gloves on."

Dad shuffles into the kitchen, his hair artfully styled by the couch. The sound of Mom's voice acts like an alarm clock on him, I guess. They smooch for a minute. Get a room, 'rents!

"What's up, funny man?" says Dad, pouring his coffee.

"Not much," I say. "Just trying to avoid cutting off any fingers this morning."

He blinks. Then he looks at the table. "Ohhh, the head saw. Sorry, bud. I brought it home to fix it, but I fell asleep."

"Why do *you* have to fix it?" asks Mom.

"Eh." He shrugs. "Spending freeze. You know the routine: state-of-the-art facility, not enough money for gloves."

"What?" I say. "Not enough money for *gloves?*"

"No." He smiles. "It's not that bad yet. Just joking. But I figured I could fix the head saw myself, so why waste time sending it out?"

Garrett and The Dog Formerly Known as Prince amble into the kitchen.

"Morning, honey," Mom says, then hurries away, taking her half-finished cup of coffee with her.

"Why is the head saw here?" asks Garrett.

I feed The Dog while Dad explains.

"Good idea," says Garrett. "Can I help?"

"Sure. I'll wait till you come home from school."

"Great!" Garrett's day is off to a happy start.

Dad leaves the room, and Garrett grabs the milk from the fridge. He chugs for a minute, then replaces the cap and wipes his mouth. "Ass-wipe," he says. "I need to get to school early, so be ready to leave in five."

I pick up my cereal bowl and drink the dregs. Then I open the fridge and grab the orange juice for a drink.

"Did you hear me?" says Garrett. "Get moving."

"Dude," I say. "You had me at Ass-wipe."

Garrett's lips curl, and against his will, he laughs.

Ah, the first laugh of the day. Those hard-won points are the sweetest.

· · · · ·

Friday evening I meet Gus at the top of Tower Hill.

We shake hands kind of awkwardly. He looks at Frosty but is too nice to comment.

"Got your helmet, I see," he says.

"Yep." I pat my bike helmet.

"And your kneepads."

"Yep." I look down at my knees.

"And your elbow pads."

"Yep." I lift my arms and bend them at the elbows.

"Good," says Gus with a straight face.

What a nice guy. I know I look like a farb, but I truly do not want to die.

"I heard from someone," he says.

"Marissa?" My heart leaps.

"No. Someone who *knows* Marissa, though. She's okay."

Why doesn't he look happier?

"What else? What did the person say? Where is she?"

He stares down the hill. "The girl told me Marissa is in Seattle."

"With—?"

"Yes."

He faces me, and all six feet three of him is full of resolve. "I'll find her," he says. "As soon as I can. And I'll make her come back with me."

"Okay," I say. "Good."

We stand there for a long time. I stare at him. He stares down the hill.

I miss her, I want to say.

But his expression keeps me silent.

We mill around, waiting for Hurtle to start.

I didn't bring my camera, of course. I was afraid it might get damaged. But now I wish I had it so I could take Gus's picture. I can always come back some other time to Hurtle and get a shot of him, but I have a feeling I'm not going to come back here again.

Gus walks his bike toward the middle of the crowd, indicating that I should follow. We end up surrounded by hurtlers.

"Shouldn't I be in the back?" I say. "I don't want to slow people down. I've never done this, you know."

"You? I'm stunned. You seem like such a risk taker," he says with a grin, and all of a sudden I see Marissa in his face. He doesn't have the same heartbroken eyes, but I see her.

Oh God. Where is she?

How did this happen?

A couple months ago I had a girlfriend and a friend who was a girl. One of them loved me. The other one needed me. And I failed them both.

I think of Gus's angel tattoo, a constant reminder of his loss. I don't need something etched into my skin to remind me. I've got tattoos on my heart.

"We're fine right here," says Gus. "This is the spot. You don't want to be in front. Obviously. But you don't want to bring up the rear, that's no fun. It's just a crawl if you're in the very back."

"But—"

"Trust me," he interrupts. "I know you're a little nervous, but once you get started, you'll love it. You don't have to scream down the hill, but you do have to ride fast enough so that the people behind you don't crash into your ass."

"I—"

"Put your helmet on."

I jam the helmet onto my head and fasten it.

"And your fear, man?"

"What?"

"Just let it go," he says.

A yell goes up from the spike-haired guy in front, and the crowd roars. I jump.

"Come on!" Gus calls, and takes off.

I stand up on the pedals to get my momentum going. People are wheeling away in front of me, and I pedal faster, envisioning the bikers behind me ramming into Frosty.

Gus whips his head around to look at me and turns back to the front, shouting, "You got it! Keep it up!"

I'm pedaling so fast I can feel wind against my cheeks, and I'm breathing hard.

Houses and yards and telephone poles blur by in my peripheral vision, but no one passes me, so I must be keeping up the right speed. I do *not* look down, because I know the ground is whipping by so fast that it will make me dizzy.

My legs and lungs are pumping, straining in a wild rhythm. I'm flying down the hill so fast my belly swoops like I'm on a roller coaster. There's a turn coming up in warp speed and I'm scared I'm going to miss it and plow into that big hedge.

I grit my teeth and let out a low animal growl as I focus on making the turn. My arms are glued to the handlebars, as if they're part of the bike. A gush of relief floods my body as I realize I'm past the turn, and I'm *not crashing*.

There's another hairpin turn almost immediately, and I start panting in an effort not to overload on adrenaline. *Don't slow down and don't crash,* my brain screams. *Just a tap on the brakes.*

I make it! I'm alive and I'm spilling and thrilling down the hill!

I know there are lots of other turns waiting for me before I get to the bottom, but right now it's a beautiful straight shot. I gasp at the wide-alive joy in my blood.

Gus lets out a guttural yell.

I feel a similar sound roaring out of my throat.

I'm practically airborne. I'm flying.

And I am not going to crash.

......BLAKE'S BROKEN HEART......

(with commentary by Blake)

MAD-SAD PLAYLIST

1) "She Hates Me"—Puddle of Mudd
Hahaha! Very cleansing.

2) "Done With You"—Papa Roach
Good old Papa Roach. Truly: we are so done.

3) "Through Glass"—Stone Sour
Starts out sad, but kicks some ass by the end. "Sitting all alone inside your head." Yeah, that's not a good place to be.

4) "It Ends Tonight"—All-American Rejects
"I'm on my own side." *Yes.* From now on, I am on my own side. Thank you, All-American Rejects!

5) "4 AM Forever"—Lostprophets
Good, sad yelling.

6) "Blurry"—Puddle of Mudd
"Everything is so messed up." Yes, my muddy friends. It is. Rage on.

7) "Already Over"—Red
This helps me get it through my head.

8) "Bring It On Home to Me"—Sam Cooke
He'll be your slave till he's in the *grave,* lady! Just give him another chance. Bring that good lovin' on home to him, okay?

9) "All Over You"—The Spill Canvas
The singer's guts are "strewn out from coast to coast." Jeez, Spill Canvas Guy, have some dignity.

10) "How's It Going to Be"—Third Eye Blind
Starts out quiet, then the music swells and the singer starts wailing.

11) "I Miss You"—blink-182
Oh God, I love the squeak of the guitar strings and the pretty piano and the killing violins, and then the singer's demands come busting out.

12) "Luminous Times"—U2

This is a cautionary tale dressed up as a love song. The more you hear Bono beg, "Hold on to love . . . love won't let you go," the more worried you get. "She is the car crash" doesn't sound like the kind of girl you should hold on to.

13) "Hemorrhage (In My Hands)"—Fuel

Anytime you talk about love and bleeding in the same sentence, it's not going to be a happy ending.

14) "Say It to Me Now"—from the motion picture soundtrack *Once*

The angriest beautiful song *ever*. Perfect ending to this playlist.

SAD-SAD PLAYLIST

1) "She's Gone"—Daryl Hall and John Oates

This song is seventies-tastic, but it's pretty good.

2) "Colors"—Amos Lee

It's so true. Colors look faded when your love is gone.

3) "I Go to Sleep"—Sia

This chick starts out sad and sedated . . . but then she turns on the wide-awake yowl and her voice captures you like a dart to the chest.

4) "Over and Over"—Nelly, featuring Tim McGraw

Great, now I have to think about her being with someone else. I didn't think of that before!

5) "The Same Boy You've Always Known"—The White Stripes

How do these people keep making such good songs with only two instruments? Except for that doorbell one, of course.

6) "Color of a Lonely Heart Is Blue"—Old 97's

The perfect sad song.

7) "The Animals Were Gone"—Damien Rice

I take it back . . . *this* is the perfect sad song. Big wall-of-sound sorrow, with strings and shit.

8) "I Fall to Pieces"—Patsy Cline

Ancient song, but Patsy pours on the heartache. She's right . . . how can you act like you were never *with* someone?

9) "I Can't Help It (If I'm Still in Love with You)"—Hank Williams

Old-timey song that makes me want to put on shitkicker boots and a cowboy hat. But I totally feel the guy.

10) "It's Over"—Roy Orbison

Another old-timey song . . . three in a row. But I kinda dig them. Roy wails!

11) "The Ocean"—The Bravery

This song is now a permanent piece of pain in my heart. The rhythm is all primal and rolling, too, just like the ocean.

12) "Here Without You"—3 Doors Down

An I-haven't-moved-on song.

13) "Crying"—k.d. lang

When the audience bursts into applause, I get goose bumps and feel like *I* might cry. Thanks a lot, Cappie!

14) "Rhapsody on a Theme of Paganini, Opus 43, Variation 18, Andante cantabile"—Van Cliburn

OMG, is Cappie trying to *kill* me? This song has no words, but somehow it still makes me want to weep uncontrollably. And here's a tip: don't rent the movie *Somewhere in Time,* which has this song in it. Now I can hardly function from tragedy! Christopher Reeve was young and strong and alive in this movie.

15) "Pictures of You"—The Cure

Old-school angst. Classic.

········· ACKNOWLEDGMENTS ·········

Fierce love to my family. They give me everything.

Literaticat, a.k.a. Jennifer Laughran, thank you for the super-strength, sugar-free agenting. Oh, and that little matter of making my lifelong dream come true.

Awesome editor Margaret Raymo—thank you for believing in my book enough to take a chance on it, and for being generous with the compliments every step of the way. Thanks, also, to the whole Houghton Mifflin Harcourt team. I look forward to thanking you all in person someday.

Sisters Michelle and Beverly are my Ideal Readers, and I adore them both. Gratitude and love also to my parents, my *first* readers.

Hard-working critique partners (Melissa Higgins, C. Lee McKenzie, and Heather Strum) deliver the most thoughtful, insightful comments a writer could wish for.

Brian McLernon (he's not really "Spike") was kind enough to read the book in manuscript form and make sure I wasn't committing photography faux pas.

Unsurpassed in the FRIEND department—I would write a letter of reference for any of them—Jo, John, Sharon, Karyn, Benita, Melissa, Laura, Laureen, and Carla. And He Who Prefers to Remain Anonymous—thank you for talking to me about cadavers, *dieners,* and beveled bullet wounds. There would be no book without you.

Real Life, Real Time local writer friends April Henry and Lisa Schroeder are indispensable. And Sara Zarr may not be local, but she kindly provides sanity checks.

Novelists need constant encouragement, so to anyone who ever told me not to give up: thank you.

Online friends have a way of becoming as indispensable as RL ones. Thanks, Debs (www.feastofawesome.com), for all the fun and feelings. Thanks also to Jo Knowles, whose 2005 JoNoWriMo+1.5

Challenge drove me to finish this book in a concentrated burst of inspiration and determination.

Untold gallons of coffee and iced tea, plus infusions of chocolate, result in happy hours of writing.

This is really my book. Wow.

BIBLIOGRAPHY

If you are interested in photography, the following books are wonderful resources.

Burke, Carolyn. *Lee Miller: A Life.* Knopf, 2005.

Govignon, Brigitte, ed. *The Abrams Encyclopedia of Photography.* Harry N. Abrams, 2004.

Hammond, Anne. *Ansel Adams: Divine Performance.* Yale University Press, 2002.

Hedgecoe, John. *The Book of Photography: Simple Techniques for Taking Better Pictures.* DK, Dorling Kindersley, 2005.

Hoy, Anne H. *The Book of Photography.* National Geographic, 2005.

Jenkinson, Mark. *The Complete Idiot's Guide to Photography Essentials.* Alpha, 2008.

Lenman, Robin, ed. *The Oxford Companion to the Photograph.* Oxford University Press, 2005.

Montier, Jean-Pierre. *Henri Cartier-Bresson and the Artless Life.* Bulfinch Press, 1996.

Newman, Cathy. *Women Photographers at National Geographic.* National Geographic, 2000.

Peterson, Bryan. *Learning to See Creatively: Design, Color & Composition* in Photography. Amphoto Books, 2003.

PHOTOgraphic Magazine and Mike Stensvold. *The Complete Idiot's Guide to Photography Like a Pro.* Alpha, 2005.

Steichen, Edward, ed. *The Family of Man. Museum of Modern Art,* 1955.